we

speak

in

storms

we

speak

in

storms

NATALIE LUND

PHILOMEL

PHILOMEL BOOKS
An imprint of Penguin Random House LLC, New York

First published in the United States of America by Philomel,
an imprint of Penguin Random House LLC, 2019.
Copyright © 2019 by Natalie Lund.

Visit us online at penguinrandomhouse.com

LIBRARY OF CONGRESS CATALOGING-IN-PUBLICATION DATA
Names: Lund, Natalie, author.
Title: We speak in storms / Natalie Lund.
Description: New York: Philomel Books, [2019] | Summary: When a tornado strikes fifty
years after another killed many teens in tiny Mercer, Illinois, some of the dead unite with
misfits Brenna, Joshua, and Callie to seek peace. | Identifiers: LCCN 2018049758 |
ISBN 9780525518006 (hardcover) | ISBN 9780525518013 (e-book)
Subjects: | CYAC: Dead—Fiction. | Interpersonal relations—Fiction. | Tornadoes—Fiction.
Classification: LCC PZ7.1.L8487 We 2019 | DDC [Fic]—dc23
LC record available at https://lccn.loc.gov/2018049758

Printed in the United States of America.
ISBN 9780525518006
1 3 5 7 9 10 8 6 4 2

Edited by Liza Kaplan.
Design by Jennifer Chung.
Text set in Winchester New ITC Std.

For my mother, who has always believed

ON OCTOBER 7, 1961

On October 7, 1961, some of us snuck from our houses, climbing onto roofs, dropping into bushes. Some of us called to our parents: *We'll be at the movies. See you later.* We ignored the sharp wind, the chill that ran along the collars of our letterman jackets and the tops of our ankle socks. We loaded the pickup beds with quilts and pillows and packs of beer stolen from our fathers' basements. Or we piled into cars with our sweethearts, unable to keep our hands still, our skin from buzzing.

We drove into the country and parked our Catalinas, Coupes, VWs, and LeSabres in neat lines, mirror to mirror, facing the two-story whitewashed wall. We checked our watches, ordered pop from the waitresses, and made final trips to the outhouse, a few of us glancing warily up at the clouds. The projectionist started *Breakfast at Tiffany's*, wobbly at first, the image gritty, and then, finally, everything was steady. Above us: our stars. We climbed into the back seats to neck with our sweethearts, happy in the shadows. Or we sprawled with our friends in the truck beds like sleeping puppies, backs on knees, shoulder blades on stomachs, legs on legs. The movie's light playing out on our faces, in our eyes.

The wind grew stronger, and those of us outside pulled the blankets up to our chins and scooted closer to one another. The rain was next, pelting the cars' steel roofs. We squeezed into truck cabs, sitting on one another's laps, or we continued to fog rolled-up windows, kissing furiously—as though we knew time was almost up.

The movie stopped. A bullhorn announced something, the voice lost in the wind. Cars started for the exit, but it jammed. Some of us watched through blurred windows and waited, thinking the storm would pass.

Then, abruptly, the rain stopped. We laughed at our fear and clamored for the projectionist to start the movie back up. We failed to notice that the night sky had become the color of jade. Even though we'd grown up in the Midwest, most of us had never seen a tornado. Not up close. Not with its great, wide spin, its tapering cone. We'd never heard the roar, the rumored freight-train scream.

Not until that moment.

We panicked, put our cars in reverse, and drove madly through the field, ignoring lanes and rights-of-way. There were crashes. Some of us spilled from our cars and sprinted for the snack bar, the outhouse, the ditches. There were those of us who screamed and those who froze, facing the tornado.

We were a whole generation of Mercer. We were sons and daughters, born at the end of our parents' war. In a few years, we were supposed to go to college, join the military, marry, or stay home to help with the farm. We were supposed to leave and come back or never leave at all. We were supposed to raise children here, love them like we were loved, teach them loyalty to the town and its lore. Our children were supposed to sneak out of houses, pile into pickups, and watch their own stars. It was supposed to be a cycle, we thought. On and on and on.

How were we to know.

1

Brenna Ortiz reclined on her bed, blowing smoke out the window and listening to the storm. Raindrops clung to the screen grate, quivering, before freckling her pillowcase and forehead. A Big One, the weatherman had said that morning. They were always predicting the next Big One. Part of living somewhere like Mercer, Illinois, with all those graves marked October 7, 1961. But there hadn't been another Big One, not really. A few wall clouds, some funnels, but nothing touched down, no fields of bodies and mangled cars. Not since that day.

It thundered, and Brenna ashed the cigarette. They were the brand Colin smoked, the kind you roll between your fingers to crush the menthol crystal. Colin was her *Person*, but Colin didn't seem to feel the same way about Brenna. *I like you, sure*, he'd said right before summer ended, *but this isn't going anywhere*. It didn't matter that they'd dated for a year; he was heading off to college in the Quad Cities, and she was only a rising junior in high school. He wanted to be with someone who was in the same *life stage* as him. In fact, he'd admitted, he'd already met someone in the same *life stage*. That phrase wasn't just about age, Brenna knew. There was something coded there, something that leaked from beneath.

Earlier that day, at school, someone had written *Brenna Ortiz = SLUT* on the bathroom door. Brenna's best friend, Amy, had written *Bitches be jealous* beneath because she liked to clap back, but Brenna knew it wouldn't make a difference. She'd been called that name since she broke up with her first boyfriend in seventh grade. It didn't matter what she'd done or hadn't done with him; *Brenna Ortiz* would always = *slut, dirty, illegal, lazy, wetback*—just like her mom. It pained Brenna to wear these labels, words affixed to her by people who couldn't look beneath her skin and didn't know the first thing about who she really was.

With Colin, though, people had looked at Brenna differently, especially her teachers. Dating Colin had made people look at her—like there was something to her, something that had attracted the sharp, witty, worldly Colin, something that might get her out of Mercer or even the Midwest. But without Colin, Brenna was back to being the poor girl who lived in the bright-yellow shotgun house by the cemetery; the mediocre student; the daughter of the Ortiz family's black sheep; the half Mexican who hung out with the goths because her hair was nearly black to begin with and the white face powder was thick enough to make her blend in. The *slut*, the *dirty*, the never good enough.

Almost in agreement, the tornado siren whined, crescendoing. Brenna's house didn't have a basement. At school, they'd practiced lining up in hallways, noses to knees, hands clasped behind heads. You had to find interior walls. You had to duck and cover. It could be the Big One. The music her older brother, Manny, was playing thumped in the living room without pause. Through the vent, she could smell cheap weed and a pizza he was baking, clearly convinced he'd live long enough to eat it.

Her phone buzzed and her heart quickened, Pavlovian. But it was her mother; it hadn't been Colin for a month now. *Tornado warning. Bring your mattress to the bathtub. Colin over? Manny home? U guys ok?*

Brenna flinched. She still hadn't told her mother about the breakup—not that she'd had many opportunities. Her mom worked nights at the gas station by the library and was asleep when Brenna woke for school. But shame kept her silent too. Colin had finally realized what everyone else already thought: she was beneath him.

Brenna rolled her head back on the pillow and looked out the window. The sky resembled Mercer's canal: oily black, with swirls of scum and sediment.

I'm fine. It's nothing, she typed, but before she hit send, something unspooled in the sky, dropping its loosened threads toward the ground. Brenna flipped onto her stomach and inched closer to the window. It was in the country, maybe a mile away, and appeared to be spinning slowly, almost lazily, like soap settling around the tub drain.

This is it, she thought, an ache pulsing in her temples. She missed Colin, yes. She felt worthless, yes. But this was more than that. This was something that made her want to press her face to the screen and seep through. She wanted to open her arms to the funnel, wanted to be like those moviegoers decades ago. She wanted the wide, wild thing to know her.

2

Joshua Calloway's window was open, even though he had to pin the sketchpad's pages down with his forearm so they wouldn't flap in the wind. Beneath his arm was a rendition of Nightcrawler. Joshua liked to draw people he knew as Marvel comic book characters, usually X-Men. His mother as Jean Grey. His science teacher, Mr. Nelson, as Beast. His little sister, Ruthie, as Storm. This Nightcrawler had Joshua's own mussed red hair, thick-framed glasses, and face—slimmed down. Nightcrawler crouched, about to spring, a tail curling up over his shoulder, his long fingers and toes splayed. Joshua had shaded Nightcrawler's skin so that the character blended into the background shadows. Being invisible was Nightcrawler's strength.

Joshua's invisibility was something different altogether.

At school, he no longer had to sandwich his comics between textbook pages. It didn't matter how long he admired the illustrated male bodies: all muscle and grimace. It didn't even matter that he'd crossed 280 on the scale. There was no one to hear the table joints squeak as he sat down, or to notice the red line that the Formica tabletop left on his stomach. Everyone's eyes skated past.

Sometimes Joshua heard words that he thought were about him: *nerd, homo, fat, fag,* but, when he looked around, no one was watching him, no one whispered into their hands or ducked behind brick columns. He was the embodiment of *the elephant in the room.*

Ruthie, who was thirteen, told him he should be glad: *At least they're not shoving you against the lockers anymore.* His mother agreed: *You've taken away their power by coming out.* And maybe he had, but he'd pictured it all going so differently. He'd still be bullied, sure, but he'd be a hero, too. Someone whom the closeted teens of Mercer looked to for inspiration. Someone who rallied supportive teachers and open-minded friends. Joshua had dreamt about it: the clubs he'd start, the connections he'd make with organizations in the nearby Quad Cities, the speeches he'd write if he and his new friends were barred from prom. But it hadn't been like that. He'd somehow descended the social ladder so much that even the bullies didn't see him. He'd become Joshua the Invisible.

The rain picked up, curling the corners of his drawing. Joshua's ears popped as he slid the window down. Changes in pressure were a sign he'd been taught to recognize in a school video. *Ears pop? Find a place to drop!* Some safety lessons were even accompanied by an animated box of popcorn, a twisted reference—in Joshua's opinion—to the drive-in tragedy of 1961.

Sure enough, the siren sounded, long and mournful, like a whale call—followed by his mother's holler from the bottom of the stairs: "Basement. Now!" Joshua knew—everyone in their hick town did—that it was the anniversary of the 1961 tornado. You'd be crazy not to take shelter.

Joshua was the last of his family to descend into the unfinished basement. Ruthie was crouched beside their mother amid the stacks of toilet paper, oversized shampoo bottles, and toothpaste that they bought in bulk, winding and unwinding a strand of hair around her fingertip. She was a redhead like Joshua, but her lashes and eyebrows were white blond and nearly invisible, rendering her perpetually surprised.

"What's up, dump truck?" she said without taking her eyes off her finger, her lips pressed into a playful smirk. They were only eighteen months apart—*practically twins*, according to their late grandfather—and Joshua wished they really were twins, so he'd have a built-in best friend and it wouldn't matter that everyone else ignored him.

"Evening, ginger ball," he said.

"Not the time, you two," their mother said, kneeling and lacing her fingers behind her head. Joshua and Ruthie both had their mother's freckles and hair, but they hadn't inherited her oversized, protruding eyeballs, which they affectionately called her *buggos*. When they were little, they'd pretended they were insect-humans birthed by her, a praying mantis, and she'd played along, trying to catch them with her long, sticklike arms.

Lawrence, Joshua's stepfather, stood with his head bowed, praying under his breath. Since Joshua had come out to his family, Lawrence had acted as though his stepson's queerness would rub off on him, ducking out of rooms and keeping his distance rather than risk being alone with Joshua. This visible discomfort, and the fact that his mother had chosen such a man, scalded Joshua inside, and he never missed an opportunity to needle the guy.

Kneeling on the floor beside his sister, Joshua clasped his hands and stage-whispered in his best preacher drawl: "Dear God, please guide me away from this path onto which I have strayed. I have impure thoughts about men."

A loud guffaw escaped Ruthie, and she clapped a hand over her mouth.

"Joshua!" their mother hissed. "Dish duty for two weeks."

Lawrence flushed as though embarrassed, but he ignored

Joshua and sat on the other side of his wife, as far from Joshua as the crowded basement would allow.

The wind howled, and a trash can clattered down the street, the casement windows shuddering in applause. Ruthie leaned into Joshua—ever so slightly. She flinched when something tore loose from their house with a shriek, and Joshua pressed back with his arm, trying to comfort her. Normally, he'd tease her for her fear, but instead he marveled at the boniness of her shoulder, how sharp it was in his flesh, how long it had been since they'd huddled close, since anyone had voluntarily touched him.

Like everyone in Mercer, Joshua had thought about whether their house would stand a chance in a tornado. Thin walls, leaky windows, doors you could probably punch a hole through. It would be a shredded pile of plastic siding when it was all finished. He didn't want to die that way, an invisible virgin beside a sister obsessed with YouTube makeup tutorials and near a man who was afraid of a fifteen-year-old's cooties. If Joshua was going to die, he wanted to be remembered like the Storm Spirits.

Everyone in town traced their history to the night at the drive-in over fifty years ago, as though it had been some great war. *My grandfather's sister, Emily; my grandmother's next-door neighbor, Kelsey; the paperboy, Terry.* Whole families were still branded lucky or cursed, depending on how many people they'd lost. Joshua's family had been lucky, though his own life hadn't been any indicator. Maybe it was time for that to change. Maybe pretending to be brave was the first step toward truly being brave.

Joshua stood up.

"Where are you going?" his mother asked sharply.

"I want to see it."

"Absolutely not. Sit down, Joshua."

"Relax. It's probably just a false alarm," he said.

"Idiot, it's the seventh!" Ruthie sounded desperate, losing the usual chill she wore like a cloak. Lawrence, characteristically, said nothing.

Joshua ignored them all and took the stairs two at a time, afraid that the too-thin bravery would leak out of him if he slowed. When he neared the top of the staircase, his mother yelled his name. If they lived through this, Joshua would be grounded, but being grounded wasn't terrible when you didn't have any friends.

He tried the living room first. All he could see were rows of their subdivision's identical houses, the sky a chalkboard green behind them. The kitchen windows at the back of the house faced town, with only a few church spires to obstruct his view of the farm-land beyond. And there, in the distance, like a wasp's nest, hung a tornado. It moved like a swarm too, somehow erratic and purpose-ful all at once.

Joshua stepped backward, away from the window. He wished he hadn't abandoned the gentle pressure of his sister's shoulder, the security of the cold concrete, his mother. Despite his body, its unruliness and mass, he really was small. Unbearably so. Like a speck. Like a louse. And no amount of empty bravery was going to change that. He spun around and quickly jogged back downstairs.

3

Callie Keller gripped the wheel tightly as she drove, her windshield wipers revealing the countryside in blurry swatches: the rain-slick cornstalks arching and bowing in the wind, the runoff pooling, black, in the ditches, the turbines blinking red in the fields beside them. In flashes of lightning, her father's face lit white, and she was struck by how old he seemed. He'd always been the stereotypical beauty of the family: tall, broad-shouldered, with pronounced Swedish cheekbones, blue eyes, and blond hair. But her mom's cancer was aging him—and not just with a few more silver strands or laugh lines. He looked as if he were trying to keep his face as frozen as possible, as if it might crack and float away if he didn't lock his jaw tightly enough.

Earlier that night, Callie had stood in front of the mirror after her shower, wondering if she'd changed since her mother's terminal diagnosis less than a year before. Ever since middle school, Callie would scrutinize her appearance, wishing she didn't share her mother's boyishness: the limp brown hair, narrow nose, nearly flat chest, wide shoulders, and too-muscular legs. But lately she felt removed, like she could study her body without wanting it to be anything else. It was just a case she was zipped inside, and it was her strategy, since cancer, to make sure the case was as empty as possible. To eat nothing. To feel nothing. To believe in nothing. It was the only way she could survive as her mother slipped further from the world.

Her father craned his neck to see the sky through the passenger window. "We should head home. The weathermen were right." Her father would only admit this kind of thing begrudgingly. Unlike most of Mercer, he didn't believe in weathermen, God, or ghosts. He was a transplant, only moving to town to marry Callie's mother.

"Aren't I supposed to practice driving in all weather conditions?" Callie asked, her palms itching with the desire to get as far away as possible. "You don't want me to drive in a storm alone for the first time, do you?"

He gave her a small smile. Did he want to get out of that house as badly as she did?

Before her mother was dying of cancer, that smile would have turned into a Dad joke with him calling her full of *Callie-cat piss and vinegar*. He'd once been King of the Puns, laughing with his hand on his belly like some slimmed-down Santa. Before her mother was dying of cancer, Callie would have turned back—back to homework and microwave popcorn at the kitchen table while her parents blared a TV movie. But this was after, so Callie kept driving farther and farther, rain pounding on the roof.

There were no streetlights in the country, and even with her brights, it was darker than normal, everything blurred by sheets of rain. Lightning flashed above them, cracking the sky with silver and purple. In the momentary flash, their surroundings were lit, bright and stark, like a photograph negative. Callie saw a white car parked on the opposite shoulder of the road. It was a classic, like something you'd see in Mercer's homecoming parade: chrome bumpers, hub-caps, fins, and tiny round headlights that reminded her of cartoon eyes. A pale face looked out the wide windshield at them.

"Do you think they need help?" Callie asked as they drove past. The sky closed back up, and she couldn't see the face anymore.

"Who?" said her father.

"The person in that car."

Her father looked over his shoulder. "I don't know, but they're probably waiting it out like we should be. Pull off the road. Flashers on."

Callie eased onto the gravel shoulder and put the car in park. She glanced in her rearview mirror. Through the rain, she couldn't see the other car's taillights. She and her father sat for a moment, listening to the rain beat against the hood.

"I should have made you turn back," Callie's father said.

Callie looked at her hands, limp now in her lap. "I should have listened the first time. I'm sorry." Since the diagnosis, she usually took the path of least resistance with her parents: admitting wrong. It meant fewer talks at her mother's bedside, fewer moments trying not to stare at the green silk scarf tied around her mother's skull, the sunken cheeks, the blank ridge where her eyebrows had been, her always-watering brown eyes.

"I need to know you'll listen to me," he said quietly. "If—when—"

"Dad. Please don't. I said I'm sorry." She couldn't let him finish; she was nauseated at all that *when* implied. This nausea was one of the reasons she'd stopped eating. It wasn't sympathy nausea per se; it had more to do with the way her mom smelled now, like the cancer had replaced something essential—something Callie used to be able to detect beneath the deodorant and shampoo. Indescribable, because it wasn't from a field or pantry. The old Callie—her dad's curious Callie-cat—would have found a word for it if she'd known there'd be a time when her mother wouldn't smell like herself anymore. Now the Callie who knew that her mother's scent was gone for good just tried to think *nothing nothing nothing* whenever she leaned in close.

"In the past, I got to be the good cop all the time. And now"—Callie's father shook his head—"I can't be."

Callie cracked a window for air, and a few droplets hit her forehead. If she stopped eating entirely, stopped feeling entirely, she could fit through a crack that small: escape.

"Okay," she said, hoping it would be enough for him, that she'd be allowed out of this conversation.

They sat for a moment in silence. The rain stopped, and the sky was the color of seaweed. The air was different now, charged. Then, a long yowl, low to high and low to high again.

The hairs on the back of Callie's neck prickled. After God had failed to protect her mother, Callie had vowed not to place her faith in anything she couldn't see. Still, she couldn't help thinking of the lore her mother and the rest of the town subscribed to—that a whole family could be cursed: Callie's grandmother's twin sister had died in the storm of 1961, her mother was dying of cancer, and now she and her father were trapped in a car during a tornado.

Then it hit her. "Isn't it the seventh today?"

Callie's dad stared straight ahead. "I guess I just want whatever time your mother has left to be—"

"Dad, the siren. Shouldn't we go?" she interrupted.

Corn, lit by Callie's headlights, began to whip—not just bending in one direction, but Hula-Hooping, tassels flashing. Then a sound she recognized: a waterfall. They'd gone on a family vacation to Niagara last summer. Callie didn't understand what the sound was doing here, but her dad's face awoke. Eyes widening and teeth exposed like he was about to whistle through them. He craned his neck again, trying to see above the corn. Callie looked too but didn't see anything.

"Tornado," he said. "Ditch. Now!"

Callie swung open the door and flung herself into the ditch beside the road. She flattened herself on her stomach, water soaking through her shirt. Her dad ran around and crouched over her, his chest pressing her head into the ditch weeds.

The roar grew louder, and Callie felt something wet plaster the back of her thigh. A sharp object glanced against her arm. She expected the shriek of metal as the car was ripped apart. It would be her fault. She was the one who'd kept driving during a storm. But she didn't feel afraid, not for the car or for her life. She was simply aware of things in a way she hadn't been before: her father's collarbone pressing into her back, the wet cotton clinging to her stomach, the pull of hair around her ears. The deafening sound of rushing water, the memory of a summer afternoon posing beside her mother while her dad held his phone up. They hadn't been sure if he was taking a photo or video, so her mother kept saying: *Now? What about now? Tell us when, David. Can you see the falls? Can you hear us over them?* The airline had lost one of her mom's bags and she was wearing Callie's clothing. A Mercer High T-shirt, soccer shorts, visor. Callie wore a different T-shirt and knock-off Ray-Bans instead of a hat. Still, she knew that she and her mother must look like twins, leaning into each other and smiling big.

But that moment, like so many others, was long gone, Callie realized. What happened above them now didn't matter. Her own death didn't scare her. It was simply a matter of closing her eyes and waiting.

THOSE OF US AT THE DRIVE-IN

Those of us at the drive-in that night, decades ago, grew up watching *The Wizard of Oz.* The movie tornado is a muted swirl of farmhouses, trees, livestock, neighbors, and the mean Miss Gulch on her bicycle. The thing is, when we were inside the funnel, we were blind. We became what we felt: the stinging shards of glass against skin, skulls knocking against steering wheels, limbs flapping wildly, hearts lodged in throats, their beats broadcasting the end: *This is it, this is it, this is it.*

We ache to tell those who came after us: *This—your pain—isn't.*

4

The sound of the tornado subsided to a distant hiss. A few drops of rain hit the back of Callie's neck. How long had they been in the ditch? In the wake of adrenaline, her body felt famished, frail, and cold. But her mind was empty, vacuumed deliciously clean. There was no funnel in sight. Only thick gray clouds swirling in the dark sky.

Her dad sat up, releasing the pressure on her head and back. "You okay?"

She nodded and scraped damp grass blades off her cheeks. He was breathing hard, like they'd been running together—something they used to do before her mom got sick, racing along the Mercer canal to the tree with the heart-shaped knot. She blinked away the memory, already yearning for that vacuumed-empty feeling she'd had just seconds before.

Callie peeled a piece of wet cardboard off her jeans and tried to stand, but her legs buckled, so she knelt instead, inhaling, willing steadiness into her muscles. Shakily, her father lifted her by the elbow. Callie took inventory of her injuries: there was a cramp in her knuckles from her balled fist, the keys biting the fleshy part of her palm, a hot trickle of blood on her arm. But she was intact. Whole.

Her father circled their car, inspecting it for damage. She looked for the other car she'd seen in the flash of lightning, but the pavement stretched behind them, empty and dark. Had the person driven away?

"That was close," her father said softly, returning to the ditch to take the keys from her. She wondered if he was thinking of her mother, how she'd die alone if they were both gone. A thought snaked into Callie: *It would be easier that way.* She held the thought, rolling it around with her tongue, clacking it against her teeth, before pushing it out of her head.

As he started the car and pulled a U-turn, they were silent. Her father's face was flushed and his hands were still shaking. Did death scare him? Had he been afraid of how much he wanted to live?

Seconds later he braked hard, pulling onto the shoulder.

"Look." He pointed to the edge of a soybean field, just inside the cone of their headlights. A great wide swatch had been ripped up less than a hundred yards from where they'd crouched in the ditch, the beans churned and tossed at the base of a turbine. "I think it touched ground here."

The hair on Callie's arms stood up, a response as automatic as her belief had been before the diagnosis. The belief that in Mercer, there were ghosts, that some houses—like her own—were haunted. That there was a God. Until there wasn't.

"Dad, it's the seventh," she said again.

At first he didn't appear to have heard, but then he nodded. "A coincidence."

"A coincidence," she repeated, mimicking his confidence, but her arms still prickled.

A few fields over from where they were parked, there'd once been cropped grass, a whitewashed wall, outhouses, and a snack shack. Now there was a cornfield with a shrine of plastic crosses and fake flowers. On Halloween, kids snuck between the rows, listening for the Storm Spirits to whisper like the moviegoers they once were. Callie had never heard them herself, but one of her cross-country friends, Arlene, had insisted on bringing a Ouija board to the field the year before—back when Callie still believed. Not ten minutes in, Callie had felt the planchette move under her fingers, spelling F-I-N-D-A-R-E-P-A-R-E-N-T-S. Callie had seen Arlene's schoolwork often enough to know that she'd been the one moving the piece across the board. The Storm Spirits, Callie had thought at the time, were probably too offended by the use of a Ouija board to bother with eager teenagers, especially those who didn't know the difference between *our* and *are*.

Callie's father didn't believe, but her mother's belief was practically a birthright. Their house, which her mother had dreamt about living in since she was a child, was one of the twelve original Victorians that lined the town square and the subject of plenty of its own ghost stories. It was one of the oldest houses in Mercer and had once been an inn. Now the phantom visitors were said to knock about, climbing stairs, slamming doors, and dropping what sounded like luggage in the empty bedrooms. Callie's father had always explained the noises as squirrel nests, drafts of air, warped doorframes, and settling foundations, but Callie had preferred her mother's explanation, had loved the way the sounds made her feel like there was an electric wire inside her stomach. She'd chase the sounds, trying to find the ghosts so that she could ask them why they'd come back.

Now the wake of the first tornado to touch down since 1961 stretched away from their car, away from Callie's house, away from her sick mother—a mysterious path beckoning.

"Let's see how far it went," she said.

"We should get back. Your mom is probably worried."

"She's probably asleep, Dad."

His face was still frozen, and she wanted it to shatter into a grin, for his mouth to form the words *Okay, Callie-cat Holmes*, but he remained silent and unmoving.

Callie opened the glove box and pulled out the flashlight her father kept there for emergencies. She swung open the passenger door. The air smelled like sulfur and freshly mown grass, and was cooler now than it had been just minutes before. Callie wished she were wearing more than a damp long-sleeve T-shirt and jeans. Behind her, the headlights flicked off and the door slammed. With her dad following, Callie started down the path, her flashlight beam bobbing, the tendrils of the shredded plants wrapping around her ankles.

Something glinted and Callie stopped, aiming her flashlight at the base of the turbine. The light reflected off a splintered mirror. It was the white car she'd seen earlier on the road. Crushed. The windshield was shattered, the car's hood was accordion-folded, the trunk had been ripped open and twisted, and the paint had cracked like an eggshell. Callie shone the light inside. The seats were white leather, wet but pristine, like they hadn't been touched. There were no signs of people. No mud on the floor mats. No balled-up Kleenexes or ice scrapers or pairs of tennis shoes. Callie tried to picture the person she'd seen earlier in the lightning flash, but her glimpse had been so quick. Had that person found a ditch too? Or were they lying hurt somewhere?

"Callie, get out from under there." Her father pointed at the turbine above. One of its blades was dangling at its side like a broken limb. "That thing could fall at any minute." He pulled his phone out of his pocket and dialed.

Ignoring him, Callie walked around the car. There was a brown Route 66 sticker shaped like the road sign on the back bumper. She shined her flashlight on the plants at her feet. Footprints led from the car to the neighboring cornfield, like maybe the person had been trying to escape or was confused and stumbling. She tried to follow them with her flashlight, but they disappeared in the darkness between the rows of corn. Was the pale-faced person watching her from the shadows? Were they hiding or did they need help?

A breeze rustled the stalks so the tassels dipped together, fronds hissing. And then Callie heard something else—winding its way under, above, and around the sounds of the corn. Her dad, still on the phone, appeared unaware. Callie took a few steps back toward him, and the sounds hushed. When she returned to the tracks, they were audible again. She stood still, waiting for a lull in the gusts, holding her breath and closing her eyes. The sounds were fast and soft, like whispers. A year ago she would've called her best friend, Leslie, a staunch believer in the town's ghost lore, and held her phone up to the air. Now she didn't know what to think. Was it just the wind? Or something more?

But the sounds grew clearer, more human. *Find them. Save them.*

Was someone playing a trick on her? The person—or people—from the white car?

"The police said we should wait in our car," her father called sharply. He'd just lectured her about not listening, but the footsteps, the words on the wind—what had caused them? There had to be an explanation.

Callie glanced one last time at the prints on the ground and walked back to her father, rubbing her arms to hide the goose bumps.

5

The tornado had returned to the sky just as lazily as it had dropped, like someone reeling in an empty hook. The clouds were still rotating slowly, a few dangling wisps the only indication there'd even been a tornado. Brenna ached with disappointment; she'd been left behind again.

As she moved back from the window, her senses returned one by one: the sting where the window screen had imprinted itself on her nose and forehead, the buzz of her phone, Manny's music still thumping, the smell of melting cheese. Her stomach growled. The school's lunch vouchers were only good for scoops of gelatinous spaghetti, canned green beans, slimy deli sandwiches, or ground meat that gave her the runs. Usually she survived on handfuls of chips she bummed off Amy, who'd been her best friend since seventh grade—back when the older boys started following her and her ample chest home and girls started snapping their gum at her.

Brenna had gravitated toward Amy and her goth friends, Dutch and Jade, because they wore black shells of apathy, zipped high to cover their throats. The costume took some practice, but soon, Brenna was able to pretend the insults rolled right off the carapace she'd built—instead of what really happened: the words bored into her, making it hard for her to understand why she even bothered.

In the kitchen, Manny was cutting his pizza with a pair of scissors, squirting red sauce onto their mother's print of *The Last Supper* tacked above the countertop. He was taller than Brenna and lighter-skinned, but he had the same limp dark hair. She cut hers at steep angles, and occasionally bleached and dyed the tips bright shades of red or pink or orange. He let his grow long, to his shoulders, and wore it in a ponytail. His hairline was receding, even though he was only twenty. Before long, he'd look just like their dad, a nearly bald white truck driver based in Houston.

Brenna snuck up beside Manny and snatched two pieces of pizza. He tried to grab her shirttail, but she pivoted away. The crust was hot and oily, and a string of cheese caught her wrist, burning her. She shuffled the pizza onto a paper towel and headed through the living room, which was painted mango orange—yet somehow still felt dank and dark. Pulga and Gordy, Manny's friends, were sprawled on the couch, and had shoved aside her mother's ceramic angel figurines to make way for their beer cans. Smoke clouded the overhead lights. Like Manny, they'd graduated from Mercer and started working in the John Deere warehouse.

"Hey," Gordy drawled at her, pausing their game and turning down the music. His eyes skimmed down her chest, but Brenna kept her face straight, her shell intact, withholding a shiver. "Like the new hair," he said.

Manny carried the pizza into the living room on a piece of cardboard. "Her hair is always new," he said. Then he turned to Brenna: "You gonna pitch in or what?"

Brenna reached into her pocket, took out a crumpled one-dollar bill, and tossed it at Manny with a smirk.

Gordy lifted the bowl to her, but she shook her head—more disgusted by putting her lips where his had been than craving a hit.

At the front door, she pulled her hooded sweatshirt on, shifting her pizza from hand to hand.

"Where are you going? There was a tornado," Gordy said.

"Yeah, you three seemed really concerned."

"Let her go. She's probably meeting Colin, right, B?" Manny sneered. Clearly, he suspected there was a reason Colin hadn't been by in over a month. Manny thought Colin was a conceited prick and that Brenna was a conceited prick for dating him. "Too good for us, B?" he'd hiss as Brenna and Colin left for shows, open mic nights, or book signings in the Cities. Amy thought Colin was stuck-up too, but she always said, *You do you,* for which Brenna was grateful.

Brenna ignored the snide remark, grabbed the car keys, and slammed the door behind her. Wind lifted her bangs, a few droplets of rain hitting her forehead. She inhaled. Their house had a way of clotting her thoughts, making her think about Colin until she couldn't breathe. Outside, away, was better.

She walked down their driveway and across the street to the Blue Light Cemetery, where the old-growth oaks sheltered all the graves etched with 1961. It wasn't just the tornado victims—the bodies of Mercer's earliest settlers had nourished those trees, their flesh and hair and bones becoming, somehow, part of the bark and branches.

Brenna picked her way around gravestones that poked from the ground like crooked teeth. Tree roots had bullied them out of their neat ranks, and some had fallen over, their splintered pieces scattered. Brenna knew each gravestone—names, dates, inscriptions. Lonely, she'd explored the graveyard when she'd first moved to Mercer, mapping the stones in her notebook.

She sank to the damp ground before her favorite, a granite stone near the oldest oak. MY SKY 1945–1961. Brenna had always loved it because it was the English for what her mother called her—mi cielo, my heaven. There was no inscription. No gender. No name. The stone was unusual in another way too; it was light pink when every other stone was white or gray. Who was this family that couldn't bear to write My Sky's real name—but picked the one stone that would stand out, that would be recognized and remembered? Gretta, the only remaining survivor of the 1961 tornado willing to talk about it, had recently told Brenna that My Sky's name was actually Celeste.

Brenna often found herself imagining what life the teen must have lived before the storm. Maybe she was a professional badminton player, or she loved miniatures, or had built her own tree house. Maybe she'd been allowed to be whoever she wanted, to write her own story. But that—Brenna knew—was not the lot for most girls from Mercer.

Brenna took the last bite of pizza and leaned back against a tree, looking up at the canopy of leaves. When the moon was out, some of the stones had a bluish tint. People said they glowed blue if the dead wanted justice, though one of her teachers said it had to do with the type of stone they'd mined in Mercer for over a century, a stone that was impossible to find in the quarries now. It depressed Brenna that things could just be gone forever. She preferred the supernatural explanation. Not that she wanted a bunch of wronged ghosts wandering around—just that she liked the idea of there being an after. If she were dead, she'd want to see Colin's pain, her parents', her grandmother's, even Manny's, but eventually people would forget—unless you glowed blue as a reminder.

Brenna hadn't grown up in Mercer like her mother, but she'd adopted the town as her own—even if it had never fully adopted her. Believing was part of blending, of belonging to her mother's hometown, to her mother. It wasn't just the cemetery. Brenna had left thrift store teacups on the steps of the historical society's museum for the poisoned Winston twins, who spent their afterlives smashing porcelain tea sets at their former house. She'd been a passenger in Dutch's car when he put it in neutral in the middle of the town's covered bridge and felt the car roll to the other side—pushed to safety, it was said, by the Clark family, who'd died there decades before. Brenna had fed Mrs. Jenson, a crow-ghost, who perched on top of the grain silo where the human Mrs. Jenson had been crushed by feed corn. Brenna had led reckless whiskey-fueled séances with Amy and Jade in the Storm Spirits' cornfield, where they draped their heads in dark scarves, adopted Eastern European accents, and lit the saint candles she'd stolen from her grandmother. The spirits never answered, but she knew that they were listening. She knew they'd make their presence known when they had something to say.

You're too good to believe that shit, Colin had said once. But she did—then and now. What did that make her?

As Brenna sat under the tree, Sky's headstone lit blue and then red and blue again. Red and blue? Not ghosts. Cops. Her mother would be furious at her if she had to leave work and bail Brenna out for something stupid like trespassing in a cemetery after dark. Brenna stood, the bark snagging her hair, ready to put her hands up like she'd seen on the news. Brown people had to assume the worst, she knew. But then she realized: the cop car was headed for the country.

If Colin were there, he'd climb into his Jeep and follow, fast, for the thrill of it, glassy-eyed from pot but never paranoid because *Fuck the man.* Said ironically, of course, because Colin loved irony and didn't have to be afraid. Part of her believed that if she followed now, chasing thrills, playacting the Brenna she'd been with him, she'd feel whole again.

Brenna swiped the mud off her ass and started back across the street to her driveway. She climbed into the gold Oldsmobile—nicknamed Golden Girl—that she shared with Manny, and cranked down the window so she could smoke. She accelerated into the country, spinning the radio dial for a news report.

When an ambulance's lights spun in her rearview mirror, Brenna pulled to the side. She let it speed ahead a few hundred yards and then she followed. It was illegal, she knew, and the thought made her lower abdomen throb. If Colin were beside her, he'd squeeze her leg, proud, his fingers lingering on the inside of her thigh. She blinked away the fantasy, a drumroll of pain in her throat.

The ambulance sped down 1800, nearing the site of the old drive-in. Brenna could map the turns in her mind, the country roads as familiar to her as the graves in Blue Light Cemetery. She drummed her fingers on the steering wheel—the first excitement she'd felt in months. Would bodies be strewn like seeds? The curse awakened? Spirits chattering? But before they reached the drive-in, the ambulance pulled onto the shoulder across from a blue sedan. Brenna flicked off her lights and pulled over too. She slouched down—in case anyone looked her way—and tried to make out what was happening. The cop car was parked in the bean field, high beams illuminating an old white car smashed against the base of a wind turbine. Brenna imagined how large the tornado must have been to lift and carry a car that far from the road. Giant, certainly, since it had also left a wide wake in the bean plants and a loose turbine blade dangling above like a half-plucked petal.

At the edge of the field, a man who looked like a father in a catalog had his arm around a girl. He was talking to a cop and gesturing at the rows of beans. The girl kept glancing over her shoulder at the field behind them. She looked familiar from school, and Brenna tried to remember her name. Brown hair. Long-sleeve T-shirt and jeans. Wide cheekbones and a too-small nose. Nondescript. *Callie.* She'd heard around school that the girl's mom was dying.

Brenna climbed out of the car, crossed the road, and edged along a flooded drainage ditch, mud squelching beneath her shoes. The wind turbines hummed in the background, a hum that sank deep, like it was settling into her marrow. She couldn't imagine living on one of the nearby farms with that constant drone.

A cop with a handlebar mustache spotted Brenna, and she felt the throb in her abdomen again, the electricity of Colin's fingers on the inside of her thigh.

"Miss," he said calmly. "Please return to your car."

"I just saw my friend here and I wanted to make sure everything was okay."

The shivering girl, Callie, blinked at Brenna, confused. She leaned into her drenched father's arm and Brenna felt a pang of jealousy. Callie seemed to trust that her father's arm would hold her up, an unthinking kind of trust.

"What happened, Callie?" she asked.

The girl startled at her name and looked up at her father, then back at Brenna.

"Someone's car got wrecked by the tornado," the father said, nodding toward the field.

"Is everyone okay?" Brenna asked.

Callie shrugged and shifted back and forth on her feet. Brenna caught her glancing over her shoulder again. What was she looking for? Was there something else back there? Something to do with the spirits?

The cop shooed Brenna with a wave of his hand.

"All right. Back to your car. We need you off the shoulder. You can catch up later."

There was something going on, something Callie had seen—Brenna knew it in her gut, where her belief in the blue stones, in the spirits of October 7, 1961, in Mrs. Jenson, the crow-ghost, nested. It made her heartbeat quicken until it thudded in her ears. She had to find a way to talk to the girl again, so she pulled off her sweatshirt and tossed it at her. "Here. You look cold. You can give this back tomorrow at school."

Back in her car, Brenna thought of her mother, of all the unanswered texts on her phone about Colin and Manny, imagined her mother panicking that she'd arrive home later to a collapsed house, her children inside.

We're okay, she tapped out because the rest was too difficult to explain.

Through the driver's-side window, Brenna watched as the police searched the field. The skinny girl held the sweatshirt in front of her like it was a foreign object. Her father said something, and she put her arms through the sleeves, pulling it half on, the hood beneath her chin. Again, Callie looked over her shoulder, like something had called to her. Brenna tried to see into the rows of corn behind the girl, her body trilling with curiosity, but the night was pitch-black. What had the girl seen?

6

In his bedroom after the all clear, Joshua flipped on the scanner he'd bought with money he'd earned from detasseling corn that summer. He liked to listen to the dispatchers' calm voices and the policemen's gruff replies as he drew. After a storm like this one, there was bound to be activity. Sure enough, the air crackled before the dispatcher spoke: *"4752, I need an event number."*

"52 here with Liam. ID 478292."

"10-4."

The radio hummed. Then a click as the dispatcher keyed her mic again.

"4964, auto accident due to tornado, 1900 E between 400 N and 500 N."

"64, go 'head."

"Caller at 452 1900 E. County EMS and Mercer fire dispatched."

"64 responding."

Joshua recognized the address; it was right near the farm where they'd lived with his grandparents six years ago. What if the tornado had hit that house? Memories fired inside him. The corn sighing through the crack of his old bedroom window, the kitchen that smelled like it had been seasoned with generations of chicken noodle soup, and the alpaca rug they'd kept in the living room that he'd rolled on like a pup. He and Ruthie had spent their afternoons roaming across the bean and cornfields to the creek. They'd made swords of cattails and minions of the crickets they caught in empty butter tubs. A large weeping willow was their portal, and they'd pass through its long branches, emerging as heroes.

But when his grandfather died and his grandmother followed a few months later, it was all gone. Just like that. He, Ruthie, and their mother moved to an apartment behind a laundromat, until, another year later, they relocated to Lawrence's subdivision of tornado bait by the interstate.

The farm was the only good thing about their town, the only place Joshua had felt free to become whoever or whatever he wanted, where he didn't have to be the overweight kid with the smudged glasses and the secret feelings he didn't understand. He needed to make sure their old house was still standing.

Joshua opened his bedroom door and listened. The television

was on in his mother's room, a reporter's voice blaring down the hall, and the computer keys were clacking away in the office. No one would notice him gone.

Outside, he looked up at the mat of gray clouds in the night sky. They were peaceful now, the air surprisingly cool. He unchained the bike he'd bought with money from blueberry picking when he was ten. It was too dark to ride, but he pedaled out of their neighborhood anyway—his knees sticking out as though he were a grasshopper— and turned onto Main Street. Downtown, only the diner, a bar, and the one-screen movie theater that had replaced the drive-in were open. A few paper cups clattered in the breeze along the curb as though racing him.

In the country, he pedaled into the wind, his quads and knees aching and his eyes burning with tears. The streetlamps were behind him, but it wasn't as dark as it had been when he was a kid on the farm. New wind turbines blinked red, like an alien army sending SOS signals to the clouds. He and Ruthie had played in real dark on the farm—not beneath the yellow glow of fast-food signs or those blinking fuckers. Their back deck was a boat at sea, the corn shuffling in the breeze the waves, the small orange cat his parrot on the shoulder. Beyond the porch light, there were sea monsters; there were the ghosts of shipwrecked pirates; there were the swimming dead. And, as a captain with the power to see into the great beyond, Joshua had defeated them all.

He pedaled toward the address he'd heard on the scanner. Rode past a barn, its wood splintered, the red paint now faded to pink, *Coca-Cola* just barely visible on the roof. It had once advertised to moviegoers on their way to the drive-in and had been a signal to Joshua when he was young that he was almost home. What were the odds of a tornado appearing at nearly the same place decades apart?

Not far from the Cola barn, Joshua saw the red-blue flicker of cop lights and a collection of headlights on the shoulder. Pickup trucks mostly, angled in different directions so they illuminated the road, the field, and the base of one of the red-blinking turbines. He knew from listening to the scanner that Mercer volunteer firefighters reported to scenes—fire or not. That they were some sort of man club, uniting for even the smallest chance at heroics.

He stopped beside a dilapidated Oldsmobile just outside the ring of light, and looked around.

In front of him, a turbine's blade was twisted and drooping. A white car—something classic like the ones in the car shows his grandfather had liked—was crushed below it. It was as if Magneto had levitated the car and thrown it. The glass was shattered. The roof and hood puckered. The trunk open and mangled. Joshua didn't see any bodies.

An ambulance was parked on the shoulder, a police car in the field across the way, the bean plants rippling like water around it. One EMT leaned on the grille and spoke into a radio. Another stood beside a policeman talking to Callie, a girl Joshua knew from pre-calc, and a blond man he presumed to be her father. No one looked injured, and he could see from the wreckage that the tornado path led west, away from his grandparents' farmhouse. Joshua relaxed his grip on the handlebars.

A little way off, a clump of plain-clothed volunteers stood on the gravel shoulder. They were all men: lean and young, the kind who wore baseball caps frayed along the brim. One stood apart from the others, arms crossed, watching. His hair was dark, longish, parted on one side and slicked to the other. He was wide-shouldered, thick-necked, stubble-chinned. Joshua wished he had his sketchpad; this man would make a perfect Wolverine—chiseled, rough, and lunging off the page. Only his clothes—a gray mechanic's jumpsuit with a red belt and blackened knees—marked him as non-mutant.

As Joshua perched there, the Oldsmobile's window rolled down beside him, emitting a wave of stale cigarettes and pot.

"Hey," a girl's voice said.

Joshua glanced behind him, sure she was talking to someone else. The girl leaned out the window. She had powdered brown skin, a pierced eyebrow, thick eyeliner, and red-tipped hair. He'd seen her around the halls, crowding the drinking fountains with the goth kids and smiling with her mouth closed, as though she were afraid to show people her teeth.

"I know you?" she asked.

"Um, I don't think so."

"Yeah, I do. You're that kid who came out."

He felt light-headed, giddy like he'd just inhaled helium. She'd known who he was and still talked to him. "I'm Joshua."

"Brenna," she said. "Why are you riding your bike in the dark?"

"I heard about the car on my scanner." He left out the part about his old farm, its magic and his fear.

She nodded as though she understood. "I followed the ambulance," she said. "News flash: Mercer is boring as hell."

"Always. Do you know what's going on?" he asked.

"Not much. There was a tornado that picked up that car over there. No one got hurt. That girl knows something more, I think, but we got interrupted."

Whatever it was, it was over. Flicking off its flashing lights, the ambulance lumbered from the shoulder and headed back toward town. The emergency workers and volunteers waved and nodded at one another, turning from the scene toward their own, undamaged, vehicles. The young guy who looked like Wolverine was already gone. Only the police cruiser remained, the policeman inside with the dome light on. Joshua wished he had brought his scanner with him so he could hear what the man was saying.

"Want a ride back to town?" Brenna asked. "That bike's so small, I bet I can fit it in back."

He realized he was smiling dumbly at her. Part of him was imagining what Lawrence would say if he found out Joshua had ridden in a car with someone who smoked pot. But another part of him was just plain happy.

"Where do you live?" Brenna asked after loading his bike.

"The Piedmont subdivision off the interstate."

"Great. I know a shortcut," she said. Rather than U-turning, they drove straight and took a sharp right onto a gravel road, the tires churning and flinging rocks. This road was even darker than the last, the air satiny and thick. Ahead, Brenna's headlight caught a sliver of pale blue.

"Hold up," Joshua said. "There's something in that field."

Brenna slowed and they crunched their way closer to the blue object. She put the car in park and climbed out. Joshua scrambled to unbuckle his seat belt, unwilling to stay in the car alone. As they pushed their way through rows of corn, he could see clearly what Brenna's headlights had illuminated: a VW bus with a robin's-egg belly and a cream top. Its bug headlights glinted, blinking like eyes. There was a spiderweb crack on the windshield and the paint was dinged, like it had been in a meteor shower instead of a tornado.

Brenna pushed aside cornstalks and squelched through the mud toward the van, seemingly unfazed by the cobwebs that were plastering her face. She pulled on the chrome door handle, flicked on her cell flashlight, and shined it into the VW's cabin.

"No one here."

"We should probably call the police," Joshua said.

"Don't you think it's weird?" Brenna asked. The cornstalks cast striped shadows across her face, but Joshua could see her eyes glittering with excitement. "A tornado touching down on the anniversary of the 1961 storm. These old cars. And you know where we are, don't you?"

It was pitch-black outside the cone of their headlights, but Joshua had been there enough to fill in the details: the overgrown driveway, the plastic flowers and crosses by the road, the neat rows of corn masking what the plot of land had once been. He'd ridden his bike there as a kid with Ruthie, never venturing into the field itself because Ruthie was terrified the spirits would follow them home. Joshua used to believe in the spirits and stories too. But he had stopped believing at a very young age—once he understood that he was gay and realized the truth about his town: that most Mercerites could believe in ghosts but were unwilling to believe that someone should be able to love, marry, and have a family with a person of the same gender. He couldn't wait to be eighteen and put Mercer in his rearview mirror, to live in a city that wasn't obsessed with stupid folklore and stuck in 1961.

"I'm sure it's just a coincidence," Joshua said.

"Come on. Really?" Brenna sounded doubtful.

"Yeah. There's got to be a simple explanation." But face-to-face with the empty VW, he couldn't think of one.

MORE THAN FIFTY YEARS AGO

More than fifty years ago, back in 1961, the police found some of us in ditches, still alive, huddled and damp and scared. They wrapped us in stiff gray blankets, drove us to the station, and handed us the phone. *Call home*, they said, and we blinked because we couldn't remember what home was.

But some of us remembered and drove there on our own, as if home were the only beacon we knew. We stumbled up steps, into worried parents' arms. All of us only wanting to be held, to be children again.

It was hours before the police sorted through those of us whose bodies were flung far and wide beneath the dry cornstalks, whose cars were overturned, braced by tree branches or smashed like toys. They cut through steel, peeled us off dashboards, pried us from between folded seats, matched our severed limbs to our torsos.

Morticians sewed us back together, plastered us with makeup, or just closed our caskets.

We are many. Fifty-four buried in 1961. Another fifty who made it home with all or most of our bodies, and countless others— friends, parents, lovers—who lived on but became ghosts anyway, always waiting, always aware of the spin. How, eventually, it stops.

7

Callie woke to the murmur of voices in the next room. The air smelled of toast—breakfast that her mom probably wouldn't eat. Usually, she was up before her parents, but she'd stayed awake late, hoping to see the face in the car and hear the whispers—if that was what they were—better in memory. *Find them. Save them.* Was it real? And who was *them*? Had someone in the field been trying to tell her something?

Last night she'd watched Joshua from pre-calc climb into an Oldsmobile beside the girl with the clunky red boots who'd given her the sweatshirt. She'd hungered for the normalcy of getting a ride from a friend. All of her friends except Leslie had faded from her life as though her mom's sickness were contagious. Or maybe Callie had pushed them away with her silence, with her avoidance of the cafeteria, of youth group, of the locker room before cross-country practice. Losing friends was another side effect of emptying.

Now Callie listened to the way her parents' voices rose and fell, unable to decipher their words. It was as though she'd awoken to something secret and fragile, like a flower that only blooms every fifty years; she might never experience it again. She squeezed her eyes shut and tried to stop the thought.

Just then there was a knocking sound, somewhere above Callie's head. She opened her eyes again and looked up at the ceiling. *Squirrels*, her father would say, but something was niggling at the back of her mind. Those sounds. That face.

It was the kind of story Callie would have loved when she was little, when she and her mom had squeezed into the armchair together before bed. Callie was never interested in library books written by someone who hadn't been to Mercer. She wanted *their* stories. Mercer stories. Her mother would always say, *But you already know them*, until Callie begged, *Tell me again, please*. Then she would comb Callie's bangs back from her forehead, kiss her right at her hairline, and begin: *Back when Mercer was no more than a few farmhouses, there was a woman named Margaret Peterson. She built this house—something no one believed a woman could do at that time. But she did, and when she was done, she opened it to everyone who stopped through Mercer, so that they could sit by her fire, eat her bread, and curl up under her blankets. And they all loved it so much that some of them never left. They built their own*

52

houses right by hers, so that they could sit by her fire, eat her bread,
and curl up under her blankets all their lives. And when they died,
they still came—Callie would interrupt to finish the story—*to sit by*
her fire, eat her bread, and curl up under her blankets.

Callie shook her head, as though she could shake away
the memory. She wasn't sure how much longer she'd live in the
Petersons' house, with its rich burgundy shutters, its scalloped
trim, its tower and cone-shaped roof that always reminded Callie
of a witch's hat. A few nights before, she'd overheard her parents
talking about the mortgage, how it was hard to manage with all the
medical bills. This house was everything to her mother. She'd even
joined the historical society—founded by Eleanor Peterson, the
great-granddaughter of Margaret Peterson. With their help, Callie's
mother had preserved the home, painting its walls and refinishing
its floors, searching every antiques shop in Illinois and Iowa for
period-appropriate furniture, and opening it for tours every year
during the town's Victorian Christmas celebration. The house was
her mother's, and Callie wanted to save it. A want that she tried to
bury deep down. Because, in this new world, wants were just as
meaningless as beliefs.

"Callie? Are you awake? Come say hi to me before you go to
school," her mother called. Bedside talks were part of their ritual
now. *You can ask me anything*, her mother always said. *This is*

your chance. During the chats, Callie would pretend to be one of the ghosts her mother believed in, floating above, knocking around just enough that her mother thought she was still there, still present, while she wished herself somewhere—anywhere—else.

Callie opened the door to find her mom propped in bed, her green scarf still on the nightstand. Callie averted her eyes. She didn't want to see the caverns of her mother's skull, the beads of her spine beneath yellowing skin.

"Morning. Want some toast?" her mother asked, nodding toward the plate beside the scarf.

Callie shook her head and took a sudden interest in the jewelry chest on the bureau, pretending to be too occupied to sit on the bed. Before the diagnosis, when Callie and her dad returned from their runs along the canal, her mom would be reading the newspaper, waiting for the coffee to brew, and eating granola that she'd baked with honey, walnuts, and raisins. She'd say *good morning* but little else as Callie and her dad kicked off their shoes and peeled off damp socks. Just the crunch of granola and the shuffling of a newspaper. No pressure to make those mornings count. Now every conversation had to matter and be meaningful because they were never certain when the goodbye might come.

"You can have that," Callie's mom said.

Callie blinked and noticed she'd threaded a string of pearls between her fingers. "That's okay," Callie said, putting it down.

"No, really. You should take it. It's yours."

Callie shook her head. "I won't ever wear it."

Her mother grimaced.

"Sorry," Callie said. "I didn't mean that. Maybe I'll keep it for special occasions." Callie made a show of holding it up to her neck and posing. In the mirror, she looked so plain, so dull in her cross-country sweatshirt and pajama pants—absurd next to the pearls. Her mother's reflection appeared happy and sad all at once, and sicker, too—her face puffy, sweaty, and grayish green.

"You look beautiful." Callie's mom opened her arms for a hug.

Holding her breath, Callie walked over and bent just enough for her mother to fold her arms around her shoulders. Callie clutched the pearls, trying not to imagine them as her mother's spine.

"Anything big happening today?" her mother asked.

Callie wondered if her mom had slept through the sirens last night, and if her dad had told her about their near-deaths or if he'd tried to spare her the worry. She pulled herself out of the hug and shook her head.

Her mom dabbed at her eyes with a tissue she kept under her watchband. "How about for your birthday Saturday? Doing anything exciting?"

Callie shook her head again.

"Are you ready to get your license?"

"I need a half hour more."

"Maybe your dad can take you out again tonight."

"Yeah," Callie said, trying to force enthusiasm. Getting her license was all she'd wanted. Before. She'd been counting the days until she was able to drive her friends to the Cities for Thai food and movies. She'd enrolled in driver's ed last fall, when her mother was healthy, or, at least, when they didn't know she was sick. Her mother had often taken her to practice in the church parking lot, sucking her cheeks and slamming an imaginary brake if Callie got too close to the curb in her turns. Back then, Callie couldn't wait to be rid of her mother and drive alone.

"What if you just sign off on the hours? It's not like they have any way to check," said Callie. All practice hours were self-reported, initialed by parents, and then submitted to the DMV after the test. It was easy to fake, and Callie knew some of her older teammates on the cross-country team had done it.

"No." Her mother's jaw tightened, a ripple of muscle beneath almost transparent skin. "Practice is important. So is integrity. Do you hear me, Cal? I want you to remember that after I'm gone." Her mother's voice did this now whenever she had a lesson to impart: got louder and louder, but also trembled, like she was cry-yelling.

"I hear you," Callie said. "Integrity." But her mind was already escaping, as it often did when her mother got this way. Instead she thought about the night before. She hadn't told her father or the cop about the whispers or the footprints. She'd just watched the cop walk back and forth near the prints, like he didn't see them at all. Why, she wondered, when they'd been so obvious to her?

8

Before school, Brenna kept the volume low on the small kitchen television, hoping not to wake her mom; she wasn't in the mood to talk. On the local news, a woman with over-bronzed skin stood in the bean field. The white car was gone, but the camera kept panning up to the turbine's broken blade.

"Not since October 7, 1961, has Mercer seen a tornado of this magnitude touch down," the woman said. The producer cut in a photo from the drive-in. The wooden movie screen was halved, the cars piled like they were in a junkyard. It was the photo that the media often used, but Brenna knew there must be more gruesome ones out there, taken before the bodies were cleared.

The reporter interviewed the cop with the handlebar mustache who'd shooed Brenna away the night before. "Who was the driver?" the reporter asked.

"We're still investigating."

"Has anyone come forward?"

"No. We're in the process of reaching out to the owner now."

No mention of the blue VW, which either meant they still hadn't discovered it or that they weren't linking it to the white car.

The desk anchors continued the story with a call-in witness. "It's gotta be connected to the drive-in," the man drawled. "A few of us heard them chattering last night."

"Who?"

"The spirits."

The anchor smiled nervously, clearly thinking she had a crazy person on her hands. The local news filmed in the nearby Quad Cities, not Mercer. People from the Cities thought themselves more cultured and rational—simply because they had Super Targets, coffee chains, and more than one screen at their movie theaters. Mercerites were probably on the phone theorizing and storytelling, or packing up their planchettes for a trip to the turbine, convinced— as Brenna was—that it was all too coincidental, that the Storm Spirits must be trying to tell them something. But what?

Her mother's door creaked open at the back of the house, and Brenna muted the TV, bracing herself for a scolding, but she heard a man's voice mutter something. Brenna dropped to the kitchen floor, hugging her knees to her chest, so she'd be hidden from view by the cabinets. She'd rather hide than have to interact with yet another of her mother's "friends." By now she'd met all sorts—the ones who gave her stickers as though she were five, the ones who tried to be her buddy and told her all about their high school escapades, or her least favorite: the ones who stared a bit too long at her chest. She preferred the ones who pretended she didn't exist.

There was no telling what sort this particular man would be, but the fact that she could hear him bumping into the walls as he made his way down the hallway didn't bode well. He paused at the kitchen, and she heard him patting himself—looking for keys? Brenna held her breath. *Don't decide to get a drink of water. Don't stop to watch the TV. Just leave.* The front door opened and closed, and Brenna exhaled. She couldn't wait to move out.

In first period, Brenna sat at her desk, bored, as Mrs. Berk explained their Spanish III project in what Brenna's grandmother called *español gringo*, slow and deliberate, enunciated so that each syllable stood alone instead of flowing gracefully from one to the next. Brenna feared her own was nearly as bad because her mother used very little Spanish at home. As a kid, her mom had been chastised for speaking Spanish in school, and her mother—Brenna's abuela— had pushed her to speak English even though she did not speak it herself, because *it's not enough just to be born here.*

It was why Brenna was taking Spanish now, because it wasn't enough to be born Chicana, either. Or to spend her childhood in Houston, where the language filled restaurants and school cafeterias. Or to hear Spanish on the phone and at holidays with her mother's family. Her tongue—no matter how much she willed it— couldn't shape the words as nimbly as her cousins'. Unfortunately, spending an hour a day reciting vocabulary she already knew with a well-meaning white lady and a bunch of white kids wasn't helping much.

Brenna pulled her phone out of her bag and rested it between her thighs. She opened a browser and typed *Mercer tornado car news*. The most recent article said that police had finally tracked down the owner of the white car: a recently dead guy named Edward Milton in Indiana. The man's daughter, the executor of his estate, hadn't noticed it was missing or stolen yet, which might explain why no driver had come forward. But if the white car was stolen, what did that mean for the VW? Two thieves?

"Brenna, tus ojos," Mrs. Berk said sharply, and Brenna shoved the phone under her ass.

A group of girls snickered. They all wore their boyfriends' letterman's jackets, black leggings, and boots that looked like paper bags. Brenna didn't begrudge them their unaffordable bag-boots. She just wondered if the girls cared that they were identical, that there was nothing except subtle shades of blondness to differentiate them. Not that Brenna's friends were much better. They made such an effort to stand out with hair color and piercings and band T-shirts that they all ended up looking the same too.

High school was about belonging, Brenna knew. A belonging that—even if she pretended she had in her friend group, or didn't want at all—was always beyond reach. She was one of just five students of color in the entire school. Three they called brown and two they called black. In Houston, when they'd lived with her father, most of her classmates identified as Native American or Hispanic or Latinx or Mexican or Salvadoran, and, even though she was half white and spoke clumsy Spanish, her skin had made her belonging visible—as visible as the black clothes, hair dye, and makeup she now wore.

"This will be worth ten percent of your grade, but you can work with partners," Mrs. Berk said in English. Heads in the room swiveled. Stage whispers. Bag-boot girls clung to the hoods of the bag-booter in front of them, like monkeys holding tails. There was an odd number of them, and the one seated across the aisle from Brenna looked around desperately, bleating like she was about to be eaten by a lion.

Brenna sank lower in her seat and picked at her cuticles. She didn't have any friends in the class.

"Does anyone else need a partner?" Mrs. Berk asked.

Brenna sighed and raised her hand. The lone booted girl moaned.

"Jane and Brenna it is," said their teacher.

Brenna tried to fortify herself for the eye-rolling, the behind-the-hand whispering.

"I'll give you the last ten minutes to work in class," Mrs. Berk said.

Partners shuffled their desks so they could face each other. Jane didn't move. She jabbed her pencil over and over at the top of her paper.

"Experimenting with pointillism?" Brenna asked.

"What?" Jane spat the *t*.

Brenna sighed and spun her desk so she was facing Jane's profile. The girl had round cheeks, pink-flushed and marbled like the cuts of meat Brenna's mother could never afford. The corner of Jane's glossy lip lifted like that of a threatened poodle.

"So what should we do?" Brenna asked.

Jane shoved her hands into her jacket pockets. "Whatever. I'll end up doing it by myself anyway."

Brenna cocked her head to the side. "Why?"

"It's not, like, a secret that you don't do work."

"I do work." She paused. "I just choose to do it differently."

"Okay. Whatever." Jane cough-laughed.

People were quick to assume that Brenna didn't care about school because she didn't always play by the rules—especially in her English classes. But it wasn't because she wasn't smart. She was a voracious reader, and being assigned a book she'd already read just meant she could enjoy something new instead. She'd picked up this habit from Colin, who'd argued that he shouldn't have to do homework if he could prove he knew how to read and write and think. Once, last spring, when Mr. Scott asked for an essay on *1984*, Brenna wrote about *Crime and Punishment* instead, just to show she could. She'd told Colin what she'd done and he'd clapped her on the shoulder, praising her like she was his pet, but Mr. Scott had given her an F. Colin had never received an F in his life.

Still, she'd approached Spanish class similarly this semester. Why would she write and perform a skit in Spanish about shopping at a mall, as they were being asked to do today, when she could try to read and translate a short story by Jorge Luis Borges?

"Look." Brenna sighed. "I'll be a good partner if you will. Why don't we meet up after school? I usually go to the Taco Bell for a snack."

"Of course you do." Jane pressed her lips together, barely containing a smile.

Brenna got the insult, of course. She was Mexican, so, tacos.

Never mind that Taco Bell wasn't even remotely similar to the food her mother's family cooked. Never mind that it was one of only six restaurant choices in Mercer, and certainly the cheapest. If Brenna responded to insults like this, people said she was overreacting—even her friends. Amy, Dutch, and Jade acted color-blind, like Brenna was exactly the same as them. They didn't really hear her, didn't really understand why she was hurt when people said things like that to her. *No, but where are you* from *from? I bet your mom is really young, right? Gross—you've eaten cow intestine? There's that fiery temper.* So Brenna had just stopped telling her friends what people said, stopped talking about her family, stopped mentioning her brownness. That, too, was part of perfecting her hard shell, part of belonging.

Truthfully, Brenna didn't want to pretend that the words didn't sting. She wanted to tip over Jane's desk. Wanted to watch her blond ponytail rainbow through the air. Wanted to hear the crack of her elbow against the linoleum.

So she stood, pulled on her backpack, and walked to the door.

"Where are you going, Ms. Ortiz?" Mrs. Berk asked.

"To the office. I feel sick." If she stayed in the room with Jane any longer, she'd end up there anyway.

9

Joshua had woken up earlier than usual—more excited for school than he'd been in years. The night before, he'd locked pinkies with Brenna like they were childhood friends, and sworn to secrecy. He'd sensed how important it was for her to believe the VW was something more than coincidence, though he was pretty certain it was all a moot point. Someone else would spot the van in daylight and report it, regardless of their promise not to say anything. Still, he'd been thrilled to share that moment with Brenna. Secrets were rare in a small town like Mercer and even rarer for someone as invisible as him. He imagined invites to sit with Brenna and her powder-faced friends at lunch and to cluster around the drinking fountain every passing period. He wasn't going to dye his hair like them, but he could paint his nails black and wear red shiny combat boots to end his invisibility. Lawrence would love that.

Before the first bell rang, the masses rushed by as usual,

clipping his elbow with their books or bumping him into the lockers. No apologies. No acknowledgment—like he was one of Mercer's ghosts. A few freshmen were talking about the tornado. One mocking his father for insisting their whole family huddle in the bathtub with a mattress over them because their relatives had been unlucky. Another claiming that God or something was sending them all a message, it being the anniversary and all. Joshua rolled his eyes at that.

As he headed for a desk at the back of Mrs. Crawley's classroom, Callie's eyes followed him. Had she seen him the night before? Did she want to tell him something? But before he could stop to ask her, Mrs. Crawley started class.

While his teacher demonstrated problems on the board, Joshua thought of the white car and the VW. His grandfather would've been devastated to see classics like that damaged. He'd always thought Joshua should draw beautiful cars—anything, really, other than *men in spandex*—but Joshua thought cars were too simple. There was no challenge. No conveying a car's tortured childhood with just facial creases and expressive eyes. No sculpting of muscles and scars with light crosshatches. But the white car from the night before somehow had an expression—in the folds of the hood, in the smashed glass. There was backstory there and maybe anguish and bravery, too.

Mrs. Crawley returned his quiz with a large red *A+* and *Excellent!* scrawled across the front. Besides drawing, math was the one thing he was good at. They'd even had him walk across the field to the high school when he was an eighth grader so he could take Algebra II. Those short, daily glimpses of high school had given him the false hope that coming out would change everything.

High schoolers brought coffee from Bean City wrapped in paper sleeves. They grew facial hair and wore makeup. They'd seemed much more sophisticated than his middle-school peers, and, while he didn't talk to them much, Joshua had assumed they were open-minded. Until the end of his eighth-grade year, he hadn't considered the fact that everyone in his middle school would advance with him; there wasn't some magic spell that turned them all into tolerant intellectuals as soon as they stepped into the high school hallways.

Joshua had decided he'd come out at school the first day of freshman year. What better time for fresh starts? That summer, he'd imagined it, the open-minded upperclassmen welcoming him: the theater kids speckled in dry paint and the band kids with their instrument cases tucked beneath their desks. Those would be his people, he suspected. In preparation, Joshua watched It Gets Better videos, teary-eyed, rehearsing the language of coming out. He played with different scenarios: just being out. No denying when assholes suggested it, but no proclamations, either. Or maybe he needed proclamations, if he was ever going to start groups and bond with other gay kids. Maybe he needed a T-shirt so he could wear his outness everywhere. Or maybe he just needed to stand up on a cafeteria table, clear his throat, and announce it. The hero. In his new, magic high school, you could do things like that.

He still hadn't decided how he'd come out by the first day, but he thought he might recognize the moment when it appeared, that there'd be a call to action, a sign.

At lunchtime that first day, he stood in line for a corn dog when he heard someone mutter: "There won't be any food left after this fat fag." Joshua spun around and saw that the voice belonged to Clayton, a fellow freshman, with greasy brown hair and a scar above his lip from a fight in seventh grade.

In middle school, Joshua would've ignored it. But not that day; it was his call to action. He would expose Clayton as the bully he was *and* come out to the school.

"What did you say?" Joshua asked loudly. "I don't think everyone heard you."

A group of upperclassmen walking by stopped and snickered. "Fight," one of them said softly, like it was a question.

Clayton, though, wasn't embarrassed by his audience. "Oh no. Did I offend the little gay boy?"

Joshua inhaled. He felt it, filling his chest and expanding there, like pride, like courage, like all the voices in the videos he'd watched. This was his moment.

"I prefer the term *queer*, actually. Or you can use the adjective *gay* as in, *He is gay*."

Clayton covered his nose and mouth with his hand. He began to laugh, but his eyes were scanning the others in line, threatening them. Joshua could almost see their scared rabbit hearts beating, each thump a warning that they should toss their heads back and laugh too: *That kid just said he's gay*. They were dominos, laughing along, falling, for their own safety.

Still, Joshua was sure that when he stepped out of line and into the cafeteria to share his announcement with everyone, he'd find his place, his people. He hadn't expected it to be easy. He'd even braced himself for physical violence, and he felt grateful—and disgusted by his gratitude—that they were only laughing.

So he filled his tray, swiped his card, and marched past the lunch lady. But somehow the news had preceded him, and Joshua felt it there, churning in the large room like a storm. His skin grew hot. The laughter and whispers roared between his temples, reverberating. He saw starbursts of light, and his hands felt as though they'd been asleep, all pins and needles. Then the tiles met him with a hard slap.

All he remembered after was a teacher's face, furrowing in concern. A coach helping him sit, then stand, then walk. A cot with a pillow that felt like plastic. A glass of orange juice and a cookie. A nurse's voice on the phone with his mom. *Hunger, probably*, she'd said, and Joshua had thought that that couldn't be truer.

The next day he pretended to be sick so his mother would let him stay home. He watched old cartoons and berated himself for his weakness. Only tightly corseted women in the 1800s fainted. Not heroes.

The day after that, he was so nervous that he threw up his breakfast on the way to the bus stop. But at school, no one laughed or stared at him again. He was so relieved, it took him another week to realize that he was being actively ignored by the entire school, like someone had made an announcement over the PA while he was gone. He'd always been an outsider, but there'd been kindnesses, too—shared pens, polite smiles, and small talk. After the fainting incident, though, even his sympathizers were too afraid of being subjected to the same bullying and subsequent invisibility. That was when Joshua started a countdown to graduation and moving out of Mercer.

Callie's name over the intercom interrupted his thoughts. He wondered if it had to do with the car the night before. Would he be called too? Did the cops want to talk to people who'd been on the scene? But then Mrs. Crawley stopped writing on the whiteboard, and everyone in the room looked at Callie.

Of course: her mother.

WE ARE WOVEN TOGETHER

We are woven together—the fifty-four who died that night, the rest who came before and after. Our memories braided into a tapestry. Threads of turquoise, mauve, ochre, periwinkle, eggshell. What's mine is ours. Is us.

We speak together—as though we have always been thus. We do not remember what it means to be an individual, to be our own. And yet, we yearn for it. We want nothing more than to be each and every one of our selves. To speak as only the I, the me. To tell our own stories. To unwind our threads. To unbreak our hearts.

But this, we know, must come at a price.

10

Before her name was called, Callie's mind was far from pre-calculus. She had tucked her phone into her lap and opened news stories, taking notes on the back of her returned quiz.

Known

- *Tornado touched down approximately 8:15 p.m., Wed., Oct. 7*
- *Anniversary of 1961 tornado*
- *Tornado path about 400 meters*
- *1959 Pontiac Catalina, white*
- *Wind turbine blade damaged*
- *Police detected no evidence of person inside car*

Unknown

- *Footprints in bean field?*
- *Car occupied at time of tornado?*
- *Face spotted during lightning flash?*
- *Same path as 1961 tornado?*
- *Whispers?*

Her name over the classroom intercom stopped her pencil. It stopped her heart, too, momentarily, and she was flooded with nausea. She was sure everyone was looking at her, but her vision narrowed, and everything became blurry. Only the door was in focus. And beyond that, she knew: the office, the phone, her dad's voice. Something had happened with her mother. Maybe it was time. Or maybe the time had already come, and she'd missed it.

When Callie arrived, the girl with the red boots and dyed hair was sitting in the office vestibule, a thermometer in her mouth. Her eyes widened at Callie, but then she waved with a flick of her wrist.

Callie swallowed. She tried to say something, maybe about the loaned sweatshirt she'd forgotten at home, but she couldn't find any words. The receptionist called her name and held out a phone.

"Dad?" Callie said, her voice a croak.

"It's Toni," her aunt said. "Your dad is at the hospital with your mom. I'm on my way to get you, okay?"

Callie nodded, numb.

"Cal?"

"Yeah. Okay. Is it—" Callie stopped herself. She felt the girl's eyes on her and couldn't speak it aloud.

Her aunt Toni understood. "No, no, hon. The chemo has just done a number on her kidneys."

Callie handed the phone back to the receptionist without saying goodbye.

"I'll write you a pass so you can collect your things," the woman at the desk said, pity unmistakable in her downturned mouth and softened eyes. "Or I can have an office aide go get them for you if that would be easier."

It was hard to care about her backpack. Someone would probably get it to her later. Her cell phone was the only thing of value, and it was in her pocket. Callie shook her head and sat down.

"Do you need anything, hon?" the woman asked. "I could get you some juice or a carton of milk or something."

"No, thanks," Callie said. So many adults called her *hon* now, like her own name wasn't gentle enough, like she needed something sweeter to protect her from what was happening.

The girl with the boots reached across a table stacked with magazines and squeezed the wooden armrest of Callie's chair. "You okay?" she asked, pushing the thermometer aside. Callie stared at the girl's knuckles. She wanted to respond, to be polite, but if she opened her mouth, she knew she'd let the tears out.

11

Every Thursday during second-period study hall, Joshua went to the school counselor. The meetings were the vice principal's suggestion, a result of the fainting incident. Secretly, he called Thursdays *gay day*, because someone, at least, was talking to him about it—even though she was being paid to do so. The counselor was a self-important, comically sincere woman. Big-bodied like him with blond bangs curled like it was the eighties. Her plump lips were always trembling because she'd brought herself to tears with some story about her own past. Still, she was a human talking to him at school.

Joshua spotted Callie and Brenna through the office's glass window. Callie's face looked paler than it had in pre-calc. Brenna had a thermometer in her mouth, but was bright-eyed and healthy-looking.

Joshua rapped on the glass outside the entrance.

"Hey," said Brenna, the thermometer turning the word to marbles.

Callie's eyes were glassy and distant.

"Is everything okay?" Joshua asked, pausing in the doorway.

Brenna took the thermometer out. "I was just getting out of class," she said. They both looked at Callie.

She brought her balled-up hands right in front of her face like she was trying to keep something from coming out of her mouth. Her eyes slipped from Joshua's forehead to his feet. It didn't seem like she was ignoring him so much as she was trying to disappear, trying to be as unobtrusive and unnoticed as possible. Joshua had spent so many years wishing his body would go unnoticed. When it finally did, it wasn't a relief; it was a new and different grief. Callie's disappearance wouldn't alleviate the devastation of losing a parent. That, Joshua knew.

"My father died when I was three," he said. "I know that 'I'm sorry' doesn't feel like enough. Or that you've heard it so much, it's probably just empty words at this point, so I won't say it, but please know that I am."

Callie's eyes locked on him then, and, for the second time in twenty-four hours, Joshua felt seen.

"Adults act like I'm going to break," she said, and Joshua wasn't surprised. Each word quivered from her lips, sounding like it might shatter on the linoleum between them. "Most people our age just pretend I don't exist anymore."

"People pretend I don't exist too, but probably for a different reason," Joshua said.

"People are trash," said Brenna.

The corners of Callie's mouth lifted into a small smile.

"I know this isn't the same thing," Brenna said, "but when my parents split up, I didn't want to talk or even think about it. So we can talk about something else if you want."

"We were all at the tornado last night," Joshua said. "That shit's crazy, right?"

"Yeah." Callie uncurled her fists and looked at her palms like she was just remembering they were there. "Did you guys see anything strange?" she asked. "Anything that—didn't make sense?"

Could they tell her about the VW? Joshua looked at Brenna and tilted his head toward Callie. She nodded, sympathy plain on her face. They'd just met the night before, but they seemed to be on the same wavelength. Something Joshua hadn't experienced with anyone but Ruthie.

"After we left last night, we found another car—an old VW bus," Joshua said. "It looked like it had taken a beating too."

Callie's eyes widened. "Was there a driver?"

"Not that we saw. Why? What did you see?" Joshua asked.

But before Callie could answer, a dark-haired woman rushed into the office, smelling of fry grease and dish soap. She was visibly Callie's relative: curveless, compact build and a small, upturned nose. Her hair, though, glittered with silver and she had dimples. At the sight of her, Callie stood like a robot, allowing herself to be hugged.

"It's going to be okay. She's fine," the woman murmured as she signed Callie out of school. Callie turned back to them, her cheeks flushed. The words came out in a rush: "I saw a person in the Pontiac during the storm, and then I found footprints leading into the cornfield. I think there was someone out there—or maybe it was a few people. I heard whispering, 'Find them. Save them.'"

Before Joshua could say anything, the relative took Callie's arm. Callie looked back over her shoulder pleadingly, like she needed Joshua and Brenna to figure it out.

The whispers could have been the wind, he thought, but combined with the abandoned cars, and another tornado on October 7, it was all just too weird. Joshua vowed to find out what was going on.

TIME ISN'T SOMETHING

Time isn't something we keep, and yet it's all we have. Dates fold on top of one another like pleats in a paper fan. Today it is December 9, 2018; it is May 12, 1954; it is November 6, 1860; it is August 30, 1903; it is October 7, 1961. It is always October 7, 1961.

It is our curse, our purgatory, our blessing to spend this time watching the living. The young, the still-spinning, their lives unfolding where ours stopped. Teenagers with pitted faces, concave chests, coltish limbs, and smiles that could clear skies. We are drawn to some more than others. Those who speak to us. Those who dream us. Those who need us.

12

Callie's aunt's car smelled overwhelmingly of French fries. Toni owned a burger joint across the river and had brought lunch for Callie.

"I figured you'd be hungry," she said, nudging the greasy bag Callie's way.

Callie shook her head. Her aunt frowned but didn't say anything. She wasn't as aware as Callie's dad was that she'd been skipping meals.

Toni looked a lot like her mom had before cancer. They both had round faces, dimples, and straight brown hair. But Toni was older and her hair was lit with tiny gray threads. Callie wondered what color her mother's hair would be if it ever grew back in. She'd read that sometimes, after chemo, blond hair grew in black, or straight hair came back curly or soft hair became wiry. She tried to remember how her mother's hair had felt when she'd clipped barrettes in it as a kid. This was something else—like her mother's scent—that she'd never know again.

Callie pushed the thought away and tried to listen to her aunt talk about acute kidney failure, how it had happened in less than twelve hours. It was amazing how quickly the body could short out. She'd seen videos of long-distance runners who were dehydrated. Their legs—so trained and toned—became like rubber, bending and wobbling. Their faces went slack as they veered off course and then collapsed. Callie had never run that hard. Her body had never said, *This is all I can do.* Her mind had never let go. Even her emptying was active, controlled.

Callie envied those seconds of giving in to the body, that sure silence and peace as a runner fell.

At the hospital, Callie slumped beside Toni in the waiting room. There were always the outdated magazines. TVs tuned to courtroom dramas and news stations. The smell of burnt coffee. At first she'd hated them, but now she preferred them to the alternative: the room where her mother was connected to machines, where Callie couldn't escape the talk of cancer and death.

When her father came to get them, she studied his face for new information, but it was frozen: square, thin-lipped, creases between his gold eyebrows. He squeezed Callie's shoulder before beckoning them down a hallway to her mother's room.

Inside, her mother was attempting to tie on her green scarf, but her hands were shaking. Toni hurried over, took the ends, and made an efficient knot. Wet-eyed, her mother reached out for Callie, who tried to freeze her own face so she wouldn't look sick, revolted. Her mother's fingertips were ice-cold. There was a new machine, sitting to the left of the bed. It had a screen, what looked like wheels of blood, and tubes leading to her mom's left arm.

"I'm sorry you had to miss school for this."

Callie shrugged. "It's no big deal."

"School is important." Her mother's voice was thin, but shrill. This was a lesson.

"I know. You're right. School is important."

"I can go home after the dialysis, but Dr. Kennedy is stopping by this afternoon."

Callie nodded. She'd only met the oncologist once, a grandfatherly man with an easy grin. Not what she'd expected from a person who'd told her parents that chemo was only going to buy them time.

"Would you guys mind if I have a minute alone with Callie?" her mother asked. Toni nodded knowingly, and her father said something about needing a pop. Callie watched them leave, hoping desperately that they'd turn around and decide it wasn't a good idea, that she wasn't old enough to be left alone with a dying mother.

Her mother patted the bed, and Callie sat at the very edge, not wanting to find out if the rest of her mom's body was as cold as her hands.

"I wanted to talk to you about what this means, Callie," she said softly.

Callie looked at the walls, white with slate-blue trim.

"My kidneys can't handle this chemo anymore, and Dr. Kennedy might want to try a different treatment to keep me alive a bit longer. But your dad and I are going to talk to him about stopping. I just want to feel a little better for a few days."

Callie's mom looked at the ceiling, and tears welled along her bottom lids. She patted her wrist, but someone had removed her watch Kleenex and she had to use her fingers to swipe away the tears. "I just want to feel a little better." It sounded like a plea to someone. Callie wondered if her mother was talking to God. Her mother's belief in God was as firm as her belief in the Storm Spirits. She'd sent Callie to the Catholic elementary school in town and expected her to attend youth group throughout middle and high school so that Callie would remain connected to her religious upbringing. But Callie had quit going. If there were a

God, he wouldn't be killing her mother. Of that, she was certain.

"So you'll go back on the chemo after a little while?" Callie asked.

Her mother exhaled slowly. "I don't think so," she said, her voice choked.

"But you won't stay alive without it," Callie said.

"Sweetie, I won't stay alive with it either."

Callie felt a cavern open up inside, like her blood was echoing against stone walls. They'd talked about this before—or, rather, her mother had talked and Callie had half listened. At some point, her mom had said, they'd decide to stop treatment. At some point, enough would be enough. *At some point*, but not today.

"You know I want to spend as much time with you and your father as I can, right? I don't want you to think I'm giving up on you—" Her mother let the tears fall. "But I just—" She was inhaling raggedly, trying to catch her breath.

Callie wanted her to stop talking, wanted everyone to just stop talking. She wished she could be a little kid again, clapping her hands over her ears and humming at the top of her lungs when her mother told her to go to her room.

"I don't want you to be mad when I'm gone, because I made this decision—"

Callie shook her head, like she was trying to get water out of her ears. *Then don't do it*, she wanted to say. *Keep fighting.* Instead: "Mom, stop. Please. I won't be."

Her mother swallowed, wiped her eyes again, and took a deep breath. "Do you have any questions? About what it will be like when I'm off the chemo?"

Callie couldn't think of any, except *How long?* And there was no way she could ever let her tongue say those words.

"It doesn't have to be about cancer, either," her mother said. "We can just talk. About boys or youth group or cross-country or whatever."

Callie knew her mother wouldn't let up until they talked. She searched for something to say that wasn't about cancer, but all she could think of were the whispers she'd heard and what Joshua and Brenna had said about finding another car. She wished they'd had a chance to finish their conversation. Her mother, the devoted Mercerite, might have insight, but she also might freak out that Callie and her dad had been in so much danger.

"Have you seen the news today?" Callie asked. "About the tornado last night?"

Her mom raised her bare brows and shook her head. "A tornado? Was anyone hurt?"

"No."

Her mother patted the bed again, beckoning Callie to lie down. "Wasn't it the seventh yesterday?"

Reluctantly, Callie lay down shoulder to shoulder with her mother. "Yeah, and it touched down near the old drive-in."

"That's unbelievable! Why didn't you guys wake me up and go to the basement?"

"Dad and I weren't home," Callie said quietly. "I was practicing."

"You were driving in it?" Her mother touched her chest—like she was checking for her heartbeat. Callie knew it was building inside her—the energy for a lecture and the fear of leaving her daughter, who clearly had so many lessons left to learn.

"We were totally fine, Mom. But maybe you can tell me the story of the whispers."

Her mother's hand fell to her side, relieved by the change in subject. "You already know this one, don't you?"

"Yes, but tell me again. Please."

Callie's mom reached over and pushed Callie's bangs off her forehead. Callie felt an ache settle into the back of her throat, a heavy knot that she couldn't swallow away.

"My friends and I went to the field one anniversary to do a séance. I was always wanting to talk to my aunt, to see how alike she and my mom were. Anyway, it started to rain, and our candles went out. We took shelter in the car, and I thought I heard voices whispering around us, but no one else heard them."

"What'd they say?" This, too, was part of the script.

"It sounded like, 'Tell them we're okay,' but it was a hundred voices talking at once, so it was hard to understand."

"Why do you think you're the only one who heard?"

"I don't know. Maybe those girls weren't there for the right reasons. They just wanted a scare. And I wanted to listen. It was when your grandparents were going through their divorce, you know. My mom was always grieving her sister, my dad was tired of fighting, and I was looking everywhere for answers."

Callie shivered at this. Was she looking for answers too? "Did you find them?"

Her mother looked at her with pity. "No, honey. But I realize now, it gave me some comfort. The idea that the departed are out there watching over us and whispering makes me think that, when I'm gone, I can still—you will still—" She blinked rapidly, tears rolling off her cheekbones onto the pillow.

"I know, Mom," Callie said softly. And, in spite of everything, she, too, allowed herself a brief flare of hope.

13

On the bus, Joshua took out his sketchpad and flipped to the white tornado car he'd drawn at lunch. It looked bare—without the expression he'd envisioned in Mrs. Crawley's class. It needed something, someone. He thought about what Callie had said, and drew the outline of a person in the driver's seat with the lightest strokes. He left the face blank.

The bus stopped to pick up the middle schoolers down the street from the high school, and Ruthie climbed on. She smiled at Joshua wryly before sitting beside a neighbor girl. They turned onto Orange Street, passing an old man who always sat on the steps, smoking a cigar, his shoulders hunched to his ears. To Joshua, he never seemed to age and yet had always been ancient. When Joshua and Ruthie were little, they'd waved madly out the bus windows, seeing who could get him to wave back. Neither of them won.

Just as Joshua returned to his sketch, the brown plastic seat back slammed into Joshua's spine—someone's knee on the other side—causing his pencil to dig into the page. He leaned against the window, trying to hold his body away from the seat. He'd taken the bus since he was in kindergarten; knee jabs weren't new, especially in Mercer's old buses where the plastic had softened or torn away to reveal the fabric beneath.

The next jab caught him as he erased the errant mark. He closed his sketchpad, took out his phone, and scooted as far forward as his knees would allow, his forehead on the seat in front of him, his stomach folded uncomfortably against his thighs.

On the *Mercer Journal's* home page, there was an image of the crashed car, the first he'd seen taken in daylight. The car's rims and tire sidewalls were white, the bumper chrome. It had sleek fins and round, shattered taillights. The dimpled roof sloped upward, so the cabin was harp-shaped. An angel car.

The caption said it was a 1959 Pontiac Catalina, allegedly stolen from the estate of the deceased Edward Milton II, of Richwood, Indiana. There was no mention of the VW bus anywhere.

Joshua typed *Edward Milton II* and *obituary* into the search bar.

Edward Milton II, 71, passed away on September 16, 2017, surrounded by family.

Milton was born on June 10, 1944, in Mercer, Illinois. He graduated from Mercer High School in 1962, worked as a firefighter, and proudly served during the Vietnam War. He moved to Richwood after inheriting his in-laws' farm. Milton was a collector of antique cars and motorcycles. He also loved baseball.

He is survived by his daughter, Monica Regent; his grandkids, Katie, Henry, and Alexis Regent; and his dog, Charlie. He was preceded in death by his wife, Carolyn.

Visitation will be from noon until the time of the service at 2:00 p.m. on September 19, 2017, at St. Benedict's Chapel. Burial will follow at Claibourne Cemetery.

Joshua drummed his finger on his knee. One of the man's cars ended up near another antique car in Mercer, his hometown, after his death. He'd heard kids gossiping about the owner being dead in Indiana, but no one had mentioned that he'd grown up here. That fact was too neat, too coincidental.

Another jab to the seat disrupted Joshua's thinking. Then two more pops in quick succession.

Enough.

Joshua stood and looked over the seat back. Tyler, Joshua's only friend in elementary school, was on the other side, a shock of dark hair sticking up from his scalp as though he'd rolled out of bed without combing it. Back when Joshua lived on the farm, they'd pretended to be Pokémon trainers in the hayloft and sorted their cards for hours under the willow.

As he got older, Tyler became lanky and lethargic, like growing his limbs took all his energy. By middle school, he'd lost interest in everything Joshua liked, including their friendship, but he'd never been particularly mean to Joshua, too nerdy to be the bullying type.

"Oh, hey, Ty. I didn't see you," Joshua said—not that seeing Tyler would've changed *his* behavior much. "Can you maybe stop doing that to the seat?" Joshua tried to sound like it was no big deal either way.

Tyler looked at the back of the seat, a few inches below Joshua's face. Joshua sank back down.

Another knee, this one dug into the seat and held, the mound of brown plastic in Joshua's spine.

"Dude, stop," Joshua said, standing again.

Tyler looked out the window as though he hadn't heard, as though Joshua were a ghost.

Joshua grabbed his bag and made his way toward the middle schoolers at the front.

"In your seat!" the bus driver yelled. Ruthie glanced at him. He rolled his eyes to signify that it was something trivial, like a fart, that had driven him forward, and she returned to her friends.

Joshua sat down next to a small middle schooler with cartoonishly large ears. He wondered if she was persecuted for them, like he'd been for his red hair and glasses and the rolls above his hips. He wanted to form a bond with this girl who was less than half his size, to tell her that superheroes were often persecuted at a young age, but even she sensed the pariah he was and scooted closer to the window, avoiding him.

Joshua felt exhausted, like he'd been trying to keep his skin as a barrier, trying to patch it and hold it up, but it was beginning to disintegrate and soon there would be nothing left to keep things in. Or out. Soon he'd really disappear.

14

Brenna went to the Taco Bell. Not that she expected Jane to show up. It was just her habit since school started, splitting cinnamon twists with her friends and leaning against cars in the parking lot. Amy was in detention, and Brenna couldn't afford to waste money, so she sat at the picnic table outside, not eating, and picked at the brown rubbery material coating the metal. She pulled out a Faulkner paperback that had been in her bag for months and smoothed the cover. Maybe she could write an essay about it in Spanish—that would be an actual challenge. Screw Mrs. Berk. And screw Jane.

She'd do her own project.

According to the receipt tucked between the pages, the book was long overdue. She had probably checked it out with Colin at the end of last school year. In fact, everything in Brenna's bag was there because of Colin. The menthol cigarettes. The emo lyrics copied on crumpled napkins. The papers marked with big Fs that reeked of his influence. Before Colin, what had she carried? She remembered the weight of one book—a fat tome called *Blonde*, a fictionalized story about Marilyn Monroe. She'd read that people ascribed all these personas to Marilyn. She was an innocent angel, a tease, a whore. No one gave her the opportunity to define herself.

The first time Colin had spoken to Brenna, it was a Friday, and she was sitting against the lockers beside Amy, that book in her lap. When Colin spotted her, there was a quick movement around his mouth and eyes, like he'd caught a smile just before it spread across his face. She'd noticed him plenty before. He was tall and slim with tight jeans and a red flannel shirt just like hers. His hair was curly, uncombed beneath a gray beanie.

"You're Manny's sister?"

"Yeah. Brenna."

He tilted his head, considering this, and looked at the book in her lap. "Such a tragedy," he said.

"I'm Amy," her friend chimed in, though Colin never even glanced in her direction.

"You're much prettier than Manny," Colin said to Brenna. "And I can tell you're smarter, too."

Brenna laughed. "It doesn't take much."

The lines along his mouth moved quickly again, and Brenna was afraid that if she blinked, she'd miss his smile.

"I think you and I have a lot in common," he said. "I'll text you." He walked away without asking for her number. Brenna's skin tingled, as though he'd traced her collarbone with his tongue, but she laughed the feeling off and rolled her eyes at Amy.

The next day, Colin's text woke her near dawn. He was outside her house with a carton of orange juice and two cans of PBR: *a hipster's mimosa*. He smiled when he said this, and it wasn't just the quick movement of muscles near his mouth, but a wide, sprawling thing, goofier than Brenna had expected, almost sheepish. They talked for hours that morning.

She learned that Colin had moved to Mercer when his father, an engineer in the Quad Cities, decided he wanted to build a house in the country. But beyond being transplants, she and Colin didn't have much else in common. They had different skin colors in a town where you could count the families of color on one hand. He wore ripped jeans with ratty T-shirts and flannels intentionally—not because he had to. Not only that, but he read Malcolm Lowry and Hunter S. Thompson and Chuck Palahniuk—authors who were *great thinkers* and wrote about the world—not just *relationships and domestic things* like the authors Brenna favored. Colin spoke confidently about Islamic extremism and housing bubbles. He'd been to Europe and on college tours.

When Brenna talked about fights with her family or feeling misunderstood by teachers, he nodded. "What I hear you saying is . . ." he'd start, supplying an interpretation for her, *of* her. And while Brenna wasn't entirely sure that was what she'd been saying, she'd trusted Colin's vision of her. Soon she realized it wasn't necessarily a vision of who she was, but of who she could be. It was a Brenna who could go to college on the East Coast, who could make something of herself—more than her grandmother and family, more than her town, expected of her.

But what had Colin seen, exactly? An eager underclassman? A project? A way to piss off his parents? Brenna never knew. That was part of the power he had over her—an interest in her that seemed unfounded, that made her feel lucky. And all along, she'd had the sense that if she didn't transform far or fast enough, he'd see through his own invention. It had taken a year, but she'd been right, and that fact made Brenna want to claw away her skin.

An hour later, when Brenna was certain that Jane had stood her up, she left Taco Bell and stopped at the cemetery on her way home to pull weeds around My Sky's stone. Gretta, who'd lost one arm to her Ford pickup during the drive-in tornado, sat on a bench. She worked for Mercer's landscaping company now, and was always in muddy overalls, galoshes, and coats with her left sleeve pinned to the elbow. She had wild, crimped gray hair and eyes sunken deep in skin the color and texture of a baseball glove. Her stump was as tan as her face, the scar tissue twisted like a balloon tie. She was famous for saying that her arm was already a ghost, that she could feel it on the other side, tugging at her. It was a rite of passage in town to ask Gretta to buy you a pack of smokes, the only price being one cigarette and listening to her story. Most were too spooked to talk to Gretta more than once, but Brenna was one of her regulars.

"Taking a break?" Brenna asked.

"Always," she said, chuckling. "Who ya visiting, girlie?"

"My Sky." Brenna pointed at the pink stone.

Gretta nodded and pulled a crushed box of clove cigarettes out of her denim pocket. She offered one to Brenna, who took it and leaned close so that Gretta could light it for her. The ritual made Brenna feel crumpled inside. Colin would always light her cigarettes, the scar on his thumb like a pink thread she wanted to wind around her tongue. While he smoked, he'd flick his lighter open and closed and go on about affordable health care and marriage equality and marijuana legalization.

"Did you know Celeste well?" Brenna asked.

Gretta took a drag, shaking her head. "I didn't even know her name until she died. That's when I figured I better get to know 'em all. Since I'll be with 'em whenever my arm wins its tug-of-war."

"You believe they're really out there and interested in us?"

"Don't you?"

"Yeah, but I just don't get it. Why would they want to watch us?"

"If you were taken too soon, wouldn't you want to watch what you'd left behind? The life you could have lived?"

"I guess."

Gretta pushed her frizzy hair away from her face and blew smoke. "I hear them whispering more than most do, you know. I guess because I should be one of them." She lifted her arm as evidence. "They're always going on about wanting to come back and how it wasn't their time yet. You know, all sorts of unresolved shit."

This was Brenna's opportunity to ask about what Callie had heard. "This girl said they were saying, 'Find them. Save them,' last night. What do you think that means?"

Gretta *hmmm*ed with her cigarette in the corner of her mouth. "Couldn't say, but it's gotta be important. It's the first tornado to touch down since 1961, and on the same date and practically in the same damn place. That's enough to make you think something's going on."

It gave Brenna the chills to hear someone else mirror her own thoughts so closely. Someone with a connection to the tornado of 1961, no less.

"And that white car on the news," Gretta continued. "I've definitely seen it before."

"Really? Where?" Brenna asked, wondering about the VW as well.

Gretta twisted her hair and tucked it behind her ear. "High school. Maybe a parade or something."

"You don't think maybe it was just a popular model?"

Gretta paused for a minute. "You're probably right." Then she leaned forward onto her knees. "But we both know it's all too coincidental."

Again, Brenna felt herself shiver.

"And that"—Gretta pointed her cigarette at Brenna—"is why we're here now. Waiting for 'em to tell us something."

Yes, Brenna realized, that was exactly what she was doing.

WE THINK STORMS ARE BEAUTIFUL

We think storms are beautiful now. The pink hints of them in sunsets. The build of them—stone gray and solemn. Then the wild bloom. The greens and purples and yellows and blacks. The crashes, the bluster, the singing wind. But that's not the only reason they are beautiful.

When it storms, our voices grow louder. Or maybe it's just that the living are more likely to be listening. Usually, it's the very old—those who long for us or who are close to joining us—who tilt their heads to the sky.

We shout then, wanting only to get our messages through, one last *I'm sorry for . . .* or *I wish I'd . . .* To our sisters and brothers, to our friends, to our parents and children—those we've left behind—we say, *Remember us.* We say, *See us.*

15

When they left the hospital, Callie asked Aunt Toni to drop her at home instead of cross-country practice; she wanted to be alone. Dr. Kennedy was probably with her parents now. She imagined what they were saying: that her mother was ready, that everything was as *in order* as it was going to be, that they wanted some time together chemo-free. It hardly mattered that no one had asked Callie what it was she wanted.

She walked the rooms of her house, which, though often silent, always felt alive. Her mother said it was because all the people passing through, back when it was an inn, had left a tiny bit of themselves behind.

Callie heard a knocking sound above her. *Squirrels*, she told herself again, but she knelt on the warm wood floor and closed her eyes, sending her thoughts to the squirrels, to the house, to the ghosts and the god she'd vowed not to believe in: *Can you give my mother back? Just that tiny bit? So she can have spirit and life and breath a little longer?*

Another knock interrupted her. This one at the front door. Callie's heart raced before she discerned a person's shape on the other side of the frosted glass. Maybe Leslie trying to figure out why Callie had left school early, skipped practice, and wasn't answering her phone? Callie stood and peeked through the side window.

An old woman stood on the porch, her hair tightly permed so that her pink scalp was visible between the curls. Her nose was wide and flat, and she wore red-framed glasses and a floral-print dress that buttoned all the way up to her collarbone. A black leather purse that looked like a bowling ball bag hung over her elbow. The woman began to fiddle with the doorknob, as though hoping the door were unlocked.

"Excuse me," Callie called through the door. "Can I help you?"

The woman looked startled and glanced behind her—as if Callie might be talking to someone else. When no one else appeared, she wrinkled her brow in the direction of the door. "Hello! Is that Cath?"

Callie felt a jolt at hearing her mother's name, and swung open the front door. The woman's irises were so blue, they reminded her of photos of the earth's oceans when taken from space.

"She's not home," Callie said. "Do you want to leave her a message?"

"Me?"

"Yes. You're here looking for her, right?"

"Oh yes. I am. I'm Ellie Vidal," the woman said. "From the"—her eyes darted around as though looking for the rest of her sentence—"the historical society."

Callie's mom hadn't been involved in the organization since she'd begun her treatment last year. A few of her friends still visited, but Callie had never seen this woman before.

"My mom is at the doctor," Callie said. That explanation made her feel calmer and more in control, like this was a regularly scheduled appointment and not her mother's kidneys failing, not her mother deciding to die.

"Oh, my poor timing! I was on an outing downtown with"— again, the woman glanced behind her—"St. Theresa's. I just wanted to talk with her about registering this house as a historic place so that the state can assist in preserving it. It's something I should have done years ago."

Callie looked past the woman for the St. Theresa's Assisted Living Center's bus and its shuffling herd of elderly. The houses lining the square and the neighboring streets were quiet—except for the distant whir of a leaf blower. Two children played on the swings in the town square park, another few pretending to direct an orchestra in the band shell, their accompanying adults seated at picnic tables, engrossed in their cell phones. There was an antique black Chevy parked nearby, similar in design to the white car from the night before; the hood was wide and flat, the cab like a half bubble on top. But no bus.

"Maybe I could wait for her and you could show me the house?" Mrs. Vidal said.

"It's actually not the best timing. Today is—" Callie tried to find the right words. *The beginning of the end? A day I'll replay for the rest of my life?* Maybe there was no word for what today was except: "Bad."

Mrs. Vidal frowned. "I'm sorry to hear that. I'll definitely get out of your hair." The purse dropped from her elbow onto the concrete. "Oh dear. Don't ever get old, Callie," the woman said. "You'll be clumsy as all get-out."

This woman knew her name too? Callie's skin crawled, but she did what she thought her mom would want her to: she stepped onto the porch and picked up the purse.

"Thank you, dear. Can I trouble you a moment more for a water? Walking really takes it out of me these days."

Callie looked down the street, half expecting her parents' sedan. When it didn't appear, she beckoned the woman to follow her inside.

Mrs. Vidal stepped over the threshold and inhaled, closing her eyes. "This house," she said. When she opened her eyes, she blinked at Callie for several seconds like she couldn't remember why she was there.

"So you've been inside before?" Callie prompted.

"Of course," the woman said as though Callie's question was foolish.

"Is it like you remember?"

The woman moved slowly into the living room, touching the furniture and dismissing each piece with a head shake. "No, it's very different. The furniture. The drapes. But it feels the same, you know?" Her voice quavered and she pulled a handkerchief from her purse, wringing the fabric in her hands. She stared up at the ceiling as though she were trying to listen for something above them with her good ear. Had this woman lived in the house? Was she related to the Peterson family who built it?

"Did you ever hear weird noises when you were here?" Callie asked.

"You mean the ghosts?"

Callie was surprised by the woman's frankness. "Yeah, I guess ghosts or whatever."

Mrs. Vidal pulled at one of her curls; her other hand worked the handkerchief into a tight ball. "I heard everything and nothing at all," she said dismissively, like Callie shouldn't ask more questions. But what did she mean? Was she saying the ghosts were real?

Callie led the woman toward the kitchen, pointing to an antique cigar chest her mother was particularly proud of and a table that had been built by the original owners—too big to remove from the room without dismantling. Mrs. Vidal traced the scratches on the oak table, as though reading braille. Callie thought about the tracks she'd tried to follow in the field, about the whispers she'd tried to understand.

"Do you remember the 1961 tornado?" she asked.

The woman looked pained and ignored the question. "Did your mother ever tell you Lincoln stayed in this house back before he was president?"

"No, ma'am," Callie said.

"You should ask her about it before—"

Before she passes. It was how both of her parents talked now—with this acceptance of the future that made Callie sick.

"—before you forget," Mrs. Vidal finished. Callie blinked at her. It was rare that someone spoke to her without implying that her mother was dying.

Callie poured a glass of filtered water and handed it to Mrs. Vidal.

"Your mom takes such great care of this house."

"She really loves it." Callie's voice cracked. She cleared her throat, hoping the woman hadn't noticed.

"I'm sure you do too," the woman said.

Callie nodded. It was love by proxy. Love for the wraparound porch her mother had painted white, for the banister she polished corn gold, for the thick windowpanes she lit with electric candles at Christmas.

The woman sank onto a barstool, dug through her purse, and pulled out a Snickers. She smiled, clearly pleased. "I thought there might be one in there. I always keep a stash," she said. "Would you like a piece?"

"No, that's okay."

"You're looking thin. Haven't been eating enough lately, have you?"

Callie shrugged. Had she met this woman before and just forgotten? "I guess I just haven't been very hungry."

"No, I suppose not. But you need to keep that energy up with all the running you do."

How on earth did she know this? Callie felt the crawling sensation again, this time along her hairline. She had to get the woman out of the house, and the easiest path was to agree, like she did with her mother. "I'll try to do better."

Mrs. Vidal fixed her sharp eyes on Callie and paused, mid-chew. "You know," she said. "I lost my husband, Fred, to cancer."

So she definitely knew Callie's mother. Why else would she have said that? "I'm s-sorry," Callie stammered, thinking of what Joshua had said about how empty those words became over time. She wished she knew what else there was to say.

"Me too. He was a good man." She chuckled as though remembering something funny he'd done. After finishing the water, she carefully folded the wrapper around the remaining Snickers and stuffed it back into her purse.

"Well, I better get going. I'll be at St. Theresa's."

Callie nodded, but she wasn't sure why she'd need to find this strange woman.

On her way to the door, Mrs. Vidal touched the buttons on the velvet dining chairs and rubbed the brass knobs on the china hutch. She stopped again in the foyer. The late-afternoon sun angled through the windows so her hair glinted like ice, her scalp the color of ripe grapefruit beneath.

"I just gotta breathe it in one more time," she said. Callie froze. It was something her mom used to say before they left for vacation, or now, for chemo appointments, a goodbye that ripped Callie to shreds inside because it suggested—as all things did now—that there wouldn't be another time.

"Bye, dear," the woman said. "See you soon."

Without answering, Callie shut the door, aware of her heart beating in her throat. It wasn't just that the woman had said Callie's mother's words. There was something about her eyes, how shrewd and knowing they seemed, but desperate, too, like she had something for Callie and needed something from her in return.

Callie drew aside one of the heavy drapes and peered out the window, watching as the strange woman climbed into the antique black Chevy. As the car pulled past her house, Callie saw that the trunk was folded in on itself, the bumper practically meeting the back window. Either she'd been rear-ended or something had dropped that car from the sky onto its taillights. Callie slid the curtain closed, her arms prickling with goose bumps.

16

Joshua usually lay in bed until his mother or hunger drove him out. It wasn't that he was asleep; he just needed to gear himself up for another day of floating, invisible, through his high school. Today breakfast was calling to him. He could hear his mother moving around her bedroom and the music Ruthie woke up to every morning—pop music that contrasted so starkly with his reluctance to face the day that it made him feel jangled inside.

Joshua settled onto the couch in their living room and ate a Pop-Tart out of its foil wrapper. From the bay windows he saw a large wild-haired young man walking down the street, carrying something gray draped over his arm. His hair wasn't slicked down, but otherwise, this man looked like the volunteer firefighter he'd seen in the mechanic's uniform after the tornado—the Wolverine. Now the man was wearing an undersized vintage Mercer FD T-shirt and too-short shorts. The thin T-shirt fabric tugging at his pecs and shoulders stopped Joshua's breath. The man's legs were equally breathtaking, with their down of black curled hairs, angular calves, and overlapping diamond-shaped quads. Even the bruise on his knee was beautiful—like a fist of smashed blackberries.

Joshua could imagine him frame by frame in a comic: glimmering claws sprouting from his knuckles, teeth baring, and shirt splitting, then the crouch and the bulging crotch shot, and finally the spring, the slash, the starburst of red and orange.

The Wolverine stopped at the foot of the driveway across the street and turned to look at Joshua's house. Joshua's heart skipped a beat, and he sank low into the couch, wondering if the man had seen him staring. Why else would he be looking this way?

"Joshua! Ruthie! I have to run. Don't be late," Joshua's mother called. He heard her footsteps on the stairs, a fast trot.

"Bye!" Ruthie yelled from upstairs.

"Bye," Joshua echoed. She waved at him as she rushed by the living room. Probably on her way to court.

"Don't forget to take out the recycling!" she shouted before the back door slammed and the garage door groaned open.

When he returned his gaze to the window, the man was gone. The front door to the house across the street was slightly ajar. No one had lived in that house for months. Maybe the Wolverine-man was moving in?

Joshua heard a heavy set of footsteps on the stairs. Not Ruthie, certainly, but Lawrence usually had first shift at the meatpacking plant and was gone long before they were awake. Joshua couldn't help rolling his eyes when Lawrence appeared, tapping his phone with his large forefinger in what seemed like frustration. The man was dressed in sweatpants and a T-shirt that emphasized his large stomach. He'd been a linebacker in high school, but over the years, his muscles had given way to fat. It wasn't loose and jiggly like Joshua's, but drum-skin tight, the belly of a pregnant woman. Lawrence's face, on the other hand, had a sort of gumminess to it, as though he were wearing a rubber mask.

"What are *you* doing home?" Joshua asked.

Lawrence jumped at the sound of Joshua's voice. He'd been so engrossed in his phone, he must not have seen Joshua in the living room. If he had, he probably would have walked right past. He was an expert at putting rooms between them. Even now he looked ready to backpedal, to rewind the tape until he was back upstairs.

"Cat got your tongue?" Joshua didn't have to censor his tone; his mother wasn't home to scold him. Lawrence always left the discipline up to her, seemingly bewildered by bad behavior—like Joshua and Ruthie were two stray dogs who'd wandered in off the street to chew on pillows and pee on carpets.

"I'm feeling sick," Lawrence said, his voice raspy. Now that Joshua thought about it, Lawrence looked even worse than usual. His eyes were bleary and ringed in dark circles. Lawrence held up his phone as though it helped explain why he was home.

"I don't think the phone is going to make you soup or diagnose your illness," Joshua said.

"I'm trying to schedule one of those walk-in appointments, but I can't get it to work."

If it had been his mother, Joshua would have taken the phone and scheduled it for her, accustomed to being the cross-generational technology interpreter in their household, but for Lawrence he just raised his eyebrows. "Did you try turning it off and back on again?" he said, his voice flat with mockery. "Or you could just call them."

Lawrence seemed to hate talking on the phone. It was as though he couldn't remember what order words were supposed to go in as soon as a device was pressed to his ear.

"No," Lawrence muttered, rubbing his eyes.

"You really don't look so good."

This, Joshua knew, would make Lawrence puff up his chest with indignation. Linebackers were supposed to be tough. Meatpackers even more so.

"You know what? I'm just going to go there." Lawrence

started for the back door as though he couldn't leave fast enough.

"Good luck with that," Joshua said.

The door to the garage slammed in answer. A moment later Lawrence reversed down the driveway, not even glancing back at the house. He probably knew that Joshua was still in the front window, daring him to make eye contact.

When Joshua finally returned his attention to the house across the street, he saw the curtains in the front bay window shift, but he couldn't make out anything beyond them. He knew the house's floor plan mirrored his own. Joshua and Ruthie had explored it a few months back when they realized the realtor had a habit of leaving the door unlocked.

Was the Wolverine-man watching him from the window? Why?

"You coming?" This time his sister's voice interrupted him. He hadn't even heard her on the stairs. Ruthie had her pink backpack that she'd covered in Sharpie doodles over one shoulder. Her almost-invisible eyebrows were raised.

Joshua glanced back at their neighbor's house. He couldn't go to school yet; he had to investigate what was going on. "Our new neighbor is going to drive me," Joshua lied. "I'm supposed to go help him out in a few minutes."

Ruthie peered over his shoulder and narrowed her eyes at the house across the street: a face he called *the camera* because it felt like she was zooming in. "We have a new neighbor?"

"Yeah, he's inside."

"The For Rent sign is still up."

Joshua shrugged. "I guess they just haven't taken it down yet."

"Do you know this person?"

"Yeah, I met him before. The other night, actually."

"Where did he come from?"

"Across town," Joshua said, though he had no clue.

"Where does he work?"

"He's a firefighter."

"Okay," she said, drawing the *a* sound out. "I'm telling Mom if you get axe-murdered or something." It was a joke, but she was biting her lip, nervous.

"Fair," he said. "But don't worry; you won't have to."

Still frowning, she let herself out the front door and started for the bus stop. He caught her looking back over her shoulder.

Joshua sat on the couch a moment longer, waiting for the squeal of the bus brakes to indicate he was truly alone and trying to make out the silhouette of a man behind the curtains.

Once the bus left, Joshua opened the front door. He became acutely aware of his big toe poking out through the hole in his Chucks, the grease smear on his glasses, the sickly sweet smell of Pop-Tarts on this breath. He crossed the street, kicking rocks. Casual. All he had to do was talk to the guy, see if he could learn more. He took a breath and rapped lightly on the door.

Silence.

Joshua pushed the door gently.

"Hello?" he called.

It was dim inside and he could see dust motes dancing in the shaft of sunlight from the open door. The air smelled musty, like old books.

A dark shape moved in the living room shadows. A man. Someone *had* been watching from the front window. Joshua took a step back, suddenly feeling exposed, like he was standing before someone who could devour him.

"H-hi. I live across the street." The man startled at the sound of Joshua's voice, as though he hadn't expected him to speak. What did such a tough-looking man have to be jumpy about?

He stepped into the entryway, his wolfish brown eyes bouncing from Joshua to his house in the distance and then back again—like he couldn't quite connect all the dots. Finally they settled somewhere near the center of Joshua's forehead. He felt the heat in his cheeks rise and knew that his embarrassment would now be visible, the red patches blossoming on his face and neck at the not-quite eye contact from, perhaps, the hottest guy he'd ever met. How old could he be? Twenty? Twenty-one?

"Are you moving in?" Joshua asked. "This house has been empty for so long."

The man was silent a moment and then nodded, shifting on his feet. Was he nervous? He spoke then, his voice gravelly and unsure of itself: "I recognize you. Saw you the other night. On the bike." Joshua's heart kicked in his chest. So this was the Wolverine! And he'd spotted Joshua with all that was going on?

"Oh. Yeah. I guess I wanted to see if I could help or something," he lied. It sounded stupid. What was he going to do on a bike built for a fifth grader?

The man nodded as though he understood.

"Do you need help moving anything?" Joshua asked.

"Nothing to move," the man said. "Isn't there somewhere you're supposed to be?"

"Yeah, but school doesn't start for another hour," Joshua lied again. "Can I come in? I want to see how much the house is like ours."

The man squinted like he didn't quite believe Joshua, but he nodded again anyway. "There's nowhere to sit or anything."

"That's okay," Joshua said a bit too eagerly.

The man gave a half-hearted tour of the first floor, gesturing vaguely at rooms and allowing Joshua to name them for him: "The living room. The dining room. The laundry room." The man moved stiffly, with a bit of a limp. Had he been injured rescuing people from the tornado?

They stopped in the kitchen. The gray object Joshua had seen the man carrying was draped over the counter. The mechanic's uniform, Joshua realized. There was a hole in the chest—no name patch—and a corner of notebook paper peeked out of the pocket.

"You seen the news about the tornado?" the man asked, still skittish, his eyes shifting from the fridge to the back windows to the linoleum floor.

Joshua tried to clip his sentences like the man. "Heard they haven't found the driver yet." Was the man trying to see what he knew? Or tell him something? "Think the driver could have gotten to a ditch before the car was picked up?" Joshua asked.

"I suppose so," Wolverine said, rubbing his stubble and musing—not a confirmation, but not a denial, either.

"You must be getting ready for work," Joshua said, pointing at the uniform.

The man grunted, but he picked up the uniform and stepped into the legs. He yanked the top half up and over his shoulders. The paper fluttered to the floor. It was old, Joshua could see, the ink faded to a light blue and the paper spotted with brown.

His new neighbor didn't seem to notice it had fallen, so Joshua bent, pretending to tie his shoe, and palmed the note. When he straightened, the man was still tucking his T-shirt in and fiddling with the zipper.

Joshua slipped the note into his pocket. "I should get to school," Joshua said, wanting only to get out of the house before the man noticed the paper was missing. "I've still got to put out the recycling."

"Okay," he said. Was it just wishful thinking, or did the man look disappointed? Joshua started back to the front door and the man limped after.

Joshua stepped outside and turned around, suddenly feeling compelled to announce his name like an idiot: "I'm Joshua, by the way."

The man smiled, a tight, close-lipped expression that was hardly more than a grimace. He didn't offer his own name and Joshua didn't ask, preferring the one he'd invented.

"Don't let them get you down, Joshua," Wolverine said just as Joshua turned to leave. He stopped and blinked at the man. Was it that obvious that he was down? It was like the man knew about Tyler and Lawrence, about the whole high school, the whole town.

"Okay," Joshua said. What else was he supposed to do?

* * *

Back inside his own house, Joshua took the note out of his pocket and smoothed it out. The handwriting was printed in all caps.

L—

I CAN'T STOP THINKING ABOUT OUR DRIVE THE OTHER NIGHT. I DON'T KNOW ABOUT YOU, BUT I DISCOVERED NEW LANDSCAPES. I NEVER EXPECTED YOU TO BE SO RIGHT.

CAN I SEE YOU AGAIN TONIGHT? I WANT TO MEMORIZE YOUR GEOGRAPHY.

—E

I never expected you to be so right? This guy had a love letter in his pocket. That was the kind of thing you'd notice missing. Joshua refolded the note. Hopefully, this guy—was he the *L* or the *E?*—would just think he'd dropped it.

Lawrence might be back sooner than expected, and Joshua didn't want to risk getting caught not in school. He dragged the recycling to the curb, unchained his bike, and looked back at the empty house. His new neighbor was at the window again, this time watching Joshua with the curtains pushed back.

The man lifted his chin at Joshua, bobbing his head back

in this way that was utterly masculine and graceful. But there was something else in the gesture too. Joshua lifted his own chin in return, sure that it was awkward and unpracticed and that he was exposing the rolls of his neck. Still, the moment felt meaningful—like a secret code, like mutual recognition. And in that instant, Joshua was certain that this man, this Wolverine, was gay.

17

B renna ordered a small iced coffee and plucked a straw from Bean City's canister. Really, she wanted to order a latte or a frappé for her Friday treat, a sweet creamy beverage that would keep her full until lunch, but she'd been broke since her summer job at the Ice Cream Palace ended.

She waited for her drink, scanning the morning patrons in line with their briefcases and shipped-in copies of the *Chicago Tribune*. One old man sat at the counter, counting change in his palm. Another had the local paper, the tornado still earning a spot above the fold. She wondered if there was anything new about the car.

She looked around further and froze, every hair on her body standing at prickly attention. Colin, *her Person*, sat at one of the tables, his back to her, brown curls peeking out from under his slouched beanie. He wore a slate-gray T-shirt with a hole in the collar. That hole—she knew—only went through the first layer of the cotton. When they were together, she'd slid her finger through and snaked it along the inside of the collar. The fabric was so soft and thin from washing that it felt like gauze. More than anything, Brenna wanted to smell the shirt: name-brand detergent with a hint of pressed wood from his dresser. The desire thrummed in her ears. She tried to think of something she could say—anything—that would give her access to the fabric. She imagined walking up and taking it between her fingers, pulling it toward her nose.

A laugh broke her staring spell, and Brenna realized there was a girl facing Colin. She had marshmallow skin and Midwestern blond hair: sun-whitened around the face, with darker golden tones along the neck and behind the ears. Brenna's own hair was thin and flat. She dyed the tips because there was nothing else to do with them, because she wanted to give people something to look at besides her crooked teeth or her well-worn clothes: baggy jeans, black ribbed tanks, half-buttoned flannels, a black zip hoodie, and red combat boots.

Brenna knew she should turn away, but she couldn't take her eyes off the girl's heart-shaped face, straightened teeth, freckles. In her throat, Brenna felt the erasure of the tiny hope she'd harbored that the Same Life Stage Girl was just a passing fling, that she'd run into Colin and have a chance to show him how mature she could be. This girl was so white, so American pie. It made

Brenna feel like a beacon in the coffee shop, like she was blinking brown.

When they'd been a couple, Colin had pretended not to hear when his younger brother joked that they better use protection because Brenna was bound to be *super fertile.* He pretended not to notice his mother glaring at Brenna as if she were going to steal something. But when they went out with his friends in the Cities, he acted like Brenna was a novelty.

"She knows all about Mexican Modernism," he'd once told a friend at the art museum, even though she certainly didn't.

"I bet your family has incredible textiles," the friend had said.

"They do," Colin had responded, which, again, was untrue.

When Brenna asked him about it later, he said he must have misremembered. "But I bet you're more of an expert than you think," he'd added. And there it was again: that shiny version of her that he wanted to believe in. That she did too.

Before her now, Colin reached out the hand with the thread-thin scar and took the girl's. The movement knocked the breath out of Brenna.

"Brenna," the barista called, holding out an iced coffee. Colin started to turn, and Brenna's breath returned in a rush. She scrambled, grabbing her coffee and shoving open the shop door to the loud clatter of bells. She was sure Colin had seen her practically tumble into the parking lot, but that didn't stop her from speed-walking to her car, squeezing the sweating plastic cup in her hand.

Someone had tucked a flyer under Golden Girl's wiper that advertised a band, the River Bandits, in bold white letters. The women on the poster were dressed in rockabilly style, all lipstick and sculpted curls. They were playing a concert that night, in the courtyard the coffee shop shared with one of the town bars.

Brenna was about to crumple the flyer and chuck it, so she could make her escape, when she saw a girl peeling that same flyer off another windshield two cars down. Her hair was blue-black, straight, with short bangs and a ponytail that curled around her neck. Her makeup was exaggerated like the women's on the poster—skin powdered, false eyelashes, and cherry-red lipstick. She wore a polka-dot top tucked into high-waisted, cropped black pants, and shiny patent-leather Mary Janes.

The girl noticed Brenna and straightened, using the flyer to shield her eyes from the sun. She was staring so directly, so unashamedly, that Brenna wondered if she'd forgotten to put on pants or something equally embarrassing.

"Hi?"

"Hey!" the girl said, coming to life with a start. "You going to this show?" When the girl smiled, the makeup cracked in rays extending from the corners of her eyes and lips. There was something off about her so-black-it's-blue hair and doll eyes, something that didn't belong in a daylit parking lot.

"I'm not twenty-one," said Brenna.

"What's that matter?" The girl crossed the empty parking spaces, walking closer. "Wait, are you Brenna Ortiz?"

"Do I know you?"

"My name is Dot. I live in the Cities, but I'm originally from here."

"Yeah? You knew my brother, Manny?"

Dot made a gesture that was half shrug, half nod.

"When'd you graduate?"

Dot's smile went lopsided. "I didn't."

"Oh, sorry."

"It's okay." Dot looped the curl of her ponytail around one finger. "Hey, you live over by the cemetery, right?"

"Yeah."

"Ever see the blue stones?" Dot asked, flashing her red-lined smile again.

The coffee shop's glass door opened with a jingle, reflecting the sun in Brenna's eyes momentarily. It was too late to duck into the car. Colin, holding the door open for the girl, looked right at Brenna. She waited for some emotion to register on his face: happiness or welcome or even discomfort. But he rubbed the back of his neck, right where the tiny collar-hole was, his face blank.

"The blue stones?" Dot repeated. "You know the ones?"

"Sorry, yeah. I've seen them." Brenna watched as Colin opened the driver's-side door and lifted himself up. He met Brenna's eyes for just a second before swinging the door shut.

"He really broke your heart, didn't he?" Dot said.

Brenna looked at Dot. The girl's observation made her shiver. "How'd you know?" she asked.

Dot's smile was lopsided again. "If it means anything, I also know you're a hundred times better than him."

Brenna blushed. "It's okay. You don't have to say that."

"Someone's gotta say something. You're beating yourself up over *that*." Dot waved her hand dismissively in the direction of his Jeep.

"He's not that bad, but thanks. I'm fine."

"Of course you are. Here." Dot slid her hand into her purse and pulled out a notebook with a lavender leather cover. She held it out for Brenna to take. "Go on."

Puzzled, Brenna looked at the notebook. "What's this for?"

"For you."

Brenna shook her head, still confused.

"It's how I process everything. You're a writer too, right? Go on. Take it." Brenna did so, and the girl waved the flyer and headed for the bar. "I'll see you at the show, Brenna Ortiz." Even the girl's walk was strong, confident. A swagger.

Brenna blinked at the notebook in her hand. There were piles of composition notebooks under her bed filled with doodles and journal entries from before she met Colin. A few poems and stories, too, that she'd entered into the *Mercer Journal*'s writing contests, earning the favor of many of her English teachers and a few blue ribbons that her mother had tacked on their fridge. Colin thought you should *live your life instead of writing about feelings.* That part of her felt so distant now, small and dark, like she was looking back at herself from the end of a long tunnel.

Something fizzed under her skin, something she hadn't felt since Colin had broken up with her—anticipation maybe, like this stranger's interest in her meant something. But she was unsettled, too, by how well the girl seemed to know her. Then she remembered Gretta's words from the cemetery and wondered: Was someone trying to tell her something?

18

Callie used to wake up earlier on Friday mornings so she could attend youth group before school. Lately she woke up early to pretend she was attending; she'd stopped going months ago. But this morning there was no one to pretend for; the house was silent. Her mother had come home from the hospital late, too tired for Callie to bother her with questions about strange old women and Lincoln.

Callie put on a T-shirt and jeans and brushed her teeth before waiting outside her mom's door. Her father emerged from their bedroom, shutting the door carefully so that it didn't click.

"She's still asleep. Ready for youth group?" He handed Callie the keys, but she didn't feel like driving anymore—not after the tornado.

"I'm tired," she said, trying to hand them back.

"Me too. But you're the one who needs more practice before tomorrow."

In the driveway, Callie settled into the driver's seat, checked her mirrors, and backed up slowly, looking over her shoulder like her mother had taught her.

Her father cleared his throat, the signal that "a talk" was coming. Callie's stomach dropped. She'd avoided a bedside chat with her mother—only to end up here.

"Mrs. Walsh called me and said you haven't shown up for youth group in a while," he said. "Which is strange, because I've been dropping you off."

Callie used to enjoy youth group and reconnecting with her classmates who'd gone to St. Malachy's Elementary. The dough-nuts were a welcome change from the Gatorade and granola she ate after her runs with her dad. And he was right: he had been dropping her off. But the past few months, Callie had instead found herself pulled to the chapel down the hall from the group room, where she could be alone. She'd kneel, hands folded and eyes lowered, until a ding on her phone reminded her it was time to walk across the soccer field to the high school. Callie didn't pray during this time, but she didn't think, either. She sank into a state of blankness, where the grumbling, nagging hunger in her stomach disappeared, where the perpetual ache for the days before her mother's illness slipped away.

"I've just been going to the chapel," Callie said. "I want to be by myself."

Her father was quiet for a moment. "I understand. That's natural. But this is important to your mom. I think she wants to know that you have a network of love and support aside from just me."

Callie felt the ache in her throat again, the kind that might explode out of her as sobs. She kept moving her eyes in the pattern her mother had taught her: *windshield, rearview, left, right, repeat.*

"And it's something you might need right now." His voice cracked. "It's something we all need. Can you try to actually go this morning? For her?"

"Yeah, okay," Callie said—only to quiet him.

When she walked into the group room, Grant, who she'd had a crush on since elementary school, was talking about the tornado. She sank into her spot next to Leslie, and her friend's mouth opened in shock at the sight of her.

"The meteorologists are full of shit," Grant was saying. "An F2 wouldn't have taken out a turbine. It had to be at least an F3."

"What do you think the 1961 one was?" Silas, another classmate, asked.

"F4, I'd bet. I'm sure the chances of it happening twice on the same date, in the same spot, *and* at the same intensity are minuscule."

"Yeah, my grandma keeps taking Dad's car and driving to the field. She's hoping that she'll hear from her sister," Silas said.

Callie thought of the whispers rustling around her, could

practically feel them on her skin now. Something *had* happened. But she wasn't any closer to figuring out what. She had to find Brenna and Joshua again and see what else they knew.

Leslie nudged her elbow. Her friend was wearing her dark curly hair in an effortless bun on top of her head. Two curls were loose, framing the thick eyebrows that always made Callie jealous.

"Aren't you going to say hi to me?" she asked.

"Sorry. Hi," Callie said, turning her attention to her last remaining friend. Since the diagnosis, Leslie offered to help cook or clean at Callie's house, she planned outings to malls and water parks, she called to check on Callie's mother. She was patient with Callie's lack of interest, but Callie knew she'd give up soon, that she'd take the apathy personally and drift off to the theater kids and band geeks like the others had.

"I can't believe you're here today," Leslie said.

"My dad made me come."

Leslie passed the box of doughnuts to Callie. At once, Callie felt hungry, dizzyingly so, and nauseated at the overly sweet smell of the cakes. There was something chemical about the scent, cloying. Callie pushed the box away, ignoring the concern stamped on Leslie's face.

"So why weren't you at practice yesterday?" Leslie asked, in a voice that suggested she was trying to be casual, and also trying to mask something underneath: More concern? Annoyance? Anger? Callie was saved from answering by Mrs. Walsh welcoming her back and asking the members to say things they liked about her. The talking stick moved around the room, Callie's peers' eyes dropped to their hands, and she listened to them describe someone she didn't know.

Callie is very caring.

She has a nice smile.

She lives her life according to Christ.

Leslie: *She's always there for you.*

Was that sarcasm in her voice?

They all looked at Callie when they finished, expecting something.

"Thank you," she said. "I'm glad I have a network of love and support at a time like this."

Mrs. Walsh nodded, pleased. "I thought we'd start today by reading John 14."

Callie listened, knowing she was supposed to take comfort in the fact that there'd be a *house of many rooms* prepared for her mother—and for herself, too—and that they'd be somehow reunited in this afterlife. But how could her mother believe that was true *and* believe that Mrs. Jenson, the Storm Spirits, and the other Mercer ghosts were lingering around? Why didn't they get to go to their own great house in the sky? It made Callie's head buzz to think about.

She stood up, murmuring something to Leslie about needing the restroom. She headed for the chapel and sank down onto a kneeler. She liked the way the old cushions depressed under her kneecaps. She folded her hands, resting her forehead against them, and tried to empty her mind of thoughts of her mother. Sometimes, to empty it, she had to imagine filling it with something else—like the cotton stuffing inside her childhood stuffed animals. But the image of cotton stuffing only reminded her of Mrs. Vidal's perm, of the eerie feeling Callie had had that the woman knew her, the house, and her mother too well.

WE REMEMBER ELEANOR ROCKING

We remember Eleanor rocking on the porch, little Celeste in her lap. Eleanor was the latest in the line of Peterson women who ran the inn. Small and wiry with blue eyes like cut glass, and frizzy yellow hair. She'd flick her eyes at those of us who toddled by, initially protective and ferocious, then softening with recognition. She'd hail us, call a few questions to our mothers from her swing, and nod firmly at their responses—like a town watchman, keeping the peace.

Back then, we didn't doubt that Celeste would grow up to be the town's hearth and home, like her mother and her mother's mother and so on. Baking rolls and scrambling eggs and flapping sheets for future Lincolns. Reciting the inherited story for any who stopped in: *You're staying where Lincoln stayed on his way to Springfield. We serve boiled oats and fresh jam every morning because that was what he ate here. He wasn't one for hotcakes or pie. No, he was a man of simple tastes.* For a few of us, it's more than just a story; we witnessed his first stop through just three years shy of his presidency. He smiled with the whole of his long face when he left the inn to debate Douglas in Galesburg. Who wouldn't want a pride like that for their daughter?

Every day around two, we'd watch Eleanor walk Celeste down Main to French Imports; her husband, a Frenchman, had escaped his homeland in the war and opened his own store in Mercer. This—a Peterson woman's marriage to a foreigner, a foreigner who *had run from the war*—was something the old folks in town scoffed at.

The couple was impervious to the talk—so in love were they with each other and Celeste. The girl's future spread before them—before all of us—as lush and green as Mercer's fields.

None of us could have known what was coming.

19

After school, Brenna thought about asking Callie to describe the person she'd seen during the tornado. Both the old Pontiac and the VW seemed like the types of cars driven by someone like Dot—Dot with the bluish-black hair and that too-powdered skin. But Brenna hadn't seen Callie all day.

Brenna skipped her usual Taco Bell trip—even though it meant arriving home before her mother left for work. She was willing to risk being asked about Colin if it meant she could dig those notebooks out from under her bed and confirm that she was a writer, like Dot had said.

Brenna's mother was in the kitchen, finishing an orange over the sink. She bit into the last slice and leaned forward so that the juices dribbled off her chin and into the basin. She was already dressed in her work clothes: black pants and a polo that said MERCER FILL STATION over the left breast. The baggy uniform rendered her short and squat instead of curvy. Her curly hair was pulled back in a bun, with tiny flyaways along her ears and the base of her neck that made her head look fuzzy, out of focus.

"Hi, mi cielo," she said. "You're home earlier than usual."

Brenna nodded, unwilling to offer an explanation.

"I got groceries."

"It's about time." Brenna riffled through the bags on the counter. Aside from oranges, her mother had bought frozen pizzas, mixed veggies, and waffles. What Brenna wouldn't give for beef shank, corn, onions, cilantro, lime, and jalapeño, ingredients for her tía's caldo de res, a hearty beef soup that Brenna craved this time of year. Her mother had never learned to cook like her older sister, Camila. In Houston, that wasn't a problem because Brenna could simply step outside and find food trucks that sold everything from tacos al pastor to elotes to pozole. Now, she had to endure her abuela or drive a half hour to a restaurant in the Quad Cities if she wanted real Mexican food.

Brenna settled for an orange. "There's nothing good," she said.

Her mother crossed her arms. "Why don't you get another job and buy your own food if you're going to be like that?"

"You have to provide food for me. Legally speaking. I'm your dependent."

"Doesn't mean you can't help out. I did when I was your age."

"You also only went to school between harvests." Brenna sank her fingernails into the orange. The rind burned the tender skin under her nails. "Besides, you told me to focus on my schoolwork, remember?"

"At least do a load of towels tonight. We don't have any clean ones."

"I can't. I'm going to a concert." Saying it out loud was the first time Brenna was sure of this.

"I thought you had schoolwork to focus on, like you said."

Brenna smirked at her mother's cleverness. "I did it already. In study hall. Plus it's a Friday."

"Well, Camila texted me that your grandmother wants to see you this weekend."

"Why? She doesn't even like us. I get called gorda even though she's the one feeding me, and you just spend all your time apologizing for not being a saint like tía Camila."

Her mother put her hands on her hips and narrowed her eyes. "What's going on, mija?"

Brenna shrugged and flicked the orange peel into the garbage can.

"Is it something with Colin?"

Brenna took a deep breath, trying to prepare herself to tell the truth, but her mom continued. "What? You think I don't know man troubles when I see them?"

Brenna felt the barb on her tongue and tried to swallow it, but it was easier to expel than the truth. "Yeah, you're right. I don't know why I'm surprised. You know man troubles, all right."

Her mother looked at the *Last Supper* print hanging under the cabinet and inhaled dramatically, probably asking God for patience. "I don't need this before work." She ran her hands under the water, grabbed her keys off the counter, and nodded toward the grocery bags. "Finish unloading those, do the towels, and no concert tonight or you're gonna need a new place to stay."

As soon as the door slammed, Brenna's bluster dissipated. Sometimes her own anger at her mother surprised her, and she felt like a spectator watching an actor on TV. Sure, she didn't like the men who'd rotated through their lives, earning her mom the town reputation that had trickled down to Brenna. And sure, she'd hated that her mother moved them to Mercer only to be half accepted back into the very family she'd run away from when she met Brenna's father. If Brenna were still in Houston, she'd see her dad more, she wouldn't be the only person of color in every class, she wouldn't be called *coco* by her cousins for being brown on the outside and white inside, and her grandmother wouldn't say *ay* and *Dios mío* because her Spanish was so terrible—even though that was partially abuela's fault to begin with. But the truth was, despite how they sometimes argued, Brenna couldn't hate her mother. Her mother, who worked tirelessly, who loved fiercely, and who had given Brenna the space to tell the truth about Colin. The space to be comforted. Brenna just hadn't taken the opportunity. She couldn't. Shame was a hot thing that split her tongue.

Brenna ate the orange, finished unloading the groceries, and then walked through each room, gathering towels. She knocked on Manny's door even though Golden Girl wasn't in the driveway. She loved going through his room when she was short on cigarettes. He tended to lose packs and then buy replacements instead of finding the old ones. Under a damp towel and some muddy jeans she found a few dollar bills—enough to buy a drink at the concert—and a half pack of cigarettes. She carried the towels to the washer and dumped them on the floor. She wanted to save the hot water for her shower later, and vowed to start the laundry before she left for the concert. If she was going to break some of her mother's rules, she might as well get the chores done first.

In her room, Brenna knelt on the floor beside her bed and shoved aside some clothes. Dot's words—*You're a writer too, right?*—were knocking on something inside her. There, stacked under her bed with their frayed spines facing out, their covers wavy from the perpetual dampness of the house, were her old notebooks. *Toby*

Merchant, the name of her seventh-grade boyfriend, was scrawled all over one. Later Brenna had scratched through each instance of his name, digging the pen tip into the soft cardboard cover, and used a thick Sharpie to write *I'm not his doll for play*, as though it were the title of that miserable year. In this notebook, she knew she'd find her first kiss. She'd find Lisle, the boy who called out her name while she was exploring the cemetery and had his penis in his hand when she turned around. In her ninth-grade notebook, she'd find a bag-boot girl named Erin, who asked her if she stuffed her bra with cotton balls, and her older cousin, Tomás, calling her *Butch Brenna*. In still another, she'd find Amy. And Dutch and Jade. She'd dye her hair and start powdering her face. She'd weed her closet down to black and red. And she'd start building her shell, one armored plate at a time.

Brenna flipped to the last entry of a journal.

I'm always between, she'd written. *Between my mom and dad. Between my friends and my cousins. Between is the loneliest place to be.*

Not much, then, had changed. Brenna climbed into bed and pulled the lavender notebook Dot had given her out of her backpack. She opened to a blank page and waited for something new to write about.

20

Joshua rode his bike home from school—glad he could avoid another incident with Tyler on the afternoon bus. He had enough to worry about. The vice principal had called him into her office at lunchtime to ask why he'd skipped first period. She'd expressed her concern for his safety, which was a joke because he was far safer with his new neighbor and riding his bike than he was at school and on the bus. His counselor also "checked in" with him by telling him a story about her own truancy. By now they must have called his mother. He imagined the orbs of her eyes growing even larger, taking over her small body so she was just a set of eyeballs glaring at him. Luckily, he wouldn't have to worry about facing her until later.

Joshua hadn't remembered that Lawrence had stayed home sick until he flung the door open and saw him on the couch in the living room next to Ruthie, who'd beaten Joshua home on the bus.

The TV was tuned to a reality show about trappers in the mountains, and Lawrence had his hands folded on his large belly, a Kleenex balled in one fist.

"Hi there, Larry," Joshua said, using the name the man hated and hoping his tone dripped with acid. Even on days when he didn't work, Lawrence still smelled of the meatpacking plant: pig blood, tangy and sharp, a smell that reminded Joshua of compost and metal all at once. Joshua pinched his nose and made a beeline for the kitchen.

"Ruthie, will you go upstairs a minute?" Lawrence said, his words both rushed and a mumble.

That stopped Joshua in his tracks. Lawrence wanted to be alone with him? When all the gayness might be floating about, unabsorbed and unhindered by other bodies? Ruthie stood and cocked her head at Joshua, eyes narrowed. He shrugged at her, but knew she'd wait at the top of the stairs so she could hear everything.

Once Ruthie was out of sight, Lawrence muted the TV and cleared his throat. "The school called me to say you skipped a class today."

"Why'd the school call you?" Joshua asked. The thought of Lawrence stuttering through a phone conversation because of him would normally have filled Joshua with pleasure, but he sensed trouble.

"Your mother didn't pick up. I think she's in court for the day." He cleared his throat again and rubbed where his jaw probably was, beneath all that thick, gummy flesh. "She doesn't know yet."

Joshua crossed his arms. "So are you going to tell her?"

"I'm still deciding." He fidgeted, picking at a callus on his thumb. "You know, I was a boy once. I get it."

"What do you get?"

"Getting in trouble. Stirring things up. Pushing buttons. Taunting folks."

Joshua narrowed his eyes at this. "So I'm stirring things up, is what you're saying. Just for the hell of it."

"For the hell of it. For attention. Doesn't matter. I'd just like a bit more respect. You show me some respect, I'll forget to tell your mom."

"You're bribing me?"

"It's not a bribe. It's an agreement."

Joshua stared at this man he had to live with, this man who didn't share a drop of his blood, who didn't know a single real thing about him. A sad, fat lump of a meatpacker afraid of a fifteen-year-old kid who was also a sad, fat lump. He had never really tried to respect or understand Joshua, so why should he return the favor?

"No deal," Joshua said. "Tell her for all I care." His throat hurt, like he'd swallowed something sharp, but he refused to cry in front of Lawrence.

Joshua rode his bike to the library, picked the only comic they had on the magazine racks—a five-year-old issue of *Indestructible Hulk*—and sat down in front of a window. Across the street was the fire station—both depressing and beautiful, like everything in town. The bronze fire bell rang only for parades now.

His new neighbor wasn't in sight.

He tried to read a few pages of the comic, but couldn't hold the storyline in his head. What he wanted to do was draw, to occupy his mind while transforming himself into something new, but he'd been too pissed to think of grabbing his backpack on the way out the door.

A group of freshmen filed past on the other side of the library window, heading—Joshua guessed—for the Mercer Fill Station. Tyler was among them, hair bed-tousled, as was Clayton—the kid responsible for Joshua's coming out and his subsequent invisibility. They were laughing, and Clayton looked amused and disinterested all at once, despite the fact that he seemed to be the focal point of the group, like the joke was an offering to him. Like Joshua, Tyler had been unpopular in middle school—but now he was part of a group that was savagely anti-popular. They went after everyone—football players, dancers, teachers. Joshua felt a needle of fear beneath his breastbone, but radiating from the pinprick was something else, something bigger and throbbing. Betrayal. For the bus. For hanging out with the likes of Clayton. He thought of Lawrence, who was surely telling his mother right now about Joshua skipping school, neglecting the part of the story where he'd tried to bribe him into good behavior. Pitting her against her own son. That was betrayal too.

Joshua stood up, leaving the Hulk on the table, and followed Tyler, Clayton, and their friends down the block. He wasn't worried they would see him. Invisibility was his superpower.

21

After school, Callie shuttled her books from her locker to her backpack. She couldn't shake Mrs. Vidal from her thoughts. She'd even typed *Ellie Vidal Mercer Illinois* into the search bar on her phone. But there were no results. Did her mother know the woman? Asking her might mean another tear-filled bedside chat. With Brenna and Joshua, though, Callie thought she might be able to talk about the whispers, the car, and the tornado. She knew she could ask them: If you hit a turbine like that, wouldn't you be hurt? How could you just disappear? After yesterday, she felt like maybe she could trust them—Joshua, who knew how to face his grief head-on, and Brenna, who knew when it was time to look away.

But Leslie rounded the corner instead of Brenna or Joshua. Her cheeks were flushed as if she were raring to argue.

"What's up?" Callie asked.

"'What's up?'" Leslie said, slurring the *s* with her braces. "What's up with *you*? You weren't at lunch or practice yesterday. Then you ditched me at youth group this morning and skipped lunch today, too."

"I didn't feel like going."

Leslie seemed to latch on to that word: *feel*. Her eyes widened, the sympathy look Callie knew well because every teacher, every neighbor, every parishioner had one. "I'm sorry. It's okay. I didn't mean to snap," she said. "Is everything all right? How's your mom?"

The inquirers never wanted the truth—not really, which was why Callie had a savage desire to share it. "My mom's kidneys failed yesterday."

"Oh God. I'm so sorry," Leslie said, her voice reminding Callie of an overripe fruit, mushy and sickly sweet. She leaned against Callie's locker. "Coach asked about you, and I just didn't know what to say."

"Am I running at the meet tomorrow?"

"You were supposed to. I don't know if he'll take you off."

Callie's calf muscles tightened, a sudden, deep ache that demanded stretches, flexing, rotation. This might be the last time her mom could come to a meet, and even as she tried not to care, she did.

"I'll talk to him," she said. Coach, like everyone else, would probably forgive her because of her mom.

"Are we doing anything tomorrow for your birthday?" Leslie asked.

"I'm getting my license."

"But are *we* doing anything?"

"I don't know. Do you want to do something?" Callie said.

"Of course I want to do something. It's my best friend's birthday."

Callie tried to smile. "What do you want to do?"

Leslie's gaze was steady, almost accusatory. "If I plan something," she said, "will you actually come?"

"Yeah," Callie said, but she knew she didn't sound convincing. She shouldered her backpack, hoping Leslie would take the hint. "Gotta find Coach. Just text me the plan. Something simple, and I'll be there." She jogged toward the athletics office, glancing over her shoulder when she reached the staircase. Leslie was still against her locker, looking small and alone. But even if Callie tried harder to be a good friend, she knew things would never be as they once were. The rift was Callie's mother, and it would only widen with time.

22

Tyler and Clayton's group stopped at the gas station. Joshua hung back to watch them. They seemed to be conferring about something. One of the girls—a stoner in Joshua's biology class—climbed onto a picnic table and reclined on her elbows, her chin up to the sun like she was tanning. Her boyfriend sat next to her, leaning forward onto his knees. Tyler, Clayton, and a girl Joshua didn't know made their way inside.

Joshua followed, ducking down an aisle and opening a news-paper to obscure his face—not that they'd even glanced in his direction when he'd walked through the door.

While Joshua scanned the news for mention of the VW—still none—the trio migrated from the snack aisle to the pops, handing Tyler the bags of chips and plastic bottles. Clayton and the girl took a sudden interest in the racks of candy bars and gum while Tyler approached the register and pointed to a pack of cigarettes behind the cashier. The stout, curly-haired woman narrowed her eyes at him and asked for an ID.

He opened his wallet and held it up to the woman, who peered at it closely, shrugged, and retrieved the pack. Clayton and the girl, still by the candy, relaxed noticeably.

So this was why an asshole who kicked seat backs had friends now: a fake ID. Joshua felt something flare inside him. Maybe it was the part of him that had stood in front of Clayton at the beginning of the year and proudly identified himself, or maybe it was something darker—angrier. He closed the freezer case and approached the counter.

"Excuse me, ma'am?" Joshua said to the cashier.

Tyler glanced back at him and then quickly away. But the glance was long enough for a lift of the eyebrow and a flash of irritation in the eyes. Clayton's lip curled into a snarl—made more intimidating by the thin scar leading to his nostril.

"He's not eighteen. None of them are," Joshua continued. "I know them from school."

The girl who'd come in with Tyler sucked her teeth, and the tips of Tyler's ears reddened, but he didn't turn around again. Clayton grabbed the girl's hand and made for the door, abandoning Tyler. Joshua smiled. That was victory enough.

"Let me see it again." The cashier beckoned for Tyler's wallet, but he pocketed it and jogged after his friends, leaving the cigarettes behind.

A wave of fear flooded Joshua. There were enough of them to hurt him. But maybe it would be a relief to feel his skin again, to know it was there because it throbbed and ached and bruised.

As expected, Clayton's group was waiting for Joshua outside, leaning on the bike rack in the alley between the gas station and the library, where someone had spray-painted a penis on the Paddington Bear mural.

Joshua approached, hands up like he was under arrest.

Tyler ran his fingers through his hair and looked down his nose at Joshua. Clayton was behind him, arms crossed like a bodyguard. It was clear that they'd decided it was Tyler's fight—probably some sort of test, so he'd officially be admitted into their ranks.

"Hey, narc, why'd you do that?" Tyler asked.

Joshua shrugged. "I could ask you the same question."

Tyler stared at him.

"On the bus?" Joshua said. "Kicking the seat."

Clayton snickered and Tyler rolled his eyes. "You owe me a pack of cigarettes," he said.

"I'm still waiting for the Black Rose Dragon you owe me. Or have you forgotten about your days as a *Yu-Gi-Oh!* collector?" Joshua asked. One of the girls snickered, on his side this time, and Clayton almost looked pleased by this development.

Tyler stood up straighter and ran one hand up his arm, like he was rolling up imaginary shirtsleeves. Joshua wanted to laugh at a script that was as familiar as his own freckles. He closed his eyes and opened his arms as if waiting for a hug, an invitation for Tyler to start the fight and get it over with.

The pain was sharp and quick.

A blaze in Joshua's nose, under his eyes, even up to the center of his forehead. Streaks of white lit the backs of his eyelids. His feet wheeled backward and he found himself on his ass, gravel embedded in his palms. Clayton was laughing, almost a cackle, like some caricature of a villain.

Unsteadily, Joshua stood and braced himself for more, but nothing came. The group started walking away, Clayton in the lead. Tyler stayed a moment longer and shook his head. "You're really pathetic. You know that, right?"

I know you are, but what am I? The refrains they'd once shouted when it was just the two of them teasing each other on his grandparents' farm. "I'm rubber; you're glue. Whatever you say bounces off me and sticks to you," Joshua said. But even he was unsure whether he was trying to rile Tyler up again or if he just wanted to remind him of the past they shared.

"What are you, ten?" said Tyler.

"No. If I were ten, we'd still be friends."

"That's not my fault. It's yours, homo." Tyler turned and followed the group.

Joshua felt something hot on his upper lip and swiped at it with his hand. Blood, but not much. Nothing was broken. Sticks and stones. He stood there, just watching, as the distance between him and Tyler expanded.

"You okay?" a voice called.

Joshua turned, startled. On the sidewalk near the firehouse, shielding his eyes from the sun, was his new neighbor: a vision of untamed hair, mountain-peak eyebrows, and hard muscles.

The man crossed the street and pulled a handkerchief out of his jumpsuit pocket. Briefly, Joshua worried that the neighbor had noticed the note missing, but the pain—now like a mask across his whole face—was too distracting to dwell on it for long.

Joshua accepted the handkerchief and blotted at his nose. He studied the guy's hands, large and tan with no ring lines. His veins looked like blue worms, alive and wriggling over his tendons.

The man tilted Joshua's head back, and Joshua could feel calluses on the pads of his hands. They were warm but dry, like he used baby powder, and Joshua didn't want the hands to stop touching him. He wanted to turn away, adjust his briefs, and make sure his baggy shirt hung loose over his fly.

"Probably going to swell. Maybe bruise some," he said.

Joshua could smell him as he leaned in. The scent wasn't what he'd expected: wood or animal hide or something musty. It was light, lemony even, which inexplicably made Joshua harden more. This was the kind of guy you wrote love notes to.

"What was that about?" his neighbor asked, interrupting Joshua's thoughts.

Joshua blinked before realizing he meant the fight. "History," he said.

His neighbor nodded, and Joshua sensed that he respected the answer.

"Do you need to call someone to come get you?"

"No. I have my bike."

"You sure? You'll be okay?"

"I'm good."

"Okay. See you around. And remember what I said: don't let 'em get you down." He lifted his chin in goodbye again, and Joshua tried to mirror the gesture with the same grace and ease.

He thought of his Pontiac drawing, the broken glass like confetti on the page. And he realized: this Wolverine didn't belong in the seat, but rather crouched on top, as though about to slice open the roof to rescue whoever, or whatever, was inside.

SOME OF US FAWNED

Some of us fawned over Luke as preteens—even though he didn't show a lick of interest in us. We'd spy on him, standing on our tiptoes in the lilac bushes, and giggle into our palms because he'd often be shirtless, flexing in front of the mirror. When he sucked in, we could see his heart beating, the skin pulsing between his ribs. We wanted to touch the triangular indentations around his collarbone, the tendons that vined up his neck, the ledge of skin his triceps made.

If we stayed long enough, he migrated from bedroom to backyard, and we'd lean against the siding of his house, still hidden by the lilac bushes. He kept three large rocks beside the oak tree, in the brambles, and he'd stand there, lifting them from his hips to his shoulders, then behind his back, then over his head until he glistened.

We don't remember Luke's mom much; she died when most

of us were little. Luke's pops, though, we knew. In the post office or diner or garage, he was always the loudest, calling actors on TV *fairies* if they had manicured nails and hair trimmed neatly above their ears. He'd say they should be shot, like horses with broken legs. He wasn't saying these things *to* us. We knew—even then—the message was for Luke, the boy who lifted rocks because his outside was the only thing he could control.

23

A door slammed somewhere in the house. Callie stopped towel-drying her hair and poked her head into the hall-way. The door to her parents' room and the guest room her father had started sleeping in were shut. All the other doors were open, except the one that led to the staircase used back when the house was an inn and home to the maid who worked there. Callie hung up her towel and started down the hall. She expected to feel the suction of air, a familiar draft, but there was nothing. She opened the maids' door, flipped on the light, and started down the two sets of stairs. The first landing led to the kitchen, and the second to the cellar—where Callie guessed the Petersons had once stored soap, clean linens, and canned goods. It now held tubs of Christmas decorations and her childhood treasures—board games, books, stuffed animals, clothes—wrapped in black plastic garbage bags so they wouldn't mildew. You could access the cellar from the outside through a set of padlocked storm doors, but they'd been repainted so many times that Callie wasn't sure they opened anymore.

When she was little, she'd tested herself, turning off the overhead light and standing in the middle of the room as long as she could with just the light from the staircase. It was even worse than standing in absolute darkness. Everything was in shadows, the hulking garbage-bagged silhouettes just visible. She'd count out loud, feeling braver and braver with each number, until something sent her running for the stairs: a footstep above her head, the shift of a reflection on a plastic bag, a branch hitting the storm door. She'd arrive, breathless, in the kitchen above or the hallway on the top floor—wherever her mother might be.

Now she pulled the cord to turn on the overhead light and picked her way around the sacks. A rubber bin of photo albums was in the middle of the floor, the self-published book by the historical society on top—a low-budget text with grainy photos and too-large typeface. *Mercer, Illinois: 1850 to the Future.* Callie traced her mother's name, listed among other members on the inside cover. There was no Ellie Vidal.

Callie flipped through the book, landing on a sketch of a young Lincoln standing in front of a house—her house. The maple tree was missing, but the porch with the spindles and the scalloped wooden siding beneath the windows was unmistakable. So Mrs. Vidal's story was true. What else was?

The book included photos of Mercer and its people from each major era, describing how events such as the Civil War and the Great Depression had impacted the town. She stopped at three pages devoted to the victims of the drive-in tornado. She scanned the list of names, pausing at Celeste Vidal. Vidal? In the photo, Celeste's hair was voluminous around the crown of her head and flipped up at the ends. Her cheeks were round, and her head was tilted so she looked to the right of the camera. Was there a resemblance to the sharp-eyed, permed woman Callie had met?

A photo on the third page of the spread was taken the morning after the tornado. There was a wide path through the center of the picture just like the one Callie had seen in the bean field. The wooden drive-in screen had been halved, splintered posts at the bottom the only evidence it had ever been wider. A few twisted car frames speckled the horizon. Along the sides of the frame were streams of cars, probably those that had been abandoned in the jam. The outer cars were shoved against the inner ones. Four seemed to float on top of the stream, probably dropped there by the tornado. Callie recognized one of the cars in the foreground. White with round headlights, fins, and whitewalls. A Pontiac with a Route 66 bumper sticker, identical to the one she'd seen the night of the tornado.

24

Brenna woke to her cell phone ringing; it was her grandmother. The notebook was still on Brenna's chest, and she checked it, hoping that her dreams had imprinted themselves there.

The pages were still empty.

"Hola, abuelita," she said.

"Are you coming this weekend, Daniela?" her grandmother asked in Spanish. She preferred Brenna's middle name, since her first name was un nombre gringo given to her by her father.

"No sé. Tengo mucha tarea," Brenna spoke slowly, willing her tongue not to trip as she lied about having a lot of homework. When she spoke Spanish to her grandmother, she knew she sounded like Mrs. Berk.

"But it has been weeks since we last saw you. Family is the most important."

"I know. It's just very busy right now with school." Going to her grandmother's was a headache. When they lived in Houston, their mom would try to save enough money to send Brenna and Manny to visit for Día de los Reyes. Now they were expected for every holiday, and it meant endless noise—TV, video games, the sputtering vent fan in the kitchen, her cousins' constant chatter, and, worst of all, her grandmother's criticisms. Usually her mom got the worst of it—for her boyfriends, her dead-end job, how she was raising her children, how she'd followed a man to Texas years ago. Tía Camila, on the other hand, was the perfect daughter. She'd been married to one man and had five perfect children, and abuela never let Brenna or her mom forget it.

As though her grandmother had read Brenna's mind, she said, "Your cousin Mariana gets straight As and she still has time for family."

"Well, she also lives with you, abuela."

Her grandmother ignored this fact. "She's making the cake for Camila's birthday next week. You'll at least come to her birthday, right?"

"Of course." Though Brenna's grandmother didn't even seem to like Brenna all that much, she seemed to have it in her head that Brenna could still be fixed—somehow—and become the Chicana she was supposed to be, if only she'd visit more often. Brenna genuinely wanted to be more connected to her heritage and liked by her grandmother, but she also wanted to be accepted for who she was now.

"Talk to your cousin Mariana. Maybe she can give you some advice on schoolwork."

"No, abuela, I have to go."

But her grandmother covered the phone and said something inaudible.

"¿Aló?" Mariana's voice was nasal and flat. She was a year younger than Brenna, but she'd skipped a grade and never let anyone forget it. Brenna was glad they went to different schools, so she wouldn't have to be in classes with her and hear even more about her failures from her grandmother. Mariana had always been the tattle of the family.

"Hi, Mari," Brenna said in English. "I was actually just about to go."

"Grandma said you had some questions about school," Mariana responded in Spanish. Brenna was sure it was because her grandmother was still standing there.

"No, I don't have any questions. Grandma just wants me to visit more."

"You just have to try a little," Mariana said—this time in English. *Try at what?* Brenna wondered. School? Spanish? At being a better granddaughter? Being Mexican?

Brenna had been trying and failing. "Okay, Mari. I'll try." She hung up without a goodbye.

After a long shower, Brenna texted Amy about joining her at the concert and then wandered into her mother's bedroom. A few work uniforms were piled on a worn velvet chair in the corner, a cross hung on the wall above the bed, a mirror on the closet door, and baptism pictures of Brenna and Manny—side by side in chipped Goodwill frames—next to the window. Her mother had tucked fronds from Palm Sunday behind each one, and they'd dried gold. The sight of that stiff frond rising from the portrait of Brenna as a chubby brown baby was depressing. Her mother probably prayed for her to be someone else—someone less angry, better at school, more responsible and polite to her grandmother—someone who Brenna couldn't find any easier than she could find Colin's version of her.

There was an old TV on the dresser, and Brenna flipped on the news, hoping she'd catch something about the tornado while she changed. She opened the closet and pulled out a black cocktail dress she'd seen her mother wear on dates. The sweetheart neckline was so tight, it shoved her mother's cleavage up and over the fabric. Brenna put it on and looked at herself. The dress was too short on her. Still, it hid what Brenna thought of as her lumpiness—the fact that she was bony in the shoulders and hips, but chubby on her sides and under her arms. Without a ratty flannel and jeans, she at least looked like someone in a different *life stage*. She put on her red boots and a studded belt, and dug through her mother's bathroom drawers for lipstick. There was a red like the color she'd seen Dot wear, but it made Brenna's teeth look yellow and even more crooked. She wiped it off and settled on thick liquid eyeliner.

". . . another car found after Wednesday's tornado," she heard the news anchor saying. Brenna stepped out of her mom's bathroom so she could see the screen. There was an image of the pale blue VW being towed from the cornfield.

Again, no driver had come forward. The VW's owners, the reporter said, were in California and had reported the vehicle stolen. The news moved on, but Brenna sank onto the corner of her mom's bed, staring at the TV. Two cars magically transported to Illinois and involved in this tornado with no drivers found? How could that be so? Brenna had to find out more.

Manny had Golden Girl, so Brenna walked downtown. The band's vocals were loud, audible from blocks away, reverberating between the brick buildings but too garbled to understand. Brenna wondered if her mother could hear them at work as she cracked open rolls of quarters, rang up packs of cigarettes, sold lotto tickets, and imagined her daughter home doing laundry. *Shit.* Brenna had forgotten to start the towels after her shower, and here she was breaking her mother's trust for the umpteenth time. But up ahead, there was a woman who'd seen under her skin, who offered a reprieve from sitting at home and thinking about Colin and Same Life Stage Girl.

At the bar, the bouncer frowned and drew *X*s on Brenna's hands when she said she was under twenty-one, but he didn't check her ID to see that she wasn't eighteen, either. The courtyard contained no more than twenty people—not that Mercer had that many high school or college grads to begin with. Most left to work in the Cities after high school and only came back once they were ready to have babies. It hit Brenna that she might see Colin here, that maybe he was back in town for the weekend, visiting his parents. She scanned the tiny clusters of concertgoers but didn't see anyone she recognized.

The lead singer was playing the guitar and wearing tuxedo pants and a bomber jacket, her hair sculpted into waves. Beside her stood a bass player in camo heels and a fro, and in the back sat a drummer in green sequins.

A couple people—probably close friends of the band—jumped along with the music, beer bottles in hand. A few sat around the fountain in the center, barefoot and sifting pennies with their toes. With Colin, she'd always known where to go, where to stand, like she was an actor hitting her marks. Now Brenna pretended to check her phone until Dot danced past, her ponytail springing over her shoulder.

"Hey!"

"Brenna Ortiz! You came! Aren't they great?"

"Yeah!"

"*I'm on top, right on top, where I wanna be,*" Dot sang. Her voice was rich and smoky, like the jazz singers of the thirties, and powerful, too. The band members' voices trailed along behind hers like kite tails.

"Whoa, you're great! You should be up there," Brenna said.

"That's the dream."

Up close, Brenna saw that black eyeliner had filled the tiny creases beside Dot's eyes. Her skin was so pale and her cheeks so powdered that Brenna wondered whether Dot might be covering something. Brenna knew all about using makeup to hide.

"Have you used the notebook yet?" Dot asked.

"I've tried, but I can't really figure out what to write."

Dot beckoned her to an empty picnic table near the back of the courtyard and pulled a green notebook out of her purse. The leather cover was so scratched and worn that it looked like a crumpled dollar bill. Dot fanned the pages, and Brenna could tell every single one was filled.

"I've never been good at saying what I feel out loud. But I can write it," she said. Dot flipped to a page and traced the lyrics written there, crooning like Nina Simone. "*Make him watch me walking away. I'm not his, not his, not his doll for play.*"

"Wait, what did you just sing?" Brenna asked, her hands suddenly icy. It was the line her seventh-grade self had written on the cover of her old notebook.

Dot sang the line again, "*I'm not his, not his, not his doll for play.*"

Brenna swallowed hard. "I wrote that same line years ago."

"Uncanny!" Dot said. Her smile had a wink to it, like they were having a conversation between the lines. Brenna just wasn't sure what about.

Brenna's phone buzzed. *We're here*, Amy had texted. She was easy to spot by the entrance, her pineapple-yellow hair sprayed stiff around her face, a black Victorian collar to her chin, her skin vampire pale. Dutch stood behind her, his hair spiked into a Mohawk and his ears gauged with black discs. He wore a Nirvana T-shirt tucked into a kilt.

"I want you to meet my friends," Brenna said, but Dot seemed to be shrinking away from her, her eyes darting to where Amy and

Dutch had stopped at the bar, probably trying to buy drinks with their fake IDs.

"I can't stick around, but I heard the band has another show tomorrow at the Alehouse on River Road. You should come, and we can chat again."

"I'd love to if I can use the car," Brenna said, embarrassed by how eager she sounded. It was hard to mask how excited she felt: like Dot knew her, the real her—however crazy that seemed.

Dot waved goodbye, each of her fingers taking a quick bow, and danced toward the stage.

Amy strolled to the picnic table, licking beer foam off the rim of her pint glass and dragging Dutch by the hand. The pair was always sort of dating, sort of not. She offered the beer to Brenna, who swallowed a sour gulp.

"Where's the girl who invited you?"

"She had to go." Brenna gestured toward the small knot of fans, but Dot, with her polka dots and patent leather, was nowhere to be seen.

A FEW OF US

A few of us remember getting a black eye from Detonator Dorothy when we played Kick the Can. She was this pigtailed, saddle-shoed girl who flattened herself in the shadow of the town square's band shell, just within sight of the red Campbell's can guarded by Bobby or Kevin or Donny or whatever dumb twerp volunteered for the job. As soon as Bobby or whoever took a step back, Dorothy would unfurl herself from her hiding spot and sprint, making this terrible shrieking sound like a bomb about to explode. The can guard always reversed his direction too late, his baby-fat cheeks wobbling, arms pumping. Her toe would connect with the can, send it clatter-rolling across the bricks, before she collided with the can guard: eyes open, elbows up, refusing to flinch.

We saw her parents fighting from the street a few times, and one of us whose bedroom windows faced the same alley as Dorothy's had seen her dad in the hallway light, a sallow scarecrow of a man, slip into her bedroom. The door closed off the light and there'd been noises in the still alley air, that same bomb shriek, but quieter, like a dog whimpering. The light in her mama's room flicked on once, but then right back out. Word of the awfulness spread quickly in Mercer.

We stopped playing Kick the Can with her. We stopped looking her in the eye.

We didn't know what else to do.

25

Joshua's mother was on the living room couch when he walked in, a file open in her lap. Her eyes were on him, wide and worried.

"What happened to you?"

"It's nothing, Mom."

"Oh, Joshy." She stood, papers sliding to the floor, and cupped his cheeks. He longed for his neighbor's hands on his face, those powder-dry calluses.

"I'm fine. Nothing's broken."

"Is this why you skipped first period this morning? Has someone been bullying you at school?"

Joshua thought about lying and saying *yes*. Maybe it would end this conversation. But he knew his mother would demand meetings with the vice principal and counselor; there'd be no end. Just the thought of that exhausted him.

"I told you before: no one pays attention to me at school, Mom. It's like I don't exist there," he said.

"Well, you certainly didn't this morning. Missing a class? What were you doing? And how did *this* happen?"

"Can't we just skip all that and go straight to my punishment?"

She looked bewildered. "I'm on your side, Joshy, but you have to tell me what's going on."

Joshua felt the urge to hurt her, to ask why she couldn't just be the supportive mom after the fact. She should have protected him all along, should have homeschooled him instead of working. But he swallowed his words; it wasn't her fault.

"Can we just talk later?" He started up the stairs. "I presume I'm grounded."

She didn't say anything in response, but Joshua recognized his mother's silence. Her gaze would be sharply focused on his back, zooming in like Ruthie's did.

In his bedroom, Joshua unfolded the stolen note next to the car drawing he'd started at school. *I want to memorize your geography.* That was passion befitting a superhero.

Joshua got lost in his drawing, sketching his neighbor as Wolverine on top of the Pontiac, about to save whoever was inside, a shadowed silhouette. It was more of a movie Wolverine than a comic book one, simple and realistic: a perfect whorl of chest hair above the sleeveless tee and glimmering adamantium claws extending from his clenched knuckles. His hair feathered out above peaked dark eyebrows. He glared from the picture with wolfish brown eyes that were more alive than anything Joshua had ever drawn before.

Holding the pencil in his teeth, he dragged an eraser across the sketchpad. He couldn't get the legs right. He tried to re-create the overlapping diamonds of his neighbor's quadriceps, the lean bulbs of his calves, but failed every time. At the bottom of the torso, Joshua sketched the crouched hind legs and bushy tail of an actual wolverine in light, wispy lines. He imagined the man prowling the fields for deer and rabbits—yellow-eyed, teeth bared, hackles raised. Joshua wanted to wear the man like a hot fur pelt on his back and become a predator himself.

And this Wolverine had noticed him? Had given him advice and held his face? Despite the aching around his eyes and at the bridge of his nose, Joshua could only feel excited.

26

Brenna woke to banging, loud, like wind catching the shutters. She sat up, sure that she'd slept through a siren, that another tornado was on its way, and kicked free of her sheets. The room was dark, so she lit her phone: 2:37 a.m.

"Brenna Daniela Ortiz!" Her mother's voice. The pounding resolved into angry knocking. Adrenaline drained into Brenna's chest, where it welled, hot.

"God, Mom, what?"

The door swung open, the knob smacking the drywall.

Her mother was still in uniform. She held a wad of black material in her hand. Brenna recognized her mother's anger because it was like her own: formidable and fast, but all wind.

"What's this?"

"I don't know," Brenna said, though she recognized the dress she'd borrowed. She must have put it back in the wrong place, or maybe it had fallen off the hanger and smelled like smoke. Her mind flicked to the towels, still piled on the floor. *Double shit.*

Her mother sucked her cheeks in. "You wore it somewhere, didn't you? To that concert?"

"I'll wash it," Brenna said.

"That's not the point. The point is you don't listen."

Her mother stepped into the room and paced. Four steps to the dresser. Four back to the closet. Faster each time, gathering force.

"I asked for one thing." Turn. Four steps. "You can't do one thing?" She sounded more hurt than angry.

"In all fairness, you asked for three."

Her mother kicked the TV tray Brenna used as a nightstand. The flimsy leg gave way, bowing to the floor. The ashtray Brenna hid under wads of Kleenex hit the carpet with a thud. Her mother nudged it with her toe and Brenna braced herself for a smoking lecture, but her voice was surprisingly soft.

"You just take and take and take and do whatever you want. You don't think of anyone else, mija."

Brenna felt this slice deep into her. "*You* don't think of anyone else," she said, a spectator of her own anger again, like she was watching it build from the other side of glass. "You pretend to be a pious Catholic because your mom wants you to and then parade men through here like this is a truck stop."

The smack caught her jaw, and her ears crackled. Brenna buried her face in her arms, preparing for a flurry of slaps, but none came. She peeked out. Her mother's work visor hid the top half of her face in shadow.

When her mother spoke, she sounded resigned. "I expect that kind of talk from *them*, but not from you." *Them*—Brenna knew—were all the Lisles, the bag-booters, and the gossips of Mercer, the kind of people who had made Brenna's seventh-grade year so miserable. Brenna still couldn't see her mother's eyes, but she knew what was next: "You got an hour to get out."

Brenna dropped her arms when the door slammed. She'd been kicked out before; it was bluster—a duet they played often: angsty teenage daughter; overworked, frustrated mother. Brenna always stayed put and, the next day, there'd be a few dollars for lunch on the counter or a clean bowl and a box of cereal. She returned the peace offering by wiping down the countertops or lighting a stick of incense so the house didn't smell so dank from Manny's weed. But this was different. It was the middle of the night, and she'd said something she couldn't take back.

Still, she wanted her mother to hurt, to feel her absence like a nail in the soft flesh of her sole. Brenna pried her cell phone charger from the wall and picked up the lavender notebook from where she'd flung it beside the bed. Maybe tonight she'd be inspired enough to start writing again. She stuffed the journal, along with some under-wear, a tank, flannel, and jeans into her backpack and pulled on her boots, not bothering to change out of the T-shirt and boxers she slept in. Her mother's door was shut, but Brenna found her purse in the kitchen. Brenna snatched the only cash—a five-dollar bill—and flung open the front door. The night was starless and chilly. Brenna took a deep breath and tried Amy's phone. No answer. Golden Girl wasn't in the driveway either, and Brenna wasn't about to call Manny.

Brenna stood at the end of her driveway. Behind her was downtown. Across the street was the cemetery, then the impound lot beyond that, which was kitty-corner from the high school, and then the great wide stretch of country. She felt like she could be wild, like she could plunge off a forest path into dark brambles, and go deeper, go through. But something tugged at her. The white car from the night of the tornado would be in the lot. And by now the VW would be there too. She could study them up close. Maybe even sleep inside one of them.

The lot kept a dog, but it was old and would bark only half-heartedly at Brenna and her friends on their way to school, wagging if someone threw a powdered doughnut or granola bar. She could see its squat white shape outside the office. It was still—probably asleep.

The high school across the way was dark, and the street was deserted, so Brenna wrapped her fingers around the chain links, forced a toe through, and hauled herself up. She rolled over the top and let herself drop. Her feet crunched on the gravel, and she expected to hear the sigh of the aged pit bull while it gathered the energy to stand, but it didn't stir.

The VW was easy to spot in a crowd of cars near the front of the lot. She walked around the powder-blue behemoth, touching each ding and spider crack she could reach. Hail, maybe? From the storm? She pulled on the doors, but they were all locked.

Brenna weaved through rows of vehicle carcasses, trying not to imagine what or who might be crouched in their shadowy interiors. She finally found the white car at the other end of the lot—right up against the fence. Brenna could see the pockmarks in the car's white paint, the places where the chrome bent, reflecting moonlight back at itself. She walked around the car until she found its name scrawled in silver. *Pontiac Catalina*. It was a musical name, begging to be chanted like a spell. The car had a Route 66 bumper sticker. From history class, she remembered that the highway stretched from Chicago to LA—a whole swath of the country that could contain clues. The interior was white leather, pristine—not cigarette-burnt and losing its spongy yellow stuffing like Golden Girl's seats. Brenna tried the doors, but they were all locked too. Strange, when she could just climb onto the hood and lower herself, feetfirst, through the shattered windshield.

She positioned herself in the driver's seat and tried to imagine the terror of being lifted in the car, having only the steering wheel to hold on to. As she sat there, Brenna felt something tugging at her again, a strong feeling that she should look for answers. She ran her fingers over the leather, checked under the seats, hoping for a drop of blood, a wallet, something the police had missed, something that would explain what was going on.

Under the passenger seat, her fingers brushed a piece of cloth wrapped around the springs. When she pulled, the fabric ripped and something came free. A grease-stained name patch: *Luke*. She thought the owner's name was Edward. She held the patch up to the moonlight, hoping it would reveal something other than grease.

Brenna tucked it into her backpack so she could study it more in daylight, and pulled out her flannel shirt and jeans. She climbed into the back seat, changed, and then reclined to look out at the cloudy night. It was too dark to write, but she held the new journal against her chest. She knew that she'd grow cold soon, that she'd be hungry in the morning, that she'd have to sneak out without being seen and find somewhere to go. But, maybe, if she fell asleep again with the journal on her chest, Brenna's heart would write her as someone new. A someone who could figure out why this Pontiac and the VW were important, and if the Storm Spirits were trying to tell them something.

MANY OF US WATCHED

Many of us watched from our porches the night Dorothy's mother chased her father out of the house with a paring knife before sobbing, hands on her knees. Detonator Dorothy, probably thirteen at the time, was barefoot with her hair mussed like she'd been asleep. She had tiptoed off the stoop to her mother, but she pushed her daughter away as though it were somehow Dorothy's fault the man was gone.

When the medics put Dorothy in the ambulance a few weeks later, she was gray-faced and purple-lipped but alive, her mother tripping alongside the stretcher in a housedress. Rumor had it that Dorothy had taped a plastic bag over her head. It was months before she returned to school.

But soon we heard the Zenith crooning every night and Dorothy humming along until her mother scolded her for "all that noise." We'd drag Mr. McLauren's porch chairs into the alley to listen, at first to the Billboard hits: Elvis, Dean Martin, the McGuire Sisters. All sugar and pop. Then Dorothy found jazz: Ella, Billie, Nina, Peggy, and Carmen. How could the same person who made that bomb-shriek sing like them?

She bought a used guitar. We watched her walk home with it, her arms wrapped around it like a newborn—though it was anything but. Its wood was almost worn through beneath the strings, the yellow varnish chipped to reveal silver. From the alley, the notes had a dusky smokiness to them that seemed to strip everything away, down to the very soul. Despite her mother's protests that it was a waste of time, Dorothy even joined the high school choir. After the bell, she hung around the cavernous choir room with its arched ceiling. And those of us who'd returned for our forgotten canteens and sheet music saw her singing at the piano, alone. It was slightly out of tune, the notes dampened, but she transformed the room into a chapel, the songs into prayer.

A few of us were hovering in the doorway, listening, the day Mr. Cannon returned for his briefcase. We ducked away, fiddling with our lockers and instrument cases. Our choir teacher was gray-haired, his face thick at the jaw, the mustache and beard widening it even more. He had the same bleary, unfocused red eyes as so many of our uncles and fathers, including Dorothy's.

"You sing like a real grown-up," he slurred at Dorothy.

"Is that a good thing?"

Mr. Cannon smiled. "Depends on whether you want to be a grown-up or not." He gestured at the piano bench. "May I?" Without waiting for a reply, Mr. Cannon climbed onto the bench, barely fitting beside Dorothy. He played something moody and slow that we'd never heard before.

"Sing," he commanded.

"I don't know the words."

"Hasn't stopped you before. I've heard you."

Dorothy's cheeks flushed.

"Go on," he said.

Dorothy made a choked sound. Mr. Cannon stopped playing and put one hand on her back and one on her abdomen. "Sit up straight. From here," he said.

She moved like a trapped cat then: spastic and fast. When the bench didn't budge, she toppled from it backward, twisting her torso and landing on her palms, then snaking her legs out behind her. She ran past, not even seeing us. Mr. Cannon, however, saw us and reddened.

"What's wrong with her?" he asked, a question everyone in town knew the answer to, including him.

We lifted our instrument cases, slammed our locker doors, and followed Dorothy. It was the least we could do.

27

It was still dark when Callie woke to the beeping of her alarm. She pulled on her cross-country uniform, the compression shorts looser than they'd been at the season opener over a month ago. The historical society's book was on her nightstand now, but she couldn't muster the excitement she'd felt in the cellar the night before. She tucked the book under her pillow.

When she went downstairs, she was surprised to find the light on in the kitchen, her father leaning against the counter with the newspaper.

"Happy birthday," he said, and pointed at a banana in the fruit bowl.

"I'm not hungry."

"Bodies are like cars, Cal."

"You should change the oil every three thousand miles?"

He didn't laugh. "They need fuel to run." He pointed at the banana again.

Callie peeled it, holding her breath so she wouldn't have to smell the sweetness. She tossed the waxy peel in the trash and remembered how her father had draped banana peels over his knuckles when she was little, pretending they were wigs for hand puppets.

Callie took a bite and tried not to gag. The banana was mealy and stringy all at once. She mashed it into paste with her molars and packed it against the roof of her mouth, where she didn't have to taste it.

"Listen, I know this isn't the best time to tell you this, but a realtor is going to come by tomorrow. A friend of your mother's. She's going to help me get the house ready for"—her father cleared his throat—"for sale. Your mom wants to be sure the house will be in good hands, you know?"

Callie opened her mouth to tell him she'd overheard them talking about it, but her voice was unable to push aside the boulder of an ache in her throat. The boulder was her mother looking for her: *Is she in the closet? No, not in the closet. Is she in the bathtub? No, not in the bathtub.* It was her mother calling *come out, come out, wherever you are* after Callie had wedged herself in the cabinet beneath the window seat or in the trunk in the attic or under the chaise or behind the curtains, her hand pressed over her mouth to suppress the giggles. Hide-and-seek could last hours if they wanted it to—the house had given them that.

The banister creaked just then, and Callie heard her mother's huffing breath, her slow, shuffling steps. Her father tossed the newspaper on the counter and headed for the staircase to help. Callie pulled out a classified page, wrapped the remaining banana, and threw it into the trash.

She thought again of the videos of marathon runners who collapsed, faces slack. Callie imagined herself as a taut string, threaded from her feet to her hips to her shoulders to her ears. Singing through the air. The harder she ran, the more tension in the string, the closer to breaking. It'd be that simple: a pluck, a twang.

Callie finished second at the meet, just behind a long-limbed girl from Ottawa. She was light-headed from hunger—her thoughts in slow motion as though stretched through molasses. As she jogged a few extra meters to cool down, she imagined the string loosening again, coiling in her gut. She coughed and heaved a dribble of yellow liquid. It was the damn banana bite, she thought. If she'd been truly empty, she wouldn't have failed at breaking.

Without waiting for Leslie and her other teammates to finish, Callie walked toward her parents. The night before in the cellar, she'd felt like she was moving toward something meaningful, but now, in the bright morning sun, that feeling was distant. Had she simply imagined it? Allowed the magic of the midnight hour to turn a coincidence into something the old Callie would have believed was significant?

Her mother wore an oversized jacket that hid how much weight she'd lost. She had on a high-quality wig Aunt Toni had bought her. *It's made from real hair*, she'd said proudly, which made Callie shudder. The wig was a warmer brown than her mother's had been, almost red. She looked like a normal mother with it on, just not Callie's.

Her father handed her a bottle of water.

"What a birthday run," her mother said. "You looked good out there."

"That had to be your best time all season," her father added.

Callie bent down, stretching her hamstrings. She'd go home with a plastic trophy, the coveted gold-girl runner, hair streaming, perched on top of a red marbled pillar. But she hardly cared. Win or lose, it was just an equation like any other. Callie ran the race at x speed. Her mother would die in y days.

28

Brenna awoke in the car, shivering, a cramp in her neck and a still-blank journal on her chest. The sky was yellow gray. Her phone was dead, but she guessed it was a little after six. The leather upholstery had grown warm around her, as though part of a living cocoon. She unfolded herself, stretched, and patted the seat. There was something special about the Pontiac Catalina, a presence that made it feel alive. Maybe the car itself had been pulling her. Maybe it had wanted her to find the name patch and understand something. But what?

The guard dog was awake at the other end of the lot, on its haunches near a dented food bowl. It was facing the trailer that served as the lot's office, panting, its tail thumping occasionally. Was someone about to emerge? Brenna unlocked the car door, tossed her bag over the fence, and started to climb. She expected to feel the slippery enamel of teeth on her ankle or hear someone shout, but she landed safely and jogged away without looking back.

Two of her five dollars went toward a cup of coffee at Bean City. Brenna wrapped her hands around the hot cup and sat at the table where Colin and Same Life Stage Girl had been. She wondered what the girl thought about. Group projects? Roommates who refused to clean their dishes? Puppet dictators in Latin America? The social significance of hip-hop? Did all of that add up to a different life stage?

Brenna plugged her phone in.

No messages. Her mother was probably still asleep.

I need Golden Girl to go to the Cities tonight, she texted Manny. *Don't tell Mom.*

Can you pick me up at Bean City when you get out of Saturday detention? she texted Amy.

She googled the owners of the VW, learning only that they looked like hippies and had bought the vehicle in the late nineties. Brenna took the name tag she'd found in the Pontiac out of her backpack to see if daylight offered more clues. It was white with a red border and had once been stitched to gray fabric. Other than that, it didn't reveal anything new.

Bored, she took a pencil out of her backpack and pushed the lead into a creamy page. She couldn't think of anything to write.

Nothing but a dot for Dot. She sipped the coffee, which felt like it was burning a hole through her empty stomach, the rabid feeling replaced by hunger.

The barista, an older woman with silver hair and penciled eyebrows, kept looking at her and narrowing her eyes. Brenna could guess what the woman saw. The shredded jean hems. The ripped backpack. Her brown skin.

Just then Joshua walked into the coffee shop, looking sleep-rumpled, like he'd slept in his clothes too. His skater shoes were untied, his jeans just as ripped as Brenna's.

"Hey," Brenna called out, loudly enough that the barista glared. She'd never seen Joshua in the coffee shop before. First the school office, now here.

Joshua waved enthusiastically. At school she'd seen him moping around the halls, tiptoeing as if he were trying not to make a dent in the world. Such yearning. She wondered if that was how she had seemed to Colin. Or to Dot. Maybe that was why she felt a connection with Joshua. Or maybe it was the tornado, the look she'd seen on his face as he pedaled up to her car. She'd recognized it: a desire to be someone, to mean something to someone else.

"What are you up to? Want to sit down?" she asked across the shop.

"My mom asked me to grab some cinnamon buns for breakfast."

"Oh okay," she said, trying not to sound desperately disappointed.

He placed his order with the barista and walked over to Brenna's table to wait. She noticed him eyeing the empty notebook in front of her.

"You okay?" he asked.

"Yeah, I'm just killing time." His left eye had a shadow under it, a purple half-moon. "What about you?"

He looked confused for a moment. "Oh, the eye. Yeah, I'm fine."

Brenna leaned across her table and whispered: "Did you hear they found the VW? It's in the impound lot now."

Joshua's eyes widened. "No. Who was driving?"

"They don't know."

"No shit. Same as with the Pontiac?"

She nodded. "The owners are in California."

"Could it be connected to the Big One?" Joshua asked.

"I think so," Brenna said just as the barista called out Joshua's order. He returned to the counter for the box of rolls. Brenna could smell the warm cinnamon and cream cheese frosting from her spot a few seats down. Her stomach groaned so loudly, she was sure the whole coffee shop had heard. She wished he'd stay.

"We should hang out. I have something I want to show you. Something I found," she said.

Joshua's eyes sparked with excitement, then fell. "Technically, I'm grounded."

Brenna nodded and tried to hide her own disappointment.

"But I could probably get away with having you over for breakfast, if you want," he said. "We could say we're working on a project."

Brenna couldn't stop herself from jumping off the stool. Together, they could theorize about the VW, the patch she'd found in the Pontiac, the whispers. Together, it seemed, was how Mercer wanted them to be.

29

Brenna's cinnamon bun disappeared before Joshua even had a chance to reheat his own in the microwave. She licked the cream cheese frosting off her fingers. He pulled down a cereal box and put it in front of her without saying anything. He hated when people pointed out how much or how quickly he ate. He watched her eat and wondered if she felt the bond between them—even though they had nothing in common except the tornado and living with just one of their birth parents.

She yawned, covering her mouth with one hand and digging into the box with the other. "Sorry, I slept in a car. The Pontiac, actually."

It took him a moment to register what she was talking about.

"Wait, what? Why?"

"My mom kicked me out and I just had this weird feeling, like I should go to the impound lot." She pulled out a patch stitched with the name *Luke* and handed it to him. "This is what I wanted to show you. I found it caught in the springs under the seat." He turned it over. It was smeared with something black, like ink or grease that had been there too long to leave residue on his fingers. Joshua remembered the hole in his neighbor's uniform, and the letter he'd stolen addressed to *L*. Could his new neighbor be this Luke? But these stains looked older, like the patch had been twisted in the springs for decades.

"Luke isn't the Pontiac owner's name," Brenna said.

"Yeah, I read that. Did you see that the owner lived in Indiana but was originally from Mercer?"

She raised her eyebrows. "So how'd his car get back here?"

"Maybe Luke drove it."

"Or maybe it was one of the owner's family members. Someone was taking a trip back to Mercer and they got caught in the storm."

"Why haven't they come forward then? To get the car back?" Joshua asked.

"Maybe they didn't make it. Died somewhere in the field. Maybe Mrs. Jenson and the other crows are eating them as we speak." Brenna's eyes were glinting in amusement.

"Maybe they stole it and don't want anyone to know," Joshua said.

"Maybe the car has a mind of its own."

"Maybe it was a ghost driving."

Brenna's face grew serious. "I'd believe it. We should see if we can find out who Luke was. Research the owner, too."

"That Edward guy? I already looked online. All I could find was his obituary." It dawned on Joshua then. Could Edward be *E*?

"Maybe we could go to the society downtown. They have records and shit," she said. "We could find out who he used to be. It's like Mr. Davis says, 'History always has answers,' ya know?"

Joshua heard Lawrence's and his mother's voices above them. Their bedroom door opened, and her footsteps were in the hallway. She was coming down, which meant he was about to get a lecture. Joshua looked at the staircase, willing it to collapse so he could stay in the kitchen with Brenna a little longer. "I'm about to be reminded that I'm grounded," he said.

"So what? I'm a runaway." Brenna grinned. "Just tell them about all the research we have to do for our 'school project.'" She made air quotes.

Joshua grinned right back.

WHEN WE WERE TEENAGERS

When we were teenagers, we loved to drive loops downtown with our elbows out the windows. We'd spot Luke bent over engines, hair damp across his forehead, face smeared with grease, his eyes on the firehouse next to his father's shop. The potbellied volunteers would be sitting in the parking lot, playing euchre and fanning themselves with their cards like Southern ladies.

Before long, we realized it was Eddie he watched for. Eddie, who waxed the fire truck and greased the ladders and changed the filters, hoping, we were sure, that he'd be allowed to fight fires. Eddie looked like the kind of movie star we'd see at the drive-in. He was Golden, shining in a white tee and jeans. If it was cold, he wore a letterman's jacket with three yellow *M*s, each with two slim gilded bars. *Varsity varsity varsity.* His hair was corn silk, his skin the fall stalks. He was prince of pleasant valleys, of farms that draped like patchwork quilts across the Midwest. When he smiled, it was a little lopsided, a little *Who—me?*

Sometimes Eddie would sling a towel over his shoulder and walk to the garage. Luke would slide beneath the car or disappear under its hood, but Eddie was undeterred. Anyone who'd been in classes with him knew he could wax poetic about baseball for hours: the leather in his hands, the ribbed stitches, the scent of soybeans heavy in the air, the red dust clinging to his pants.

The less perceptive among us considered them unlikely friends: the greaser and the jock. But the rest of us saw it: the spark there. The way Luke's eyes widened when Eddie came near, like a horse about to bolt. Eddie, who is among us now, saw it too.

Connie, Luke's girlfriend, was the oblivious one. Luke had a habit of racing off to see her as soon as Eddie wandered back to his post at the firehouse. Connie whispered to some of us what happened on those nights: the steamed car windows, her hand on his cock, her mouth on his neck. And him still wanting more, more, like nothing was enough.

When Eddie's dad gave him the Pontiac, we all salivated, circling it with our fingertips brushing the paint. Eddie would pop the hood and we'd make appreciative sounds, though we didn't know much about cars. Only Luke did, and so we looked to him, waited for his reaction. But he only grunted when Eddie waved him over.

One day Eddie said: "Something's off. Can you take a look?" Luke, skittish as always, took a step back from the proffered keys. Our chins dropped. If they'd been offered to us, we would have snatched them from his fingers.

Finally Luke took them and Eddie slid into the passenger seat and they were off, fast, toward the empty countryside. We knew this drive into the sunset was only the beginning.

30

Callie climbed into the driver's seat, hugging the historical society's book and the paper license she'd been temporarily issued. Now she could drive without her parents. Now, when she was losing her mother anyway.

The car smelled like her—not the old smell, but the new, nauseating one. Earlier, she'd been asleep in the passenger seat, gurgling that smell into the upholstery while Callie and her father waited in line at the DMV. She'd woken up when they'd returned to the car, but had been unable to complete her sentences, repeating *happy* over and over. Callie wasn't sure if she meant *Happy birthday* or *I'm happy for you.*

Callie's phone buzzed in her pocket and jolted her to the present. It was Leslie, whom she'd managed to avoid at the meet. *Ready for birthday fun?* Followed by another: *Meet me at Giovanni's in an hour!*

Callie looked at the time—it was two thirty—but didn't respond, her father's rules about texting and driving ringing between her temples. *I don't want you to become one of those PSAs,* he'd said once. Listening to this one rule was the least Callie could do.

At the museum, she parked on the street and tucked the book under her arm. She wasn't sure exactly what she intended to do there. Find out if Mrs. Vidal and Celeste were related? Find out if the Pontiac she'd seen in the photo of the 1961 storm was the same as the one she'd seen the night of the tornado? It was just an excuse not to think about her mother—like everything she did now.

The docent, Mrs. Greenley, greeted her warmly. Callie knew her from every elementary school trip they'd taken, where she'd repeated the tale of the poisoned Winston twins, who loved to smash china and had grown up in the house now occupied by the museum. She was unchanged, her back curved like a shepherd's hook, forcing her to crane her head upward. It made Callie want to roll her shoulders back and stretch her own neck.

She said hello back and forced a smile for Mrs. Greenley before wandering around the familiar display cases. They contained bone china ringed in blue, brooches with glass stones, inventories of the founding settlers' livestock, Bibles with family names inscribed on the first pages, and letters in a script Callie was barely able to decipher. All of the cases were made of shatterproof glass, supposedly to protect the historic artifacts from the Winston twins and their penchant for smashing. Callie had always guessed that it had more to do with the living—distant relatives wanting to reclaim their stake in Mercer's history, children wanting something pretty to call their own, teens wanting to leave their mark on something. Would Callie have had a destructive phase if it weren't for her mother's illness? Would she still?

"I heard your class is doing research on the sixties," Mrs. Greenley said, interrupting her thoughts. "Some of your classmates are already here."

Callie's mind whirled. Her classmates? Had she been assigned a history project and forgotten?

"Come. Come. We have more records downstairs."

She followed Mrs. Greenley to the basement. Hundreds of white cardboard boxes lined the rows of shelves. Joshua sat at a table in the center of the room, lit by green banker's lamps. Brenna sat beside him, her dark hair with the flame-tipped ends curtaining her face. Callie felt at once glad and confused to see them.

"Here they are, dear," Mrs. Greenley said. Joshua looked up, his bruised face registering Callie. He tapped Brenna's arm. She pushed her hair back behind her ear and nodded, like she'd expected Callie all along.

31

Y ou're here about the car, aren't you?" Brenna asked as Callie
sank into a chair beside her.

Callie nodded.

"Us too," Joshua said. "Brenna found a patch with the name
Luke in the Pontiac, so we're looking for something—anything—that
connects the name Luke to the car."

"You got into the Pontiac?" Callie's wan face arranged itself
into something like interest.

"Yeah, she's a badass like that," Joshua said. "No big deal."

Brenna felt herself flush. She wasn't used to being admired.

"Where's the car?"

"At the impound lot. The VW we found is there too. They
don't know how it got stuck in the storm either."

"So what can I do?" Callie asked.

"Grab a box and dig in."

Brenna pushed a box toward Callie and stood to grab another. She allowed her hand to hover over the boxes the old lady had pointed out until she felt the tug beneath her ribs again, like she had in the impound lot. She was about to find something big. She slid the box off the shelf and opened the lid.

Yearbooks.

She flipped through rows and rows of individual portraits, of clubs and teams on risers. There was a choir in knee-length robes. She recognized the girl front and center, standing on the lowest riser, and the pronounced gap between her shoulders and the boys on either side. Brenna brought the book to her nose. The girl's skin was pale, washed-out in the old image. She wasn't wearing makeup. She didn't have bangs, or they were pinned back, but the heart-shaped face, the large eyes, the ponytail curled over her shoulder—they were familiar.

She counted the names in the caption, stopping at the fifth: *Dorothy Healy*. Dot. Brenna's stomach shifted. She wanted to vomit, but she also felt hungry, ravenous. This was definitely the same person. Dorothy Healy had crossed back and was visiting Brenna, of all people.

But if Gretta was right, and the spirits were trying to communicate, what on earth was Dot trying to tell her?

Joshua started with the obituaries from the night of the 1961 tornado, looking for other Miltons, relatives of Edward Milton who may have been driving the Pontiac. There weren't any.

Brenna told him to check the police logs, so he pulled them off the shelf and began flipping through each one. Most were typewritten reports in plastic page protectors, but a few were handwritten notes on blue-lined paper. Joshua tilted the pages to read the chicken scratch.

Eddie Milton. The name was scrawled like an afterthought on the top corner of one page. Joshua inhaled sharply. The Pontiac owner was at the drive-in that night.

Eddie had reported his friend Luke Winters missing. He'd told the officer he'd last seen Luke heading in the direction of the snack bar. The officer underlined Luke's name twice and wrote a question mark. *Luke*, the name on the patch. *L* and *E*—just as he'd guessed. The hair stood up on Joshua's neck. How was this possible?

Brenna handed him a yearbook with a spread of candid photos of Fall Fest.

"The car," she said, but Joshua didn't pay attention to the Pontiac, or to the young version of the owner, Eddie Milton, sitting on the hood, smiling widely with a letterman's jacket unbuttoned to reveal the Mercer FD emblem on his chest. All he saw was a young man who was identical to his Wolverine neighbor, except his hair was gelled back and his facial hair was faint. The man's arms were crossed and he leaned against the car confidently, his eyes bright and amused, teasing whoever was taking the photo. *Alumnus Luke Winters and junior Edward Milton II join the Fall Fest parade*, the caption said.

Joshua slammed the book shut, his heart thudding in his chest. "No," he said. All Mercer's backward beliefs came hurtling at him—Mrs. Jenson, the bridge, Blue Light Cemetery—everything he'd grown up with but had sworn off because the town had refused to accept him. If he admitted they were right about ghosts, did it mean they were right about him? No, of course not. But the situation didn't make sense. Unless the man in the yearbook was his neighbor's relative. Maybe the picture was of the guy's grandfather. Maybe he was the one who'd gone missing during the storm.

Brenna was watching him, chewing on the red-dyed ends of her hair. "You met one too, didn't you."

It was a statement not a question, but Joshua didn't know how to answer. He looked at Callie, who held an obituary, her mouth opening and closing like a fish reeled onto a boat.

Brenna craned her neck to see it. "You've met Celeste Vidal?" she asked. "I visit her headstone sometimes."

Callie shook her head. "No. Not Celeste. The mother who's listed as a survivor. She came to my house—" She shook her head. "It doesn't make sense. None of it does."

Brenna slid off her chair and sat cross-legged on the concrete floor. She held out a hand for each of them. Joshua was surprised by her hand, how comforting it was, how easily Callie sank beside Brenna too.

"Some weird shit is happening to us," Brenna said. "And we have to figure out why."

At this, Joshua felt a rush of excitement beneath his skin, as though his cells were gathering there, preparing to rebuild him as someone needed, someone new, someone seen.

33

Callie clutched the obituary in her free hand. She'd be listed as a survivor soon. Her father, too. How could living on after her mother be considered *surviving*? How, when she was barely even surviving now?

Callie felt something awaken in her, its eyes dazed and blinking. It dared her to keep going, to interrogate her surroundings. Why was she in a basement, holding the hand of a girl she'd only met days ago? Why did she hear whispers? Why did it seem as though her house was trying to tell her something? Why was an old woman asking her about Lincoln? Why was her mother— She had to say it aloud.

"I'm so scared for my mom to—" The word was stuck there, behind that boulder in her throat. She pushed, wedged it aside, so that enough air could get through—enough for the word: *die.*

Brenna met her eyes and held the gaze. "I know," she said, and it felt better to Callie than all the mumbled "Oh, hon"s and "Sweetheart"s and "Prayers" and "I'm sorry"s she'd heard over the last few months. It felt like relief.

Callie exhaled.

34

As she held Callie's hand, the adrenaline drained from Brenna, leaving a cold prickle on the back of her neck. Otherworldly beings weren't as terrifying as the thought of her own mother's death. Imagining her gone was like imagining a tear in the force that tethered Brenna to earth, like floating into cold darkness. Yeah, they fought, but she couldn't imagine life without her mother in it.

"Let's get out of here. It's stuffy. And you look like you've seen a ghost." She tugged gently at Callie's bird-boned hand, hoping for a smile. Instead Callie laughed—a surprising bark of a noise. Joshua's eyebrows shot up at the unexpected sound, and he began to laugh too, his laugh huffing off the roof of his mouth. Brenna couldn't help grinning.

When the laughter had died down, Joshua spoke first.

"Shouldn't we, I don't know, look for more evidence? I mean, dead people walking on Earth? It's ludicrous, right? We're just going nuts like the rest of this town."

Brenna looked pointedly at Callie, who had fallen silent and was reshelving boxes.

"Yeah, okay. Let's get out of here," Joshua said, stuffing the police log into his jeans pocket. Brenna closed the yearbook and tucked it back into the box.

Together, they climbed the stairs of the historical society and stood on the front porch. Brenna shielded her eyes. In the bright sun, the whole thing seemed implausible. And yet she was certain she'd seen Dot in that photo. "Who are your"—Brenna paused, searching for the right word—"visitors?"

"I don't know about 'visitors,'" Joshua said. "But there's this mechanic dude I saw the night of the tornado. The next day, he was watching my house from across the street, and he said this weird thing to me. He said, 'Don't let them get you down,' like he knew me. I definitely saw someone who looked like him in the photo, but maybe this guy just has a relative who died in the tornado years ago and who looks just like him." Brenna raised her eyebrows. "I know, I know. When I say it out loud, it sounds crazy. But so does the alternative that he's . . . dead."

"What about you?" Brenna asked, turning toward Callie.

"Ellie Vidal, Celeste's mother," she said. "I mean, it's possible

214

her daughter died in the tornado and she's still alive. The math could work, I guess. But she knew stuff about me just like yours did, Joshua—my house and my mother—and I'm pretty sure we don't know her."

"Mine knows me too," Brenna said. "She gave me a notebook the first time we met and told me I was a writer even though I haven't written in a while. I think I saw her picture in that old yearbook too."

They all stood in silence for a minute. Each of them lost in thought.

"So now what? What do we do?" Joshua finally asked, rocking backward and forward on his heels. He was spinning out, Brenna could tell.

That photo of Dot had chilled her. She'd seen far too many horror movies with girls like herself dragged into a hellmouth, possessed, or murdered for defying some understood but unstated rule: too much sex, doing drugs, not being white. But Dot's presence had never felt dangerous. It was comforting.

"Maybe we ask them," Callie answered—so long after Joshua had asked the question that Brenna had forgotten it.

"Ask them what? Like, 'Hey, are you alive?'" Joshua said.

Callie shrugged. "I guess so."

"And then what do we do?"

Brenna thought about what Gretta said. "We listen. Maybe they're trying to tell us something."

"We listen," Joshua repeated, rocking even more violently, about to launch off his toes and into the sky.

"What are you thinking?" Brenna asked.

"We need to tell someone," he said.

"Like who?"

"I don't know. Someone in charge. I mean, if this is true, and that's a big if, it's huge. Like, talk-show huge. Everyone in the town is going to want a piece of them. A piece of us."

Callie shuddered.

"I don't think it's come to that yet. Let's just start with what Callie suggested," Brenna said. The thought of talking to Dot again made her skin crawl with excitement and fear. Even if she'd believed in the Winston sisters wreaking havoc on the town's china, and Mrs. Jenson pecking grains from Mercerites' palms for eternity, she'd never been face-to-face with the truth before. Belief, surprisingly, was easier. "I think we have to figure out why. Like, why us and why now?"

Callie's phone buzzed. "Oh shit. I have to go," she said.

"Are you okay? Is it your mom?" Joshua asked. Brenna shot him a look.

"No, it's my birthday."

The girl turned and jogged toward a car on the street. "Happy birthday," Brenna called after her.

"And don't forget to ask your"—Joshua paused—"stranger?"

"Storm Spirit," Brenna corrected, savoring the name. For so long, it had been part of a legend she'd believed. Now it seemed closer to the truth.

DAYS AGO

Days ago, right after the storm, we realized it wasn't just our voices that crossed through. The excitement is still ruffling through us. We billow.

But.

We didn't all cross back. So we are angry, and this feeling careens. It ricochets.

Only *they* made it through. Only *they* dropped onto Earth like *The Wizard of Oz*'s pigtailed Dorothy. The chosen who get to meet those who speak to us, dream us, need us.

Even worse, their thoughts are not ours anymore. The ones who fell are separate, individual again, plucked from us because only they could answer, because their aches paralleled those below. How can they survive without us? How do they remember how to live? Will they stay forever?

We who remain, we worry, watch, and want.

35

Callie had forgotten Leslie. The girl who'd held her hand on the first day of kindergarten and made up a song because Callie was crying about missing her mom. She'd never wanted a birthday celebration less in her life, but Callie knew what she had to do.

I'm on my way. Sorry got held up with Mom, she texted as she climbed into the car.

In the rearview mirror, she saw Brenna and Joshua talking outside the museum. Callie wanted to be with them, figuring out what was going on, who their visitors really were, and why this was happening to them. Joshua and Brenna spoke to her with a directness, with an ease, that comforted her. That made it simpler to forget about her mom—and to remember, too. And now, something inside her—the something that was her mother, that was Mercer—had woken up. It was buzzing beneath her skin, crawling from limb to limb. Could their visitors really be ghosts? How, when Callie no longer believed?

Leslie met Callie in the parking lot of Giovanni's, holding a black bandanna. Her smile was so big, so angry, the metal braces around her back molars were visible, but Callie trusted she'd still be herself—cloyingly sweet—if only because it was Callie's birthday.

"Turn around," she said, holding up the bandanna.

"Leslie, I thought this was going to be low-key."

"Turn around." Her voice was sharp.

Callie complied and Leslie tied the bandanna over her eyes. It smelled like Leslie's house: browned butter and vanilla. Callie tried to remind herself that this was for Leslie. Leslie who played her flute at St. Theresa's Assisted Living Center at Christmas. Leslie who spent her spring breaks painting houses for Habitat. Leslie who handmade thank-you cards. Callie tried to concentrate on the softness of her hand, the smell of garlic and melted cheese, as Leslie led her through the restaurant.

"Surprise!" voices shouted, and Callie pulled the blindfold down over her nose, blinking in the green-shaded light. Her friends from church and cross-country were seated at a long table, Mrs. Walsh, Leslie's mother, and Callie's father among them. Her stomach sank; if her father was here, then Leslie knew she'd lied about being held up with her mom.

Everyone just smiled at her, waiting for something. Her father was smiling too, but his eyes were slits, the lines underneath like angry parentheses.

Mrs. Walsh clapped her hands and walked around the table to hug Callie. Her perfume was too strong, like she'd bathed in Easter incense. "Happy birthday," she said. "Forgive us; we ordered a few appetizers because we were starving."

"I'm sorry. I got held up," Callie said, but her voice came out tinny, robotic. "This is really nice." She shot Leslie a look that she hoped said everything: *Why did you do this, I didn't want this, I refuse to feel guilty.* Then to her father, pleading: *I didn't know.*

A seat beside her old crush, Grant, was open—like this, too, was a gift from Leslie. Callie sat, unrolled the cloth napkin, and put it on her lap.

"Your dad told us the race went well," Mrs. Walsh said from her end of the table. "And you got your license?"

Callie nodded.

Mrs. Walsh seemed to be waiting for her to say more, but Callie looked pointedly at her silverware.

Grant handed her a platter of cold garlic knots. She took one, pulled it into two doughy threads, dunked them in marinara sauce, and then dropped them onto her plate.

"Are you—okay?" he asked, pushing aside floppy chestnut hair.

"Yeah," Callie said. "It's just been a weird day and this was—"

"Too much?"

"Way too much. Did she really plan this overnight?"

"Yeah, she sent a group text. Said things were rough with—you know—and you needed it."

He handed her a pitcher of pop. The ice was almost melted and it looked flat, like even the carbonation didn't want to be there. It made Callie inexplicably angry.

She picked up one of the strands of her garlic knot. She wanted to find Mrs. Vidal at St. Theresa's—or search online for information. Something other than sitting here, thinking what a bad friend she was, what a bad daughter. Her stomach grumbled, hungry. Always that gnawing feeling that she had to battle to empty herself. The garlic smell reminded her of her father's zucchini lasagna, of guacamole on taco nights, of delivery pizzas she'd shared with her mother when her dad had had to work late. Unable to resist, she bit the knot. It was doughy in the center, undercooked and wet, like paste. She spit it into the napkin and tucked it into her pocket.

"Excuse me," she muttered, though no one was paying attention to her now.

In the bathroom, Callie planted her elbows on the tiles and splashed water on her face. She looked at her reflection, at the droplets funneling down her nose and the tip of her chin. The skin under her eyes was purple, like someone's ink fingerprints on her face. Then the door opened behind her and Leslie appeared, her cheeks flushed.

"We want to order pizzas. People are hungry and some have to leave soon."

"Okay. Go ahead."

"What do you want to order?" Leslie asked.

"Whatever."

"It's your birthday. You should decide."

"I don't care. I'm not even hungry. Pepperoni's good. Cheese is good."

"You show up an hour late. You lie about your mother. You say you're not hungry. Are you going to leave early too? Maybe flake red pepper into our eyeballs on your way out?"

Callie sighed and steadied her voice. "I'm sorry I was late and that I lied. I really am. But something crazy is happening."

"I don't care. You haven't even said thanks."

Callie's fingers tightened around the ridge of the basin, like they were cramping. Was that what this was about?

"Honestly, I haven't said thanks because I'm not thankful. I didn't ask for this party. I didn't want to do anything. And I only go to church group because my dad makes me." She thought of Brenna, of how her simple *I know* had been enough. "I mean, let's be honest. This is more for you than it is for me. You want to be the girl everyone is indebted to. Who's going to bring you soup when you're sick? Leslie. Who will do your laundry when your family is falling apart? Leslie. Who's never going to let you forget it? Leslie."

"What's wrong with you?" Leslie hissed, tears in her eyes.

"Oh, I don't know. It's my last birthday with my mother." Callie leaned over the sink again, aware she wasn't going to have her mother as an excuse much longer, aware that there'd be an after—no matter how empty she made her life now. She let the water run scalding, let it burn so much that then it stopped burning. When she looked up again, Leslie was gone.

Leslie and her mother's chairs were empty when Callie emerged from the bathroom. Her father's fingers were steepled in front of him.

I'm sorry, she mouthed. He shook his head and pointed at Leslie's seat. Callie pulled out her phone and texted: *I'm sorry I said all that. You've been nothing but there for me.*

Leslie did not reply.

MOST OF US DIDN'T

Most of us didn't understand at the time why we repeatedly saw Frederic burying blood-splotched sheets and Eleanor's night-clothes beneath the Crimson King maple in front of the inn. Now we know Eleanor needed something to bury, something to point to. There, a miscarried child, right where the roots arch above the soil.

Frederic bought a spaniel puppy for his daughter because she had no siblings to play with. The puppy was clumsy, tripping on its bunny-like ears and new long legs. Its fur was curly around its face and along its tummy. Some of us came over to tumble into the grass with it, to feel its hot tongue on our cheeks. And we loved Celeste, too, for her bright cheeriness like fizzy water. She was wide-boned, limbs nicked and bruised from playing hard. She'd flush from her neck to her strawberry-blond hair.

When we used the bathroom, we'd glimpse Eleanor eating rolls of antacids like they were Life Savers. Her already frizzy hair stood out straight from her head, and there were patches of it missing, like she'd been tugging at it. The inn closed around that time so Eleanor could rest. Our parents gossiped about it endlessly, using the words *depressed* and *barren*, and we pictured tracts of winter cornfields, a stubble of cracked stalks.

Celeste, who is one of us too, didn't remember the antacids or the sheets beneath the trees. Only freedom. Only playing with her whole heart. Now, like us, there is so much more she understands.

The day the spaniel dug at the roots of the maple, Celeste was washing up for lunch and had left the puppy in our care. Even though we didn't yet know why, those of us who were Celeste's playmates knew that the mound was sacred. We called at the puppy to stop, but it kicked dirt between its hind legs with mad excitement. Eleanor appeared in the kitchen window, pale-faced and wild, and we scattered. From the park, we watched her stumble to the garage and emerge with the same shovel Frederic had used to bury the linens. She dragged it behind her like a red wagon, leaving a wake in the grass.

The puppy bowed, its paws stretched toward her, its rear and wagging tail in the air, like they were about to play. Eleanor lifted the shovel, her arms visibly shaking, and swung. The flat side of the shovel connected with the dog's jaw. It yelped, high-pitched and almost human, before staggering sideways and collapsing. Eleanor dropped the shovel and cupped her cheeks, covering her eyes with her fingertips.

Just then, Celeste appeared on the doorstep, and our hearts went out to her, our happy friend.

"Is lunch ready?" Celeste called. She didn't know what had happened.

Eleanor uncovered her eyes. The dog was on its feet again with its head tilted at an angle that seemed off, uncomfortable. It licked her calf and slunk toward Celeste. From that day on, the spaniel walked with its head cocked, as though wondering what it had done wrong.

Those of us who saw kept the secret until we no longer had secrets to keep.

36

On the walk home from the museum, Joshua bubbled with nervous energy. He wanted to investigate now so he could disprove the legends, but he was terrified, too. What if they were true? In some movies, ghosts were dangerous—deadly, even. Or worse, his biggest fear: that he'd finally found a gay man in this shit town, someone to look up to and learn from, and he was dead.

Joshua's mother emerged from the house as he was checking the mailbox to see if his latest comics had arrived. Her red hair was down, but kinked where it had been wound up in a bun. Cake a little dirt under her fingernails, add some calluses to her hands, and she'd look just like she had on his grandparents' farm. The thought flooded him with warmth.

"How's the project?" she asked. He straightened up, recognizing her fake casualness. This was the talk he'd managed to delay the day before.

"It went good," he said.

"Brenna seems"—his mother squinted, as though searching for a word in the distance—"interesting."

"She's nice," he said defensively.

His mother put up her hands and lowered them, like she was closing a briefcase. "All I meant is, she's very different from you."

Joshua kicked a crab apple. It skittered across the lawn and stopped at the edge of the driveway. "Not that different."

"Okay. I look forward to getting to know her better then." Her voice was gentle, probably the same voice she used with the kids amid abuse cases and custody battles. "Listen, we need to talk. Lawrence told me about yesterday."

It was sunny, but the storm a few days before had chilled the air.

Joshua narrowed his eyes. "What exactly did he say?"

"He's worried about you. I know you don't have the highest opinion of him, but he does care about you."

"I'm sure," Joshua said.

"Don't be surly. Let's sit."

He looked at the grass suspiciously.

"It's not that damp. Come on."

They sat side by side on the curb.

"So why did you skip your morning class yesterday?"

Joshua glanced across the street. He didn't need this right now. He needed to talk to Luke to find out who he was. He couldn't let Brenna and Callie down. "I didn't want to ride the bus," he said. "So I rode my bike."

"Why?"

Joshua pointed at his bruise. "Things like this happen." It was a half-truth.

Tears welled in his mother's eyes. She dabbed at them with her denim sleeve.

"Oh, Mom, don't cry. Stop. I'm fine."

She shook her head. "I didn't listen to you about school. I've been so busy."

Joshua felt his own tears, hot and sudden. It was Tyler. It was his mother. It was Callie's grief. It was the yearbook, the police report, and the name patch battling with the worldview he'd finally settled on, that he'd grown to trust, because Mercer's had let him down. He wanted to crawl into his mother's lap. Like when his grandfather died and they'd moved into that apartment that always smelled of laundry detergent and rumbled with the dryers below. Their mother would sit on the bare floor, pull him and his sister onto each knee, and play feel-good cartoons on her laptop. It had been the three of them against the world that year, and he craved it now, how knit he'd felt to them.

"I'm not going to brush this off," she said. "I promise you that I'm calling the school Monday morning, and I'm going to drive you there myself."

"You don't have to do that." He wondered if Tyler's parents would be called in for a meeting, if he'd have to unravel his lies and pick out the truths in front of everyone.

"Yes, I do," she said. "It's my job as your mom."

It occurred to Joshua that it must have been so hard for his mother, too—to have been largely on her own with him and Ruthie.

"You've done good, Mom. This isn't your fault." He reached out for her hand, but once it was in his own, he felt awkward—self-conscious—and dropped it.

She wiped her eyes again and cleared her throat. "As part of doing better as your mother, I need to hold you responsible for your actions. You're still grounded and have chores, but I'd like you to spend some time with Lawrence. Do you hear me?"

Joshua wanted to roll his eyes at this, to blurt out Lawrence's attempted bribe or the fact that Lawrence didn't want to spend time with him, but he just nodded.

She patted his knee, stood, and wiped damp blades of grass off her backside. "You can start by cleaning your room." She leaned down and plucked a dead leaf that was stuck to her foot. "And raking."

Joshua's heart sank. There'd be no escaping to investigate Luke. Not under her watch. Dutifully, he followed his mother inside and opened the kitchen door that led to the garage. Lawrence was at his workbench, drilling holes in a piece of wood, gold flecks of pulp like pencil shavings coating his arms. Joshua bit off his fingernail and spit the sliver onto the mat. He and Lawrence had barely said a word to each other all day. People said tension was thick, but Joshua thought silence was too: sliceable.

"Hey, Larry."

Lawrence started at Joshua's voice, the drill whining as he lifted it.

Joshua put his hands up. "Don't shoot."

Flushed, Lawrence wiped his face and set the drill down. "What do you need, Josh?" he asked, sounding more tired than embarrassed by Joshua's presence.

"Just the rake." Joshua pointed at the wall where the rake hung. Something flitted across Lawrence's face. Disappointment? Joshua certainly wasn't going to apologize for storming out the other day, if that was what his stepdad was expecting. But maybe he could cross *Spend time with Lawrence* off the chore list, for his mother's sake. "Do you need help or anything?"

Lawrence tilted his head, like he had to process the question from a different angle. "You want to help me?"

"Yeah. I don't know. Just if you need it, I guess."

"Have you used these tools before?" he asked, gesturing to his workbench.

Joshua's instinct was to make Lawrence squirm: *Gay men know how to handle tools, Larry.* Or, alternatively, he could snap back: *You're so closed-minded that you can't even conceive a gay kid might know what a hammer is.* But he thought of his mother crying, of taking her hand and it not feeling right anymore—not like those moments she'd drawn him onto her lap when he was little and rested her chin on his shoulder. He could play nice. He could be bigger than this petty, gum-faced man.

"You could teach me," Joshua said.

Lawrence dropped his eyes to the pulp on the table before him. He was probably trying to figure out a way to avoid spending time with Joshua, which was more than fine. He could still tell his mother he'd tried.

Lawrence coughed into his fist. "Well, I guess you could run to the hardware store with me in a few minutes. I'm making your mom a wine rack for our anniversary."

Joshua tried to hide his surprise. Maybe his mother had talked to Lawrence, too, convinced him to spend more time in the same room with his stepson—no matter how uncomfortable it was.

"Okay," Joshua said.

"Okay," Lawrence repeated.

Joshua felt generous-hearted, forgiving, and a little bit hope-ful. If he could face the Lawrences of the world, maybe he could face the Tylers, too, and all the others at school. Maybe he could be a hero yet.

37

Usually Brenna drove on the interstate to the Cities, but today she felt too nervous, like she needed the slowness of country roads, rows of corn and pig barns, to think. Brenna needed to find out why Dot was here, why she haunted Brenna—if *haunted* was even the word for it. According to the legends, the Winston twins smashed china because they were angry and wanted the injustice known. The Clarks pushed cars to safety because they didn't want others to die how they had. And Mrs. Jenson's story kept kids from playing in grain silos—lest they end up buried too. But what was Dot's reason? And why did the voices tell Callie to *Find them. Save them*?

Brenna wanted to know the truth, but she also didn't. She felt better around Dot—like she had something to learn from her, and why question that?

She rolled down the windows to light a cigarette. The speed

limit dropped for the bridge, the cars bottlenecking, so she was forced to take in the slate-gray expanse of water, the tracks along the banks, the riverboat casinos like tiered wedding cakes.

She'd picked up the car from Manny, but had ignored four texts from her mother. There'd been dozens of messages and calls since her mom realized she'd left, but she'd ignored them all. Brenna wasn't sure what she'd do after the show. Another night in a car—even if it was Golden Girl—made her nerves jangle. She'd been so tired and hungry all day.

Amy had loaned her a few dollars, and she had just enough time to swing by Raul's, her favorite place in the Cities, for actual tacos—shaved pork nested in corn tortillas and topped with cilantro, onions, and lime.

After dinner, the navigation on her phone led her to a row of bars next to an old railroad bridge with rusted trusses.

In the parking lot, Brenna turned off Golden Girl and sat for a moment. Callie's and Joshua's numbers were in her phone now, and they'd each texted that their families had held them up from investigating. She wished they were with her now, or that they'd invite her to spend the night at their homes after the concert.

A few rows from Golden Girl there was a blue Jeep—just like Colin's. She'd been so excited about the prospect of seeing Dot again that she hadn't even considered she was on Colin's turf now.

It was a weekend; he'd be out like every other college kid in the Cities.

She watched the venue door, trying to see past the bouncer. Dot was inside. Answers were inside. And they weren't just about Dot but about Brenna herself—why she mattered. There must be a reason, if a Storm Spirit had chosen her. Or was that a crazy thought? Besides, Jeeps were common; there was no reason to be nervous.

She marched up to the bouncer, accepted the black *X*s on her hands, and went inside. Another band was finishing their set, and Brenna sat on a barstool near the back, surveying the crowd. Hipsters mostly: beards and tight pants and granny glasses. Definitely Colin's crowd. Brenna tugged at the dress she'd borrowed from Amy. It was made of artificial black lace, some polyester blend: cheap and undoubtedly flammable. She'd practically ignite under the stage lights.

After the first band cleared the stage, the house lights went up and roadies began shuttling equipment to and from the stage. Brenna hopped off her stool to squeeze to the front, hoping to find Dot.

"Excuse me," she muttered over and over again, elbowing her way toward the stage, swimming through the stench of booze, cigarettes, and sweat. A wave of menthol smokes and something woody hit her.

"Bren."

She looked up into Colin's face.

"Oh. Hey. I—" All the blood rushed to Brenna's head and pounded in her ears. What words were supposed to go next?

Colin wore a stretched gray sweater, gray beanie, black jeans, and boots, like he'd stepped out of one of the black-and-white filters on her phone. His curls were wet with sweat and sticking to his cheeks and neck. She wanted to brush them away and lick the salt off her fingers. Same Life Stage Girl was nowhere in sight.

A group surged behind Brenna, propelling her into Colin. He was warm and his scent was dizzying. She heard him inhale too. What, she wondered, was her smell? The powder makeup dusted along the collar of Amy's dress? Cilantro and onions?

The tide of people receded and Brenna was back on her heels, feeling suddenly cold, like she'd climbed out of a pool without a towel.

"Sorry," she said, but she wasn't. That old thing was between them, like a spiderweb—fragile, delicate, nearly invisible, but glimmering in just the right light.

"How's it going?" Colin asked.

She wanted to tell him about Dot. It was practically bursting from her, but he had never believed in that kind of thing. It felt like she would be giving away an important piece of herself. "I've been kicked out," she said instead. She sought his dark eyes, bloodshot but still sparkling. He used to listen to her complaints about her mother and repeat "I hear you" before he launched into a story about his own parents. The stories never compared—not really—but that "I hear you" had felt like enough.

He frowned. "God, your mom is such a bitch. You're better off on your own anyway." Brenna raised her eyebrows. He still had confidence in her—or at least, the *her* he'd cast her as.

"How's school?" Brenna asked.

Colin shrugged. "I mean, it's more of the same. But once I'm done with these general classes, I'll get into something real."

"Like what?"

"Philosophy, art, sociology. You know, stuff that makes you think." He rolled up the loose sleeves of his sweater, but they slid back down to his wrists.

Brenna nodded.

"Have you thought about college? What you'll do?"

"Not really." Brenna's parents had not gone to college. Nor had Manny or any of her older cousins. What was it like to grow up in a family like Colin's, where college was just a given?

"You'll figure it out." He looked at her in that way that made her aware of her exposed skin, of bareness. She shivered.

He cleared his throat. "Hey, you want to get out of here? Catch up?" he asked. There was a tiny part of Brenna shaking its head. It wanted her to remember his betrayal.

"What about your girlfriend?" she asked, but her voice didn't rise above the crowd and instrument tuning.

"What?" Colin leaned in, cupping his hand next to his ear. She wasn't even touching him, but it felt like his body was sending off solar flares, like its heat was licking her.

Just then Dot walked out onstage in the same polka dots and blocky Mary Janes. The roadies moved around her—never addressing her—a dance of shadows around a shining woman. She took center stage, under the lights, and closed her eyes. If Brenna tunneled through the crowd and reached up to grab Dot's ankle, would it be cold? Would there be something sinister in her eyes as she looked down from the stage? Or would it make her stronger because Dot knew the real her? If she opened her eyes and met Brenna's gaze, Brenna vowed she would have the courage to stay, to confront the truth.

"Bren?" Colin asked, stepping closer. His heat and scent made her hungry, a humming want. And the wanting offered safety if only because she knew it, recognized it as her own.

"Do you see her?" Brenna asked.

Colin wrinkled his brow. "Who?"

"In the polka dots."

He turned toward the stage and then shook his head. "Who are you talking about?"

Could no one see Dot but Brenna? As if in response, Dot's eyes fluttered open. She scanned the crowd. Brenna waved her arms above her head and tried to get Dot's attention. *See me*, Brenna pleaded, but Dot turned and walked from the stage.

"Who are you waving at?" Colin asked, squinting at the stage.

"Never mind," Brenna said. "Forget it. Let's go."

Colin waved at his friends before encircling her wrist with his forefinger and thumb. He tugged lightly, but enough that whatever Brenna had assembled of herself, whichever version she was in that moment, gave way.

38

After everyone left, Callie and her dad sat on opposite ends of a table littered with green cloth napkins, red frosted glasses, and crumbles of parmesan. The piece of pepperoni pizza Callie had forced down in the face of her father's disappointment burned in her stomach and chest. She wanted to vomit, and Leslie still hadn't texted back.

"Before you even start in on me," Callie said, "I blew up at Leslie because I didn't want a party and she didn't listen."

Without a word, her dad folded his napkin, stood up, and headed for the exit.

Callie jogged after him.

"Are you going to tell Mom?" She couldn't handle another bedside lesson.

He pushed open the door and let it swing behind him. Callie caught it with her forearm and followed. "Dad?"

"Callie, this isn't just about Leslie." He spun around, and she could see the artery in his temple pulsing. "Your mother asked me the other day why you don't want to hug her anymore. I shouldn't have to tell you that she needs you more than ever right now. That every hug is precious. That you're hurting her feelings." His voice cracked then, an anguished sound that wrenched everything inside her to the surface. All at once, Callie felt guilty and wretched and angry and sorry and just so sad.

Under the weight of it all, Callie's legs became rubber. She sank to the pavement and leaned back against the sturdy brick building. Everything was tinged with gray—the parking lot, the sky, her dad. Her eyelids felt leaden. A cold sweat prickled her hairline. Was this the short-circuit she'd wished for?

Her father said something about her needing counseling. But his voice was distant, as though he were calling to her from the next room. He needed some time to think, he said, to cool off. Counseling? Time? Had she messed up that badly? Had she pushed away the only other person still by her side?

She allowed her eyelids to close for a second. Just one. They were so heavy. *Open*, she had to think. And then finally managed to, but he was gone. How much time had passed? Did it matter? It was her fault he'd left. Her fault her mother was hurting. *Open*, she thought again. *Open*.

EVENTUALLY OUR TOWN WATCHMAN

Eventually our town watchman, Eleanor, returned to her post. The inn reopened. The antacids, the sheets beneath the maple, and the shovel faded from our minds. When Celeste took the bus home, the spaniel—white-faced and rheumy-eyed—trotted out to greet her. Celeste always invited her friends in, and we'd sit in the kitchen doing our homework while Eleanor washed dishes, stirred sauces, and tossed salads with her sleeves rolled up to her elbows, her apron hanging on her like a bib because she refused to knot the ties. Our mothers told us not to get in her way while she worked, but we were confident she liked having us there. She'd put out butter crackers and cheese balls rolled in nuts. And while the conversations between her and Celeste were halting and awkward, she chatted easily with us.

One afternoon, not long before the tornado, some of us were over at the Vidals' house, preparing for the homecoming dance.

We stood in the kitchen in pajamas, our hair in curlers. Celeste's eyelids were painted blue, which only accentuated the fact that she had blue circles under her eyes. Celeste was the girl who did everything: bowling league, student council, waitressing at the drive-in.

Eleanor had set out a plate of apple slices and carrot sticks for us, but Celeste kept reaching over the counter for a pinch of cheese her mother had shredded for a lasagna.

Eleanor swatted her hand away with a *tsk* sound. Celeste was heavier than most of us, heavier than her mother, certainly. Pleasantly round, with a fullness that matched her flushed cheeks and bright hair.

Eleanor went back to straightening a layer of noodles and ladling meat sauce on top. "My Sky," she said softly, as though not wanting us to hear. "I worry that working at the drive-in while school is in session is too much for you."

Celeste picked at one of her cuticles. "Are you and Papa going to pay for college then?"

Eleanor sighed. She was always trying to convince Celeste that she didn't need college to run a successful business like the inn. "Maybe I could pay you a little for working here," Eleanor responded instead. We stopped munching on our carrots to listen.

"I'm not cleaning up a stranger's hair in the drain."

"I think you'll find that cleaning can be relaxing, that it feels good to make something neat for others."

"Doubtful."

"And I can teach you to cook." Eleanor—we knew—had learned how to cook from her own mother, and her mother had learned from her mother before her, and so on. We'd eaten scrambled eggs sprinkled with fresh-cut chives, ingredients that descended from Margaret Peterson's first chickens and herbs. Because Eleanor had been depressed for so long, Celeste hadn't ever learned to cook spaghetti, create luminaries to light the sidewalk in the winter, or tuck the sheets around the corner of the mattress the proper way like her mom. Eleanor seemed to want to make up for the lost lessons, to have her daughter by her side—no matter how stilted their conversations.

Celeste used her pink-painted fingernail to scrape at something on the counter. "Don't you want more for me?"

Her mother was silent. We began to think she wouldn't answer, but she finally said: "I just want you to be happy."

Celeste smiled at this, as though she'd won an argument, but we think she misinterpreted her mother's response. The inn, we knew, made Eleanor happy. Why wouldn't she want that for her daughter?

"You're just looking a little peaky," Mrs. Vidal said.

Celeste reached for the bowl of cheese again.

"And all that sugar and salt." Eleanor pulled the bowl out of her daughter's reach. We sat back in our seats, embarrassed, as though we'd spotted our neighbor's torn underwear on the clothesline.

Celeste's eyes narrowed. "Oh, I see. You think I look tired and fat."

"I just want you to be happy," Eleanor repeated.

"Jeez Louise, Mom. I am happy. You can't leave well enough alone." Celeste stood. "Let's go to Mary's to finish getting ready," she said to us.

Celeste's father stepped into the kitchen, a corsage in his hand. "How are you, mes chéries?" he asked.

"Tu lui demandes!" Celeste said, pushing her way through the door to the foyer. The few of us who spoke French knew she'd said, "Why don't you ask her?"; the rest of us knew only that tone. The spaniel groaned to its feet and padded after. We murmured our thank-yous and apologies, and retreated from the kitchen.

Later we stood in the city park and our mothers took photographs of us leaning chastely into our dates, poking one another with corsage pins, and linking arms with our friends.

Eleanor watched from the porch as Celeste, in a dress the color of a spring sky, spun from group to group with a smile that seemed a bit too huge, as though she wanted her mother to see it from across the street, wanted to jab her with its sharp joy. Too proud, her mother remained on the porch, her camera inside— undoubtedly consoling herself that there'd be another year, another dance, another chance to photograph her daughter.

39

The smell of wood struck Joshua when the sliding glass doors parted. He hadn't been to the hardware store since his grandfather had passed away. His grandfather had always released Joshua and Ruthie into the spruce-scented warehouse with only a reminder not to steal. It was that farm-freedom, tucked into everyday errands, that he missed. They'd fan out the paint strips and rename them—*onion, cicada, tentacle*—climb into the display bathtubs, and knock on the sample doors, taking turns being the salesman of plungers, doorknobs, and palmfuls of screws. Joshua wanted to gather it all to him, to hold it against his chest, but he forced the memories back down. They settled in his stomach, solid as fruit pits.

Lawrence pulled a crumpled receipt out of his pocket and smoothed it out. Impatient to be home and learning more about Luke, Joshua drummed his thumbs on his thighs. Lawrence began pushing the cart, muttering, "Wood first." Joshua trailed behind, grinning at the potential joke. Without Ruthie as an audience, there wasn't much of a point. Plus, this errand was for his mother, for the way she'd hugged her knees in the grass.

They made their way to the back of the store, and Lawrence eyed the display.

"I need a two-by-four and a two-by-six."

He reached for a pale-blond board that Joshua and Ruthie probably would have named *plain Jane*.

"I can't really imagine that in the kitchen," Joshua said.

"Oh. Yeah. I don't know much about this kind of thing," Lawrence said. Joshua wondered if he was blushing because he was reminded Joshua was gay, and therefore, in his tiny mind, more likely to know about design, or if it was something else—shame at not knowing, not understanding.

Joshua shrugged. "I don't either. But maybe you could use a stain? So it's darker. You know, like warmer."

Lawrence nodded, and Joshua led him down an aisle to the stains.

As they reviewed the options, Joshua heard a voice, its vowels drawn out and thin with exhaustion or annoyance. A second voice—a booming, jolly one that Joshua hadn't heard in years—answered. Tyler and his father.

Mercer had a way of producing the people you loathed at

the most inopportune times. Joshua wanted both to hide behind Lawrence's large frame and to show himself, proving he was unaffected by bullying, that he was out doing what other boys did with their fathers. Instead he did nothing, inspecting the colors as closely as he could: *mahogany, light oak, cherry, walnut.* Tyler wouldn't bother talking to him, but his father was a wild card, as interested and engaged in his role as town alderman as Tyler was disinterested in everything except, apparently, smoking.

Tyler and his father rounded the corner and started down the aisle, Tyler's eyes on his phone.

"Hey, look who it is!" his father called out. "Joshua Calloway."

Joshua's shoulders tensed, and he turned away from the stain samples. He'd refuse to smile—at least he could do that.

Without looking up, Tyler shoved his hands in his pockets. "That's not him," he said, his voice a snarl.

Really? Joshua thought. Tyler was going to take a "mistaken identity" approach? Or maybe he meant it literally. That Joshua wasn't the Joshua Calloway they knew anymore—the straight boy who played Pokémon in the hayloft.

Lawrence hovered behind Joshua, emanating nervousness like heat. It occurred to Joshua then that maybe his stepdad was shy. That was why he fumbled awkwardly on the phone and only ordered online. Joshua felt himself softening a little more toward the man.

"Course it is, Tyler. Hi, I'm Victor Barrett," Tyler's father said, reaching toward Lawrence for a handshake. "You must be Joshua's stepdad. Tyler and him are good friends."

Lawrence wiped his hand on his T-shirt and shook the man's hand. "Lawrence," he mumbled.

"Why haven't I seen you around?" Mr. Barrett asked Joshua.

Joshua shrugged and Tyler smirked, tapping out a message on his phone. It was probably to Clayton, his companion asshole.

Nodding like he'd had the greatest idea in the world, Mr. Barrett said, "You should all come over next weekend. Get both families together."

Joshua expected Lawrence to blush and fumble for a response, but his eyes narrowed and he was looking back and forth between Tyler and Joshua, figuring it out. "Is that the kid who did it?" Lawrence asked Joshua, almost under his breath. Joshua had to give him credit. Maybe former linebackers were smarter than they looked.

"Did what?" Mr. Barrett asked.

"Dad," Tyler said sharply.

"The shiner on Josh's face."

"Excuse me. Are you accusing my son of punching your son?"

"I am," Lawrence said, and Joshua felt amazed at the way the two men seemed to elongate their necks and lift their chests, like strutting roosters. Even more than that, he was amazed that Lawrence hadn't corrected the word *son*.

"There's got to be more of a story here," Mr. Barrett said.

"There ain't. Your kid picks on Josh."

"They're friends. Why would he do that?"

Say it, Joshua thought. *Tell him why.* Lawrence flushed. "It's not a fair fight."

"Not fair?" Tyler's father said, angry now. "Your kid could crush my son just by looking at him."

With his eyes finally on Joshua's face, Tyler stage-whispered, "It's because he's a faggot, Dad."

Joshua felt punched by the word, its guttural *g*'s, the arcane heaviness of it. Mr. Barrett looked like he was choking on his own tongue. Lawrence was still red-faced with shame or anger. Joshua wasn't sure which.

Defend me, Joshua thought. *All you have to say is "Don't use that word."*

But Lawrence said nothing.

"Come on," Mr. Barrett said, swinging the cart around and heading back down the aisle. Tyler looked smug, as though they were back in the barn and he'd just won a battle with his Pokémon. Lawrence's fists were balled, but he just stood there, unwilling—or unable—to enter the fray again.

Joshua smacked the stain display so the sample strips fluttered to the ground like falling leaves.

"Josh, what the heck?" Lawrence said, grunting as he squatted to catch them. Joshua headed for the sliding doors, glad they'd close behind him, sealing Lawrence, Tyler, and his dad in that wood-scented case.

40

"Are we going to your place?" Brenna asked when she and Colin were outside. She wanted to know what his room was like now that he didn't live with his parents. Did he hang posters? Did he bother to fold clothes? His parents' house was new compared to hers, the walls white and decorated with wooden letters that spelled *love, hope,* and *trust.* Colin once rearranged them: *thrust, lope, ove.*

He shook his head. "Roommates." He led her across the bike path, down the riverbank, and under the railroad bridge. They were in the shadows then, blocked from the view of the parking lot and path. Up close, the river was the color of eggplant and smelled dank, like laundry left in the washer too long. She shivered.

Colin flipped open his cigarette carton and pulled out a joint and his Zippo. He clinked it open, the flame illuminating the scar on his thumb. Brenna wanted to put his thumb in her mouth, to taste his skin, dirt and copper and salt. He lit the joint, taking one puff, and then handed it to her. She took two hits, wanting to be relaxed, as cool and collected as him, when in truth her body was buzzing with anticipation and her mind was reeling.

"So besides stuff with your mom, anything new?" he asked.

She knew Colin would think her expedition to the museum was childish, that her discovery was ludicrous. She held the smoke in and shook her head.

"Mr. Forester still being a dick in gym?" He smiled, as falsely self-conscious and sheepish as always.

Nodding, she passed the joint back. "I hear he is. I don't have him this year."

Colin inhaled and tilted his head back, smoke curling out of his nose. Lanky, narrow-faced, with those charcoal eyes, he reminded her of a disheveled dragon.

"Does Kahn still say, 'If you're bored, you're boring'?" he asked.

"Of course." She took the joint out of his pinched fingers.

"And Mrs. Castle still has her pink fanny pack?"

"Oh yes."

"Damn, I miss that place."

"Really?"

He sighed. "My roommates suck. I thought part of being an

adult was getting to do whatever you want, whenever you want, but I can't because they're always in the apartment."

"So you'd rather be living with your parents?"

He shrugged. "At least they were too busy to care what I did." His mom had certainly cared about Colin hanging out with Brenna, but she didn't bother to correct him. He would probably say that Brenna was too sensitive. Colin reached out and encircled her wrist again, as though measuring it. His finger and thumb overlapped. He kissed her ear first, so softly, she wasn't entirely sure it had happened.

She'd forgotten how, exactly, kissing him felt, how it worked: teeth, tongue, saliva, lip pressure. The kiss felt new and familiar all at once. Her muscles clenched and relaxed, and there was a pulsing sensation in their wake, aftershocks.

He cupped her jaw but quickly slid his palm along the side of her neck. Despite the pot fog forming in her mind, she was aware of how large his hand was against her neck, of how much pressure was being applied to her throat—something he'd never done before—but she couldn't form any thought or feeling about this. It just was.

With his mouth and hands, he pushed her downward and back, lowering himself on top of her. A rock dug into her scalp. She shifted and another knuckled her spine.

"Ow," she said.

He kissed her harder.

"Ow," she said again, louder.

"What?"

"The rocks. And it's too cold. Let's go to the car."

He shook his head and looked around. He pulled her to her feet and pinned her against the crossbeams of the bridge, working his hips against her pelvis. He brought her hand down to the crotch of his jeans. The fabric was hot and grossly damp.

This wasn't how it was supposed to be. Not with her *Person* after so much time apart. They were just supposed to remember each other and slip back into their old rhythm. She wanted to make it better. She needed to. She wrapped her arms around his waist, bit his lip, and then sucked his neck. He caught her hand and put it back on his crotch, pressing her fingers against the teeth of the zipper.

This pissed her off, but she pulled it down anyway, undid the button, and wriggled her fingers through the flap of his briefs. He moaned and she rolled her eyes to the bridge's dark underbelly, trying to make out its structure as she moved her hand.

He spun her so her back was to him and held her hip with one hand while snaking the other around her front. He hissed in her ear: "Just like you like it." Brenna didn't remember ever telling him that. Was this something else he'd invented for her? His finger was too insistent, too fast, like he was ringing a doorbell repeatedly. He sank his teeth into the lacy shoulder of her dress. It didn't feel familiar, but maybe she was just remembering it all wrong, how good it had felt.

She looked out through the crossbeams at the empty gray stretch of bike path, at the factory in the distance, and she realized—she finally understood—it wasn't her he was fucking. It had never been her.

Afterward, they walked back to the parking lot and stood beside Golden Girl awkwardly, Colin pushing up his ridiculously loose sleeves again.

"It was nice to see you finally," he said.

"You saw me at Bean City."

His face went blank.

"Yesterday morning, remember?"

"Oh yeah."

"'Oh yeah'?"

"What do you want me to say, Bren? Yes, I remember seeing you."

"You're not—I don't know—sorry for barely acknowledging me?"

"I was with Tara. It would have been awkward."

Tara, so that was her name. Tara with the teeth. Tara the

Midwestern blond. *Tara.* Brenna kept rolling it over her tongue. It was earthy, hippie, like granola and ukuleles. "Are you still?"

"With her? I guess. Kind of."

"You guess? Gee, she's lucky. Is that what you told her about me a few months ago? 'Yeah, there's this other girl I'm *kind of* seeing. *I guess.*'"

He rolled his eyes. "Haven't we been through this before? What do you want me to say?"

"Let's start with why you came on to me if you're still with her."

"We're pals, too, Bren. Or we were. I miss that."

Brenna wasn't sure if it was the pot, but this struck her as hilarious. "Pals?" she snorted. "We were just pals for an entire year?"

Colin pushed his sleeves up. She wished she had a pair of scissors to snip them off at the elbows. This image made her laugh even harder. Harsh, dry laughter, like heaving.

"I should probably find my friends," he said. He stuck his first two fingers together and waved them—a sideways salute or a misshapen peace sign. Whatever it was, it was wrong.

Brenna sank onto the pavement, half laughing and half sobbing. She felt like a barnacle scraped off his hull, awash, at sea. But finally she was free.

DETONATOR DOROTHY DROPPED

Detonator Dorothy dropped out of school and started to work at the same diner as her mother. She said it was to help her mom with rent, but we wondered if it was to save money for a move to the Cities, for recording time, for a demo. Something her mom would surely hate.

The early risers among us would order a short stack and Dorothy would swing by with a coffeepot—eyes blank, unseeing. The name *Dot* was printed on her tag, as if she were someone new. She'd hum, filling the saltshakers and ketchup bottles, and we'd remember the choir room, how lucky we'd been to overhear.

Only a few of us were at the diner the day the stranger came in. He was brown-skinned and black-haired at a time when that was unheard of in Mercer. He wore a suit made of finer material than any of us had ever touched. When Dorothy hummed by with the coffeepot, he watched her, eyes glittering.

The next time she passed by, he pinched the corner of her yellow sleeve between his thumb and forefinger. We watched her twist away from him and slam the coffeepot down on his table.

The man flinched. "I—I heard you singing." He spoke with a slight accent.

Dorothy raised her eyebrows, a clear *So what?*

"What song was that?" he asked.

"Did you need more coffee?"

He shook his head. "I'd just like to hear more." When she stared at him in reply, he offered: "It's my business."

"Your business," she repeated.

"I manage a band, Rock-a-Gals, that needs a new front girl. You interested?" He took a card out of his wallet, tapped it on its edge, and slid it to her. "Tomorrow. Three p.m."

We recognized the mistrust on her face, knew it came from her father, from Mr. Cannon. But she took the card and the coffeepot without answering, and swung by one of our tables—already back to her songs.

The next day, at the close of her shift, she emerged from the diner bathroom in a red crinoline skirt and heels. One of the bus-boys saw her pocket a paring knife—just like the one her mother had wielded the night her father had left—before hopping on the bus to the Cities.

A few of us had been to Rock-a-Gals shows and knew Beth, the brunette with a red bandanna tied around her temples; Bex, the bleach-blond with tattoos; and Kitty, with thick eyebrows and faint black hair on her upper lip. On the record, they wore matching pedal pushers, white button-up blouses, and red lipstick. The fabric tugged across their biceps and chests, lean muscles built from carrying all the equipment and practicing in airless garages.

None of us knows what happened except that she got the gig. But we like to think she auditioned as though she were alone in that cavernous choir room. Singing only for herself.

41

The temperature dropped while Brenna sat in the parking lot, waiting for the River Bandits to finish their set. Her teeth were chattering, but she didn't think she could move. This was where the sea had swept her, and this was where she'd be until something new scraped her loose.

After the crowd spilled out, Dot finally appeared, her ponytail loose. She spotted Brenna and waved. Brenna was too depleted from her encounter with Colin, from the shivering, to confront a ghost, but she couldn't run, either. She wondered if this was why the women in those horror films died—they were too exhausted by men, by trying to be what they wanted.

"Hey, I looked all over for you," Dot called. "Did you catch the show?"

Brenna shook her head.

"Oh." Dot sounded disappointed. She sank down next to Brenna, unbuckled her Mary Janes, and kicked them off. "That's the best feeling in the world, isn't it?" she asked, curling and extending her toes over and over. Brenna wondered why they weren't painted, like everything else on Dot's person. The tiny pearl toenails seemed like the most human, most earthly part of Dot.

"Are you dead?" Brenna whispered, stunned that the words had even made their way out.

Dot rubbed her left ear. "What? Sorry, still deaf from the concert."

Brenna buried her head in her knees. She was too drained to explain, to repeat her question, to formulate new ones. "Never mind," she said. Then Dot's warm hand was on hers, squeezing. Who knew ghosts could be so warm?

"Is there anything I can do to help?"

"I need a place to stay. Just for the night," Brenna said, surprising herself again.

"Aren't you expected home?"

"My mom kicked me out."

"Oh, Brenna. Why?"

"For going to your concert last night when she told me not to."

Dot bit her lip and looked worried.

It was a manipulative thing to say, Brenna realized. "Actually, it's more complicated than that," she corrected, rubbing her eyes with her palms. In the darkness, she felt nauseated, unmoored. "It was a mistake."

"Mistakes help us figure out who we are becoming," Dot said.

Brenna thought about that for a moment. "Was it easy for you?" she asked. "To figure out who you were becoming?"

Dot laughed. "I'm not sure I ever got to become, but I did get to make something beautiful for a little while. Be easy on yourself, Brenna. Try going home and talking to your mom. I know you're missed."

"How can you know that? You don't know me."

"I do, actually," Dot said, peeling away her false eyelashes. They curled in her palm like centipedes. "You're an excellent daughter and friend. You're strong and brave and smart."

Could Brenna be all those things if no one else believed them—least of all her?

"What about this," said Dot. "I'll give you my address, and if going home doesn't work, you can come to my house. Okay?"

Brenna opened her eyes, and her vision of Dot was speckled with tiny bursts of light. She wasn't a ghost but a guardian angel.

* * *

At home just after midnight, Brenna made herself dry toast and sat at the counter. The lavender notebook was still in her bag. She fanned out the pages and tried again, this time somewhere in the middle in case it was simply the beginning that scared her.

She wrote *I don't know what to write*, repeating the sentence over and over until she'd filled that page and the next. Eventually, something relinquished its hold on her—Colin, maybe—and she wrote the words *I'm not enough, except when I am. I'm not your love, never again.* She imagined Dot singing them, her voice dusky and low, a mic held close to her lips.

The gravel crunched on the driveway then, and her mother's brakes squeaked: a familiar sound. Brenna closed the notebook.

"Manny?" her mother called as she stepped into the living room.

"It's me," Brenna said.

Her mother's footsteps were quick then, and, before Brenna could brace herself, she was wrapped in arms, pliable and warm and smelling of cinnamon. Her mother rocked her gently, lulling her like when they'd floated the Guadalupe River on inner tubes and Brenna had drifted in and out of sleep, sun-drunk and happy. Before her parents had split up, before the move to Mercer, before she began to think she wasn't enough.

Switch-quick, her mother pushed back and smacked Brenna

lightly with her gas station visor. "I've been praying and praying. Where were you?"

"You kicked me out."

"It was just an expression. You know that."

"It doesn't ever feel like just an expression," Brenna said. The truth was like cracking open a shell.

Her mother put her hand on her chest, a pledge. "You can always come home, mija," she said. "Hell, look at Manny."

"Manny's your boy."

"So?"

"Boys are the beloved."

Her mother smacked her with the visor again, playfully. "Where'd you get that idea?"

"Everywhere, mami."

Her mother pressed her lips together and then nodded. "Boys really got it easier, don't they?"

Brenna smiled.

"Speaking of boys." Her mother cleared her throat. "I called Colin's parents, looking for you."

"What? Why?"

"I was worried sick."

Brenna clamped her teeth so hard that pain shot into her jaw.

"His mom said she hasn't seen you in over a month. She was a real pendeja about it too. You still with him?"

"No." Brenna thought again of his lazy salute and that word: *pals*.

"Ay, mi cielo." Another rocking hug. "I'm sorry," her mother whispered, mouth right against Brenna's ear. "Why didn't you tell me?"

Brenna wiped her nose on her sleeve and shrugged. "I guess I thought you'd say I made a stupid mistake by being with him in the first place."

Her mother laughed and shook her head. "You're right. You were too good for him. That boy was always saying our house smelled funny. Everyone knew he was an asshole. Manny, Amy, all of them."

"Amy?"

"Yeah, she'd come into the station and we'd talk."

"You gossiped about my boyfriend with my best friend?"

She squeezed Brenna's shoulders. "What could I do? You weren't talking to me."

"It's not like you consult me on your boyfriends," Brenna said.

Her mother rolled her eyes. "Always you on the men I date."

"Well, they're not exactly winners, are they?" Immediately Brenna wished she could suction the words back inside so she didn't get smacked for real, but her mother just sighed.

"I won't apologize for living my life as I have. Sure, some men were mistakes, but it's got to be okay to make mistakes, mija."

Brenna remembered the words she'd heard earlier that day. *Mistakes help us figure out who we are becoming*, Dot had said.

"When you and Camila tried talking to the Storm Spirits as kids, did they ever answer?"

"The wind answered. But maybe that's just their way. Why do you ask?"

Brenna hesitated. Could she tell her mother about the Pontiac and the VW? About Dot and the others? She grew up in Mercer; she might even believe Brenna.

But before Brenna could answer, her mother went on. "What's that Shakespeare quote I always liked from Mrs. King's class? 'There's more in heaven and earth, Horatio, than are dreamt of in your philosophy.'"

Brenna thought about this. "So you think there's even more than the stories Mercerites tell?"

"There has to be. The universe is a big, big place."

It was comforting to think the universe was so big that Brenna could find a place where she didn't have to wear her shell, where she didn't have to perform, or shut off parts of herself.

It seemed like years since Brenna had spent the night in the mysterious old car. "I need to sleep," she said, already turning toward her bedroom.

"Good night, Horatio." Her mother caught her hand and squeezed it just like Dot had in the parking lot. And Brenna, who'd just an hour ago been sea-swept, now felt steady, anchored, home.

42

Joshua woke to the garage door opening below his room. It was probably Lawrence headed to church, alone, like every Sunday. He wondered if the man felt lonely in the family he'd married into, where no one liked him except Joshua's mother, and she was too busy or too disinterested to join him in the things he enjoyed: motorcycles and church and fast-food lunches. Joshua wasn't as pissed at him as he'd wanted to be after he'd failed to defend Joshua in the hardware store. Even in the car on the way home, Joshua had simply pretended to sulk, crossing his arms and staring out at the cornfields. Whatever had softened him toward Lawrence before the encounter with Tyler was still there.

Joshua kicked off his covers and checked his phone.

A group message from Brenna, sent after midnight: *Long story but I didn't get to ask Dot a lot of questions.*

Callie hadn't responded.

Joshua typed: *I'll get to mine today.*

He pushed aside his blinds, and cold air seeped through the window cracks. Fall, when it finally arrived, felt like catching your breath.

The house across the street was still—not that he'd seen any movement since Friday. Joshua pulled out his sketchpad and thumbed through. When he came to the Wolverine drawing, he picked up his pencil. He darkened the lines of the animal legs, shaded fur and tendons, and then drew black claws at the end of each splayed toe. The legs were bent mid-spring, as though he were leaping off the car. It was one of his best drawings, he thought.

"Joshy?" his mother called, knocking.

He snapped the pad closed, his heart beating fast, as though he'd been caught masturbating. "Come in."

She swung open the door and leaned against the frame, appraising his room.

"I know, I know," he said. "I still have to clean."

"And rake. Did you do anything after our talk yesterday?"

"I ran to the hardware store with Lawrence."

"I heard. He said you were helpful." Joshua listened for sarcasm, for an indication that Lawrence had tattled on him yet again, but she seemed sincere.

"Where you heading off to?" he asked, looking at her floral dress.

"Nolan's baby shower," she said, patting her hair. "These chores will be done when I get back?"

"Yes, ma'am."

She pursed her lips like she was going to say more, like another scolding was on its way, but she just nodded instead and closed the door.

Joshua slid the stolen love letter into his pocket, kicked his laundry pile into the closet, and shoved old worksheets, notebooks, and a few textbooks into his backpack. He straightened the covers on his bed. It looked clean enough.

The garage door closed below, and Joshua peeked out the blinds as his mother backed down the driveway.

Downstairs, Ruthie was on the tweed couch with her headphones in and a history book open on her lap. "I'm going to rake," he called.

She pulled out one earbud and raised her barely there brows.

"I'm going to rake the yard," he repeated.

"Why are you telling me, red 'stache?"

"So you know I did my chores in case Mom asks later."

She narrowed her eyes, zooming in on him. "What's really going on?"

"Mom's mad, so I have to rake."

"That's not what I mean." Ruthie waited for Joshua to respond. But he didn't. "We talked Friday morning, remember? The same day the school said you skipped."

"I told you: I was helping the guy across the street."

"What guy?"

"Our new neighbor!"

"Who are you talking about? No one has lived in that house for months."

So Ruthie had never seen him. Had anyone else? "Well, there's someone now," Joshua said—less firmly than he would have liked. He didn't want to let her in on his secret. "And I was helping him and just lost track of time."

"Should I tell Mom that?"

"Why would you?"

"It seems like it might be important." The tone was flippant, a challenge, but she looked worried.

"It's not. Just stay out of it, okay?"

Ruthie gave him a mischievous look. "What are you going to give me?"

"My undying affection?"

"Allowance this month and next."

Joshua rolled his eyes, but he was nervous. Ruthie was sharp and loyal enough to their mom to tell. And what would his mom do if she found out how he was spending his time? He couldn't risk it.

"Fine. But this month only."

"Deal. Pleasure doing business with you." She smirked and pushed her earbud back in.

Joshua headed to the garage.

43

In the car on the way home from their Sunday grocery trip, Callie wanted to say something to her dad: to make promises and swear to be a better friend and daughter and agree to go to counseling, as he'd suggested after the birthday party. She could feel his anger, compressed, in the small space of the car, but she couldn't gather the oxygen, couldn't arrange the syllables. She was still exhausted. She wasn't sure how long she'd sat outside the pizza place the day before, after her dad left. At some point, she'd gathered herself enough to drive home, to climb the stairs, to drop into bed.

Before they left for the store that morning, her father had stood watching while she gagged down toast and jam *for energy*. She threw it up moments later in the bathroom. It was the first time she'd done that, and she sat in the car, rolling the word *bulimic* around like marbles in her mouth. It didn't seem to describe her. This, her emptying, was something else entirely.

Now, before they stepped over the threshold of their house with their grocery bags, her father inhaled, squaring his shoulders like he was gathering the courage to go in. She thought she could see his face setting, a key turning, weights adjusting.

"I've got to vacuum," he said. "You put away the groceries and go see your mother."

When Callie arrived upstairs, her mother was reclining in bed, earbuds connected to her phone on the nightstand. Reading tired her out too much now, so she listened to podcasts and audiobooks with her eyes glazed over. Callie could never tell if she was awake and listening, or if she used the podcasts as a way to check out, to empty herself, like Callie.

"Mom," Callie called softly. The glaze receded and her mother's eyes opened wider.

"I didn't hear you guys come home," she said. She shimmied into a sitting position, the scarf loosening until its tail dangled beside her ear like a stray piece of hair. If it had been hair, Callie would have reached over and brushed it away. Now she couldn't make herself touch the green fabric, for fear of brushing her mother's skin accidentally, of feeling that coldness again. She thought of the anguish in her father's voice the day before. *Open*, she reminded herself again.

"I never got a chance to ask you how the party was yesterday," her mother said, patting the bed beside her. "I really wanted to go, but it was that or the meet, and, well, you know how much I miss being outside." Then she laughed. "I wish I could say I missed pizza, too."

"It was okay," Callie said, perching on the edge of the bed. Below, she heard the vacuum switch on. The roar moved quickly, rumbling over rugs, whining in corners, like her father was communicating his anger through that, too. "I was late. I sort of forgot."

"Oh, Callie. You didn't forget. You just didn't prioritize friendship." The lessons again. "Parties aren't just for the person being celebrated, you know. You need friends like Leslie when things like this happen." She gestured at her body, a lump under the comforter.

Callie felt shame, dull and gauze-wrapped, but there all the same. And then the question Callie had avoided asking—*how long?*—bolted off her tongue, like it had been waiting for shame to clear its path.

"Dr. Kennedy said a month maybe," her mother said quietly. "But it could be much faster. We need to prepare for it to be faster."

Callie remembered her father saying that same phrase—*We need to prepare for it to be faster*—when he'd sat her down about the terminal prognosis last winter. She had just returned from a run. The kitchen was overheated, and she'd kicked off her shoes, peeled off her track pants, and stood in her spandex shorts, listening to the house.

Her father came down the stairs, and she'd been aware of something slightly different about his face, something off—though maybe that memory had been reshaped later, after she was asked to sit on the kitchen stool, her shorts slipping on the lacquered wood. He stood across the island from her and told her they'd determined chemo and radiation would only help to lengthen her mother's life—maybe as much as a year, but that they should prepare for it to be faster. He and her mother had decided, given Callie's age, that another year was worth the discomfort of treatment. Callie wondered now if they felt the same way, if these past ten months had been worth it. Especially since Callie had spent them emptying herself of everything, including her mother.

"Where's Mom?" Callie had demanded at the time, words that felt like an ice pick in her throat.

Her father had calmly explained that she was on a walk, that she'd asked that he be the one who dealt in bad news from now on.

Callie shook her head. "No," she said. It was a *no* to her mother's walk, a *no* to her father's calmness, a *no* to the cancer.

Then Callie heard the familiar jingle of her mother's many key chains and the door swung open with a thwack. Her mother stood in the threshold, knocking her boots against the doorframe, snow falling onto the mat. She was flushed from the cold, hair full of static from her hat. Callie ran to the door and threw herself into her mom's arms. Her mother stumbled backward and then regained her balance, still strong enough to hold her daughter. And then she laughed, like laughter was the only logical response to the inevitability and hopelessness of it all. That was the exact moment that Callie had begun to build cocoons around her feelings, to empty herself of them.

Only a few days after the announcement, Callie's mother initiated the daily talks. The first being, what to expect when your mother is dying. Callie had counted the intricate plaster designs on the ceiling, wondered at their floral patterns, who had made them and why.

Now, ten months later, she still didn't have the answer, but something inside her was loosening.

"What do you think will happen after?" she asked.

Her mom smiled sadly. "I don't know. Maybe I'll become a beautiful mourning dove—I'd rather that than an ugly crow like Mrs. Jenson. And I'll sing to you from the window, be your early bird."

"How early are we talking?"

"Hmm. Four or five a.m."

Callie laughed—an easy laugh that reminded her of laughing beside Joshua and Brenna in the historical society basement. Her mother smiled in reply.

"Mom, you don't know a Mrs. Vidal, do you? From the historical society?"

Her mother frowned and shook her head. The confirmation made the skin on Callie's forearms buzz again. The little germ of belief that had reawakened the day before was pushing its way through the soil. This strange woman might truly be related to both of the tornados that had struck Mercer.

"She said Lincoln stayed in this house. And I found an illustration of him here, back when it was an inn, in that book the historical society made."

It was the first time Callie had seen her mother's eyes light up in months. "Really?" For once, Callie felt something too. She jogged to her room and returned, carrying the book she'd found in the cellar in front of her like a gift.

She climbed back into the bed, this time allowing herself to sink against her mother's shoulder. Callie flipped through the book and pointed at the sketch of Lincoln.

"Look at that," her mother said, her voice soft. "It sure is our house. I can't believe I never noticed that before."

"We're a part of history."

Her mom smiled. "Let me show *you* something." Her mother flipped to the final chapter, "The Future," which discussed planned renovations to the town park and the building of a new middle school—projects that had since been completed. "Do you recognize anyone?"

In one of the photos, there was a girl playing in the park's sandbox in a purple corduroy jacket—a jacket that was probably stored somewhere in the cellar beneath them. Callie's hair was blonder back then, and she held something blurry and red above her head, menacingly almost, as though she were about to strike the ground hard. Callie knew that her mother must have been the one taking the photo, sitting on a nearby park bench, her hair still long, her face much fuller.

Callie wrapped her arm around her mother, trying to make up for all the skipped or stiff hugs in one squeeze. With her other hand, she put a finger on the photo, holding herself and her mother in that moment forever.

44

When Brenna awoke later that Sunday morning, she thought of Colin, his stupid sleeves and his stupid salute, which made her blood boil all over again. Then she thought of Dot. Of writing in the notebook. What relief it had been. The night before, Dot had all but admitted she was a ghost: *I'm not sure I ever got to become.*

Brenna dressed, layering her flannel with a hoodie, and knocked on her mother's door to tell her she was running an errand.

Dot's address was near the church Brenna's grandmother attended, on a street lined with maples flaring red and orange. Her home was a blue warehouse muraled by street artists. Brenna wandered around the building, looking for a normal door, but there wasn't one. She knocked on a tin garage door.

"Who's there?" Dot called.

"It's Brenna. I hope it's okay I'm here?"

The door slid open. Dot stood beneath it in the same clothes she'd been wearing every time Brenna had seen her. Her hair was grease-glossy and pillow-flattened, her makeup nearly gone. In the morning light, she appeared younger—maybe a year or two older than Brenna at most. And underneath the remaining powder, there were hints of bruises, a yellow thumbprint above the bridge of her nose, a plum crescent under her right eye. Were they bruises from the tornado?

"You're always welcome," Dot said. Brenna stepped into a dim space and Dot lowered the garage door behind them. What little light there was filtered in through two rectangular windows near the roof. If this was going to turn into a horror movie, the location was perfect.

"I don't have electricity," Dot said, using a lighter to ignite a candle. "Sorry if it's a little chilly."

The loft was empty of furniture except for a bare air mattress and a beaten recliner, its chocolate leather scratched away in patches, revealing salmon-pink material below. There was a guitar scarred with holes, resting on a stand, and sheet music fanned across the floor.

"You just moved in?" Brenna asked, sinking onto the edge of the air mattress. It dipped under her weight.

Dot nodded and sat on the floor, her knees folded to her chest. "I just found this place abandoned. And it's perfect." She sighed. "This is the life I've always wanted. A musician's life."

Dot's assurance in who she was and what she wanted was striking. Could Brenna just start calling herself a writer? Would that be enough?

"Everything went well with your mom last night?" Dot asked.

"Yeah. Thanks for making me go home. I was in a bad place."

"Just stuff with your mom?"

"That and"—Brenna swallowed—"I slept with Colin. The boy you saw in the Jeep that day we met."

"Oh yes," she said knowingly. "Are you okay?"

Brenna shrugged and nodded at the same time. That scraped-free feeling in the parking lot had felt like a big, albeit painful, step toward okay.

"I started singing and writing music because I had this storm inside," Dot said. "Because sometimes it hurt so much that it was hard to go on. When one notebook was filled, I started the next. I needed an outlet, a way to express myself. You have to let yourself out, Brenna."

"I'm trying. I started writing last night."

Dot grinned. "What'd you write?"

"Lyrics maybe. I don't know."

"I don't always know right away either," Dot said.

"But you figure it out?"

She smiled. "Usually."

Brenna took a deep breath, readying herself for the confirmation she needed. "Dot, I found a picture of you in a yearbook. You're Dorothy Healy. Right?"

At her name, Dot's eyes welled with tears. "I was," she said softly.

Brenna swallowed a few times, hoping to calm her stomach. The truth—admitted so freely—made her feel nauseated, even after years of believing in whispering spirits and ghost birds. "Was?"

"I have Dorothy Healy's memories, but I have everyone else's, too."

"What do you mean *everyone else's*?"

"There are many of us—those who died that night, during the tornado, and those who died on other nights. It's hard to keep yourself straight, to be who you were before."

"But what are you doing here?"

"I don't know. Trying to be a musician? That's what I was doing before the storm. The purple notebook was supposed to be for my next chapter with the Rock-a-Gals. But when I saw you in the parking lot last week and you saw me, I felt like there was some other reason I had it with me, some other reason I was back."

"Something to do with me?"

Dot nodded. "Before, when I was—beyond—I'd watch you and think, *How dare they make her feel like less and that her life doesn't have value?* It took me so long to realize that my life was valuable, that I was worth more than what everyone thought they knew about me. I wanted you to have a better shot than I did." Brenna remembered lying on her bed while the tornado approached, how she'd yearned to be known and remembered like the Storm Spirits, a story lit blue. Even though it was only days ago, Brenna felt like she was remembering someone else's history.

"And music helped you realize all that?"

"It did."

Brenna was calmer now, her heartbeat slowing. "I wondered if the two tornados were connected," she said. "Especially after the old cars they found."

"The cars?"

"Yeah, there were two cars that must have been carried by the tornado."

Dot closed her eyes like she was trying to concentrate. "I remember the storm, I think. And my face hitting the steering wheel. It might be the first thing I remember. Or I might be remembering the other one, the one I—"

Brenna nodded; she understood not completing that sentence. "What do you remember next?"

"Corn. As tall as the VW."

"The VW?" Brenna could hear her own heartbeat.

"My dad's bus. It was too damaged to drive, so I just left it there in the field. I'm not sure if it's still there."

Brenna couldn't contain her excitement. "No, but I know exactly where it is."

MANY OF US REMEMBER

Many of us remember watching, slack-jawed, from our stoops and driveways the day Detonator Dorothy's father returned. He emerged from a van we'd never seen before. He was as tall, stick-slim, and sallow as we remembered, except his face had bloated and cracked like dried mud in the years of his absence.

Dorothy was the one to open the door, and we tried to read her face. Shock? Terror? Anger?

"Dotty," he said, opening his arms for a hug, but it was all wrong, like he was telling a tall tale about the size of a fish: *It was this big.* She didn't step into his arms. He waited, his arms hanging, until her mother appeared behind Dorothy, in the doorframe.

We remember being shocked by how pleased she looked. It was as though she hadn't been the one chasing him with a knife, screaming *You pervert* as he peeled away four years before.

He leaned in and, with a wet-sounding smack, kissed Dorothy's mother on the cheek. Dorothy cringed and slid outside—freer to escape if she needed. She stood barefoot on the pavement.

"Run," those of us there whispered, and her toes curled like she'd heard us.

"You look swell," her father said, glancing at Dorothy and her mother, as though the compliment was for them both.

Dorothy took another step back—more space between them.

"I came because I wanted to give you something, since I haven't been around much." He said this as though leaving were his idea, like he hadn't been chased out by her mother's knife.

"I got this van, and I see you still only have the Wayfarer." Dorothy turned her head and looked at the vehicle behind her. The Rock-a-Gals had their first show with their new front girl coming up. Bands need vans.

"We don't need another car, Elmer," her mother said.

Dorothy's eyes fixed on her mother and she made a face that we were sure meant: *See me for once. Really see me.*

"Well, you can sell it or something. For the money," he said.

"I'll take it," Dorothy said, her voice louder than we expected. Bold.

"What do you need a van for?" her mother snapped. Maybe she hadn't told her mother about the Rock-a-Gals yet.

But he offered the keys on his palm. "It's yours," he said. We held our breaths. She reached for them, and he snapped his hand closed, grasping her fingers before she could grab the keys. She looked at her mother desperately, as though she wanted to be saved again.

"Can Dotty and I have a moment?" he asked her mother.

Now, finally, a look of doubt passed over her mother's face, but it blew past like a cloud. She nodded and backed into the house.

"I don't know what your mother told you back then," he said. "About why I left. I'm sure you know now that kids have big imaginations. They make things into something they're not."

Dorothy wrenched her fingers free, but he continued talking: "And I'd like it if you would come to a better understanding now. So we can be in each other's lives."

She looked so terrified, some of us were afraid she'd snap and grab the bat the neighbor boy had left in the yard. Instead she plugged her ears, sank onto her knees, and shrieked like she had as a girl, a sound that raked our bones. He didn't try to speak again. He dropped the keys in the grass and started down the street on foot, heading for the train station.

45

When her mother drifted to sleep, Callie shut herself in her bedroom. Her father was still cleaning, slamming cabinet doors and kitchen drawers. She organized her school binder, opening and closing the three rings with satisfying clinks in response to her father's slams. *You aren't eating.* Clink. *You're a terrible friend.* Clink. *You're a worse daughter.* Clink. *You might be talking to dead people.* Clink.

Callie needed to go to St. Theresa's, but the only way she was getting out of the house was a school-related excuse. Or her mother.

Downstairs, her father was wiping off the ceiling fan from a ladder in the kitchen. Fuzzy clumps of dust floated down, gathering on the counter and floor. Callie wanted to point out that he'd just have to vacuum again, but she wondered if that was what he wanted: another excuse to roar through the house.

"Mom asked for more frankincense," she said, trying to keep

her face stony. She was lying again. And all for what? A creepy old woman?

He looked down at her, gold eyebrows raised. "I thought Toni brought more by the other day. I'll go check the nightstand."

"She's asleep, Dad."

He sighed and returned to the fan, swiping another gray clump. "You can help me clean for the realtor when you get back."

Callie felt the knot in her throat again, pulsing like it had its own heartbeat. "There's nothing we can do to keep this place? Like, what if I got a job? Or maybe Toni can help. Please."

Her father looked down at her, the fan casting strange shadows across his face. "I don't think so, Cal," he said, his voice cracking. "I'm sorry."

Entering St. Theresa's lobby made Callie feel like she was diving into a bowl of wedding mints. Curtains in baby-duck yellow, couches in pale blue, tiles marbled with spring green and pink.

"Can I help you?" a woman seated at the front desk asked. She looked old enough to be a resident herself.

"I'm looking for someone who lives here," Callie said.

The woman smiled with pity, clearly thinking Callie was some lost granddaughter.

"What's the name, dearie?" she asked.

"Ellie Vidal."

The woman frowned and typed something into her computer. "Spell it for me?"

"*V-i-d-a-l.*" She wondered if Ellie was short for Eleanor or Ellen.

"No, I'm sorry. I can't find that name."

"Okay. Thanks, anyway. Do you mind if I sit and make a phone call?" If Mrs. Vidal had ever been involved in the society, Mrs. Greenley—the museum docent—would know her.

The woman smiled pityingly again. Callie used her phone to search for the historical society's number.

"Mrs. Greenley, this is Callie Keller. I was in the museum yesterday, working on a school project."

"Of course, of course, Cath's girl," the woman said.

Callie cringed at her mother's name. How much longer would people call her that—even though it would never cease to be true? "Yeah. Uh, my mother was hoping you could do us a favor. I'm looking for the address of a society member: Ellie Vidal. Mom has something to send her." This was the second time in an hour that Callie had used her mom's cancer as an excuse for lying.

"Yes, let me see what I can do." She huffed into the phone like she was climbing a staircase. "What was the name again?"

"Ellie Vidal."

"I'm embarrassed to say I thought she'd passed quite some time ago. She bequeathed an antique car to the society, and we sold it to a collector, I believe. But I can see if we still have her information on file." Passed away? An antique car? So was it true?

While Mrs. Greenley was puffing away, Mrs. Vidal rounded the corner into the lobby, wearing the same floral dress, her perm slightly looser than before, her eyes just as sharp. "Callie!" she said, waving excitedly. "It's so great to see you."

Callie waved back. "Never mind, Mrs. Greenley. Thanks for your help." She hung up without waiting for a reply.

"Come, dear, there's never anyone in the game room at this time," Mrs. Vidal said.

Callie glanced back at the desk, but the receptionist had walked away. Callie followed Mrs. Vidal down the hall.

"I was just looking for you," Callie said.

"Usually I'm pretty easy to find. I don't move very fast." She chuckled and led Callie into a room carpeted in pale pink. The walls were white with pink candy stripes, like this was a baby's nursery and not a place where humans able to formulate opinions and speak might live. There were four tables in the room, each of which was topped with an unfinished jigsaw puzzle.

Mrs. Vidal sat down at a table and gestured for Callie to

do so as well. The outside edges of the puzzle had already been assembled and sat like an empty frame. The remaining pieces had been sorted by color into piles.

Callie picked up a puzzle piece and tried it before setting it back down and taking another, smiling when it locked into place.

"Brava," Mrs. Vidal said.

Callie reached for another piece. She couldn't remember the last time she'd done a puzzle like this, and she was glad, because it had probably been with her mother, like everything else in her life.

"How's your mother?" Mrs. Vidal asked as if she'd read Callie's mind.

"She's okay," Callie said carefully. "But I asked her, Mrs. Vidal, and she doesn't know you."

Mrs. Vidal's eyebrows rose above the red frames of her glasses, but she didn't respond. Callie decided to try a different approach. "Do you go by another name?"

"What do you mean, dearie?"

"I didn't find anything when I searched online for you, and the woman in the lobby said Ellie Vidal wasn't a resident here."

Mrs. Vidal's strikingly blue eyes met hers. "My name is Eleanor Peterson. I went by Vidal, but I never legally changed my name to my husband's. Too much busywork." She flitted her hand dismissively. Callie felt the buzzing, hopeful belief sprout further—not just beneath the skin on her arms, but under her cheeks, her stomach, all the way along her spine.

"You're the Eleanor Peterson who founded the historical society? Whose ancestors built the house I live in?"

Mrs. Vidal smiled. "You must be good at puzzles."

"So you remember when it was an inn?"

"Oh, of course. But so would anyone my age," Mrs. Vidal said.

"If you don't mind my asking, why'd you sell the house?"

Mrs. Vidal cupped a puzzle piece in her palm. "We lost my daughter, Celeste," she said softly. "And it felt as though every sound was her trying to speak to us. It was just too hard." She shook her head. "Frederic found good enough owners—the Gallaghers, who had it before your family—but I've regretted it ever since."

Callie's breath caught in her throat. So she was definitely Celeste's mother, but Mrs. Greenley had said Mrs. Vidal had passed away and bequeathed an antique car. Callie had to be sure that this newly awakened thing prickling her spine wasn't a false hope, wouldn't fail her.

"Mrs. Vidal, are you—" Callie swallowed, gathering her courage. "Are you a spirit?"

"A spirit," Mrs. Vidal repeated, as though puzzling out the word. "The house spirits spend all their time knocking about. Am I just knocking about?"

Callie shook her head.

"I didn't think so. But maybe what your question really is—the crux of it all—is have I died? And the answer is yes."

Callie's hearing went out, her ears humming, her mind swimming, dizzy—everything else distant and tinny. When the sound returned to Callie, it was loud and hard, like Mrs. Vidal had thrown bricks. She swallowed, recovering herself, tried to put her thoughts in order. So it was true. And if Mrs. Vidal could die and return, what did that mean for Callie's mother?

"I didn't want to scare you, so I lied about living at St. Theresa's. I mean, it's where I used to live. Before. But I lied about *living* here now. I've just been visiting, wandering, talking to those who can hear me."

Callie wasn't sure what to say. What could someone say after their world had been turned upside down? Or maybe it had simply been righted? "We might have to sell the house too," she blurted.

Mrs. Vidal pushed her glasses down the bridge of her nose and looked over the top. "What? Why?"

"The doctor bills, I guess. And without my mom working, they can't afford the mortgage."

"Well, we have to do something."

"My dad will try to find a good buyer."

"We were lucky with the Gallaghers. And again with your

family, but we may not get lucky a third time." The woman's eyes glittered with tears, which only enhanced their sharpness. "It's home. It's where I last saw my mother. And my daughter. Someone else might tear it down."

Callie looked down at the picture on the puzzle box, smiling faces leaning over the white table, an old couple at the center, a turkey on its platter, and all she saw was her mother with a bucket of soapy water, running a mop over the floorboards. Her mother wrapping her hand in masking tape to pull hairs off the heavy drapes. Her mother trying a lamp in three different positions, each time looking at Callie with a hopeful smile—*here?* Her mother *was* the house, golden and chestnut and warm. The thought seared beneath her breastbone.

"I have an idea," Mrs. Vidal said. "We'll sell my car."

The black car Mrs. Vidal had driven away had looked battered. Had it been crushed in the tornado like the Pontiac? "I'm not sure it's worth much, Mrs. Vidal."

"Of course. It's a classic, but they towed it the other day."

"Who is *they*?"

"This place." She waved her hand at the room around them. "I overheard them talking about how the car didn't have a parking pass and they couldn't locate the owner. Of course, I couldn't stop them. They can't see me like you can. Did you drive here?"

"Yes."

"Well, then let's go find it."

Callie shook her head. "I'd be happy to help you find it, Mrs. Vidal. But you're not going to sell it for my family. If anything, we'll sell ours. I can take the bus and Mom—" Callie inhaled.

"Your mother doesn't need a car anymore," Mrs. Vidal finished, her blue eyes unblinking.

Callie exhaled and nodded.

"Let's get my car. I insist," she said. Callie agreed, if only to spend more time with the woman. Mrs. Vidal understood dying and what came after.

46

Joshua raked right in front of the bay window, so he'd be seen by Ruthie, and then worked his way to the side of the house, outside her periphery. He dropped the rake, walked a few houses down, jogged across the street, and then snuck up behind his neighbor's house.

He'd spent so much time trying to keep Ruthie from figuring out what he was up to that he hadn't considered what he'd say to the Wolverine. For all he knew, the man might laugh in Joshua's face, dismissing him as a crazy kid. But Joshua had too many questions. Was he dead? A Storm Spirit? More important, how on earth could Joshua survive the next four years in Mercer? How could he stop the town from getting him down?

Joshua knocked on the back door. No response. He cupped his hands over his eyes and peered through the kitchen window. The house was as empty as before.

Where else could the man have gone? The only other place Joshua had seen him was outside the firehouse.

Even though he'd memorized every word, Joshua pulled the love letter out of his pocket for clues.

I discovered new landscapes.

Something clicked inside Joshua. For that kind of love, you went back. The Wolverine would be at the Pontiac.

Without bothering to be stealthy, Joshua ran to the apple tree and unchained his bike. He swung a leg over and pedaled madly down the driveway. Out of the corner of his eye, he thought he saw the curtains move in his own house. Another month's allowance for Ruthie.

Joshua lowered the gear and spun his feet quickly, ignoring the sweat that tickled the backs of his knees. He was biking the same path as he had after the storm—except now he wasn't fighting wind or the fear that his grandparents' house had been demolished by a tornado. He was going to see if love survived even death.

SOME OF US HEARD

Some of us heard Connie sobbing in home ec because Luke had broken up with her. We expected Eddie to follow suit and dump his sweetheart, Carolyn, a flautist in the marching band. Luke even bought a Route 66 bumper sticker for Eddie's Pontiac. There was talk they'd drive west together, end up in Hollywood, where we'd heard it was safer for people like them. Eddie, with his golden allure, could act on the big screen. Luke could work on the cars of the famous.

It was—we all agreed—time for them to leave; they were getting sloppy with their secret. We'd spotted the Pontiac just outside town after dark, shadows moving behind fogged glass. We knew it wasn't Carolyn, whose preacher daddy demanded a nine-o'clock curfew. We'd also seen the hole in Luke's jumpsuit, right at the heart, and smirked at the explanation that it had been snagged in the wash.

Not long before the night of the storm, a few of us were

downtown for lunch, drinking floats and eating fries on the hoods of our cars. Eddie pulled into Luke's shop, Carolyn in the passenger seat. We crept closer, pretending to admire the Pontiac. Luke slid out from beneath the car he was working on, squinting into the sun. When he registered Carolyn, he made a face like he'd been bitten.

Eddie chirruped a *hello* and Luke stared, still on his back, his face hard.

"Join us for lunch," Eddie said as though it was the most natural thing to have his two lovers together.

"He looks busy," we heard Carolyn say. There was panic in her voice. Standing there, between the two men, it had to be dawning on her: the nights Eddie didn't call after her curfew, the sour sweat smell in his car, the frequent visits to the mechanic. Eddie was still smiling, but his brow was crinkled now, like he didn't understand anything at all.

Without answering, Luke slid back under the car. This heartbreak—not even our own—was one of our last memories.

47

The impound lot doubled as a junkyard, with towers of junked cars along the back acres—a rusted skyline—and impounded cars sprawling like suburbs in neat rows toward the street. Some of the impounded vehicles were pristine, glistening—towed from Main Street shops and bars. Others were crushed and crunched, flagged with tape for police investigation.

Joshua pedaled slowly past the VW. It seemed a brighter, cheerier blue than it had in the cornfield. He would have guessed that someone had given it a bath—if it weren't for the mud caked on the tires. The Pontiac was down the fence line, the lot pit bull snoring nearby. Joshua pedaled over, dropped his bike, and wrapped his fingers around the fence links. It was the closest he'd been to the car, and he thought of his grandfather, how he would've walked around it, whistling through his teeth.

Something moved inside. It was his neighbor's head, just

visible above the passenger seat. Joshua's instinct had been right, and seeing the man in the Pontiac felt like everything was now in place. He thought of his sketch, of the ghostly outline he'd left in the driver's seat. Was Eddie supposed to be there?

His neighbor's eyes were visible in the cracked passenger mirror, and Joshua couldn't tell if they were meeting his gaze, or if the fractures meant that the man was staring at the clouds or the black-top or the yellow stone high school behind him. *Be brave*, Joshua told himself, and his mind flitted to Brenna, like she was whispering in his ear, hand cupped over her mouth to hide her teeth.

"Hi," Joshua said. The man's head jerked and he straightened in the seat. "I'm sorry. I thought you might be here. I just had a few questions."

The man was silent, but Joshua pressed on.

"Is your name Luke Winters?"

"Yep," he said.

Joshua's skin felt like pins and needles—almost like it had before he'd fainted. "Were you in the tornado? In 1961? Did you— did you die?"

"Yes," the man said softly—almost a whisper.

Joshua felt himself flush from his toes to his forehead. This was what a born-Mercerite like Joshua should have believed all along, and the truth felt like coming home, like waking to the sound of cornstalks, opening his bedroom door to the smell of his grandmother's pancakes, of padding across the alpaca rug to the kitchen—sweet and familiar. As much as he hated Mercer, he loved the stories that had cracked open his imagination as a child, he loved that farm, he loved his grandparents and sister and mother. *They* were his home.

"I grew up on Orange Street. In that brick house with the green shutters," Luke continued. The house with the cigar-smoking man who'd never waved at Ruthie and Joshua? "My father still lives there," Luke said, as though reading Joshua's mind. "Luke Senior."

"Can he see you?" Joshua asked.

"Doesn't seem to," Luke said. "After you saw me, I was going every day, hoping. Not sure why I bother. He never accepted me when I was your age. Don't expect he's changed."

Joshua thought of Lawrence, of the way he'd ducked out of rooms, but also of the way he'd squared his chest at Tyler's father. Mercerites could change. Hell, he'd changed, hadn't he? He was doing it right now.

"I have something of yours," Joshua said, his heart rocketing against his rib cage. Luke might be furious when he found out Joshua had stolen the letter, but Joshua knew he had to return it.

Luke got out of the car and walked over so they were face-to-face, with only the links separating them. Joshua handed him the folded square of paper, and Luke stiffened, like he was willing all his muscles to hold his skeleton together.

Joshua understood then that Eddie was Luke's eclipse, something bright and dark that he couldn't look at directly. Maybe he'd even died before he had the chance to come out—a thought that made Joshua ache.

"This was Eddie's car, right?"

"Yes," the man said, still staring at the letter in his palm as though it might explode.

"And you loved—the car?" Joshua asked, hoping the implication was clear.

"Yes," he said.

"But then the tornado?"

"I don't remember much about that night. I thought being in the car might help me understand why I'm back."

"And has it?"

Luke met Joshua's eyes, and the contact didn't feel animal-skittish now, but direct and meaningful—like it was the only way Luke knew how to say: *You. I'm here because of you.*

48

The attendant monitoring the gate to the lot slid open his booth window when Callie pulled up.

"Tell him we're here to get the 1957 Chevrolet Coupe," Mrs. Vidal said.

Callie repeated the message to the curly-haired man in the stocking cap. He never even glanced past Callie at the woman in the passenger seat. "One moment," he said, frowning at his screen and sliding his window shut again.

Mrs. Vidal raised her eyebrows and smiled at Callie. "It seems we wait," she said. "Do you have any questions?"

Mrs. Vidal probably meant questions about the fact that she was a spirit, but it was the same thing Callie's mother had asked her on the day her kidneys failed. Now Callie was with someone who knew what it meant to die, someone who wasn't her mother.

"What will it be like? The dying, I mean," Callie asked.

Mrs. Vidal nodded sagely. "It's different for everyone." She cleared her throat. "For me, it was fast—a stroke. My vision went blurry, my limbs went numb, and when I called for help, I couldn't make the word, couldn't put the sounds in the right order. I don't remember feeling pain. Just being in the Chevy one moment, and then being part of the others the next." She gestured vaguely at the space around them, as though the spirits were everywhere. "Frederic's death was slower. He stopped eating. His skin looked so yellow and tight, I thought it was going to pop and all his tumors would spill out. He was in pain, so they kept him on his side and turned him over every few hours. He'd wail each time, like he was being tortured. I tried to help him drink water, but he usually threw it up. I'd have to blot the mess off the pillow. He wasn't conscious much at the end, and when he was, he'd ask confusing things, like where the people on TV were. He thought they were real, that they were relatives from France who he was supposed to remember and didn't." It was brutally matter-of-fact—how Mrs. Vidal talked about her husband. Her sharp gaze was directed at the gate, the cars beyond. "There's this point when they'll tell you she's actively dying, which is a hoot because we all are—dying, I mean. Even you, young as you are. Your cells are at it right now."

Callie followed Mrs. Vidal's gaze, trying to see past the cars that were flattened and stacked along the horizon. If Mrs. Vidal could be here, right now, talking to her so frankly years after her daughter's death, after her husband's, Callie could sit at her mother's bed and hold that icy hand and be the daughter her mother deserved.

"And after?"

"After is the hardest part for the living," she said. "After Celeste, I stopped eating. I didn't go to the funeral. I sold the house where she'd grown up, where I'd grown up. It took me years to realize that, in pushing the pain away, I was pushing her away—everything I had left of her. You have to preserve. You have to do work—to think of the person and remember, to reread the essays she wrote for class, to cook the foods she loved, to look at the photos you took. And as a town, we have to do that too. That's why I started the society. It's the history of this place that keeps it alive."

"Why didn't you register the house as historic back then?"

"The Gallaghers didn't want me to. They thought the state would meddle if they tried to make changes to the property. And then your mother bought it, and I knew it was in good hands."

Thinking of her mother, Callie was about to ask what the afterlife was like for the dead, but the attendant slid open his window again, interrupting Mrs. Vidal. "You own the car?" he asked.

"No," Callie said. "My grandmother does."

"Do you have the title or other proof of ownership?"

Callie shook her head.

"Sorry," the man said. "No dice."

"See if he'll at least let us go look at it," Mrs. Vidal said. "Maybe we can break it out of here."

Breaking the car out and selling it was not remotely an option, but Callie was curious and Mrs. Vidal was set on going inside. "Can I check and see if my grandpa's pipe is in the car? He really loved that thing, and he just passed."

The man frowned, but perhaps Callie looked tragic enough that he nodded. "All right. You can go in now, but you'll need to come back with the title and what you owe to get the car off the lot."

The attendant gave them the spot number and pointed. Callie parked on the street and Mrs. Vidal took her arm as they crossed into the lot. Callie expected her to lean, but Mrs. Vidal remained upright and steady, almost dragging Callie along.

Up close, the damage was even worse than Callie had first thought. The taillights were shattered. The rear end crumpled.

"It looks like it's going to be harder to sell than I thought," Mrs. Vidal said, stroking one of the fins. Callie had expected this, and still the disappointment flooded her. How could she save the house?

"You know, it was at the drive-in that night," Mrs. Vidal said. "My daughter took it to work. I never saw the damage. Frederic kept it in a storage facility. I was a lot more nervous back then, and he was very protective."

"Why didn't he just sell it?"

She shrugged. "I guess he kept it for the same reason I couldn't keep the house. Because it reminded him of her. He'd work on it on the weekends. Trying to restore it. I didn't go see it until after he died. I thought I'd sell it then, but I couldn't help climbing inside. It reminded me of all the places we'd go as a family: church, the grocery store, Starved Rock State Park. I started visiting it regularly after I moved into St. Theresa's. I even wrote it into my will, so the historical society could sell it for operating costs. I was inside it, thinking of Celeste and Frederic, when I had the stroke. And then there I was the other day, inside it again during this terrible storm just like the one when—" She closed her eyes and shuddered. "When it was over, I drove it into town. I kept having this feeling that I needed to look after the house, make sure it would be preserved, and look after you, too."

"Why me?" Callie managed to ask, but she sounded winded, like she'd just finished a run.

Mrs. Vidal stared at Callie, the lines in her forehead forming Vs, like flying geese. Then she spoke slowly as though she were discovering each word, tasting it for the first time. "My memories are tangled. Some are mine and some seem to belong to the others. But I do remember watching you grow up. And you've been worrying me lately; you're buried deep down."

Callie imagined herself in a hole, pulling down handfuls of dirt, scraping until it cascaded like a shower. It was safer in the suffocating dark. That was why she'd collapsed to the pavement after her father wrenched her and her feelings to the surface in Giovanni's parking lot. Underground, she'd forgotten how to breathe.

49

As Brenna neared the impound lot, she spotted a shock of red hair. It was Joshua, leaning against the fence near the Pontiac, talking as though there was someone on the other side. His ghost? Brenna threw Golden Girl in park and beckoned Dot to follow her.

"Hey, Josh. I want you to meet Dot."

He turned, and Brenna watched him scan the air beside her without finding Dot.

"Nice to meet you," he said anyway, and gestured toward the Pontiac. "This is Luke."

Brenna smiled toward the Pontiac, hoping that Luke—wherever he was—knew she was glad to have him there. "Do you guys know each other? Can you see each other?" Brenna asked.

"I don't see anyone except the redhead," Dot said. "But I have this familiar feeling, like when you're with someone you've known your whole life, and you don't have to say anything to understand each other."

"I wanted to show Dot the VW," Brenna said to Joshua, and she pointed toward the end of the lot that was closer to the cemetery. Dot was already marching to where the blue VW leaned on its flat tire on the other side of the fence, the chrome still glinting. Brenna followed, Joshua trailing her, and possibly Luke, too. Before Brenna realized what was happening, Dot bent and dug into the grass along the sidewalk, ripping up a fistful of soil and sod. She chucked it, but the dirt diffused in the air before it hit the bus. That didn't stop her from grabbing another fistful. And another. The pit bull waddled over, wagging his tail, and snapped at the flying dirt clumps like he was trying to catch tennis balls.

"I shouldn't have accepted it from *him*," Dot spat. Brenna stopped mid-step. Behind her, Joshua did the same.

"If I hadn't taken it, we wouldn't have—" Dot grabbed another clump of dirt and grass. This time, some hit the bus and crumbled between its headlights. Brenna wondered what this man had done to Dot and what the VW had to do with it all.

"Here." Though he couldn't see Dot, Joshua held a small piece of broken concrete on his palm like he was feeding Mrs. Jenson. Dot took the concrete, and Joshua's face bloomed with wonder. He grinned at his empty hand.

Dot launched the concrete over the fence. It bounced off the roof of the bus with a disappointing thud. Brenna found a larger piece of cracked concrete and levered it from the soil with a stick. She handed it to Dot, and this time, the projectile hit the windshield with a satisfying crack. Dot's chest was heaving, and she bent over her knees to catch her breath.

Behind them, a car pulled up and idled. Brenna spun around, afraid it was a cop. How would they explain this?

"Hey, you guys." Callie was in the driver's seat. "I'm here with Mrs. Vidal," Callie said, waving at the empty seat beside her. Brenna couldn't help laughing, a gleeful, bubbling sound. Again and again, she, Callie, and Joshua were being pulled together, and now all three of them were here with their Storm Spirits in tow.

Maybe Mercer really was a magical place.

"I think it's time we heard your stories," she said. And as each spirit spoke, Callie, Brenna, and Joshua repeated so all could hear.

From Luke, a story of a forbidden life and love. Joshua's expression was grave, for it was his history too—the fight to be seen, to take up space.

From Mrs. Vidal, a life of losses, beaded together. They dangled before Callie, heavy and near.

From Dot, unimaginable trauma and a cold, lonely depression that tugged at her like a moon. Brenna knew that moon, had felt it orbiting closer and closer. But for Dot, there'd been the relief of music and art and friends. Finally, now, Brenna felt that too.

FOR MANY OF US

For many of us, our worst day was October 7, 1961, when the tornado ripped through our town, our lives. But the day itself started out so ordinary. Bowls of creamed wheat with baked apples, a pancake glazed with melted butter and warm syrup, an egg or two with fried bacon. Then there was dusting, sweeping, and hanging clothes to dry. There were speech meets and babysitting. Homework and busing tables. Play rehearsals and apprenticing with fathers and feeding livestock. At lunch, many of us were together, drinking floats on the hoods of our cars or the tops of picnic tables in the town square, under Eleanor's watchful eye. We thought of the square as our place, never considering that our parents wanted that for us—the town's heart to be ours.

After lunch, there were books to read, cars to wax, lawns to mow, cards to play, cash registers to balance. Most of us ate dinner with our families, filled our stomachs with pork chops and chicken thighs and beef shoulders, animals that were born and raised just down the road. We teased siblings. We were silenced by fathers' stern gazes. Before the drive-in, we helped mothers soak pots and bathe brothers and read stories.

There's such sweetness in ordinary, in the calm before a storm.

50

At the lunch table, Callie was pinching pieces of bread with her forefinger and thumb until the sandwich looked like it had been pecked by a flock of birds. Joshua found it difficult to watch her shrinking into herself, dense and dark like a dying star. It was another reason he admired Brenna; she could look directly at Callie, and at him, without flinching.

"I wonder why Mrs. Vidal, and not Celeste, is visiting me," Callie said suddenly. "You two have visitors who were actually in the tornado. Mine had a whole life afterward."

"Maybe she's exactly what you need," Joshua said quietly, almost under his breath. "Maybe that's why all three of them are here. Because only they can help us, because we need them."

Joshua could feel Callie's need from across the table, could feel it pulling at him, at everything around them: his crumpled napkin and deli paper, the din of lunchroom chatter, the light.

What was it he needed? What could stoic, gruff Luke possibly give him? But Joshua already knew the answer. *Don't let them get you down.* He had to do what he'd planned when he started high school: start the support groups, rally, date, go to prom—everything Eddie had turned away from and lost, everything Luke had needed too. Joshua wouldn't run because people refused to see him, wouldn't wait for another tornado to disappear inside. What he could do—what he needed to do—was make himself impossible to ignore.

Callie's hands continued to crawl spider-fast over her sandwich, but Brenna appeared to be musing, her eyes on the water-stained cafeteria ceiling. "What happens when we don't need them anymore?" Brenna asked. "Will they return to wherever they came from?"

Joshua's stomach plummeted. Would Luke leave if Joshua did the things he planned and so badly wanted? Brenna's face portrayed a similar fear. Only Callie, still so lost in her grief, didn't react to the question.

51

At Taco Bell, Amy was braiding Jade's hair, piling it high like the wigs of eighteenth-century women. Jade was the most beautiful person Brenna knew—with green eyes, silky black hair that fell to her ass, and tiny stick-and-poke tattoos she'd etched into her skin. Even now, she was digging into the back of her hand with a pen, fashioning something that looked like a galaxy, which was both hard to watch and hard not to. Both of her friends were completely unaware of what was going on inside Brenna, of what had happened over the past several days. Brenna took out her lavender notebook. For Dot, writing was putting words to feelings, putting on paper what couldn't be expressed out loud.

Could it do the same for her?

I am Brenna Daniela Ortiz, the in-between. I used to be afraid of being between, of being caught in

*the middle and crushed. But between is a space
too, a room of my own. Between, I can see my
grandmother, who wants us to be happy, successful,
and part of the family, but is unable to expand her
vision of what that might look like and is unable to
forgive. I can see my mother, my solid foundation,
who loves with her whole self and wants only love
in return. I can see my friends, so wrapped in their
shells that they are blind. I can see Colin, the fraud
and narcissist. I can see Dot, the artist who was
never heard. And I can see myself. A writer.*

When Brenna arrived home from Taco Bell, her mother's car was still in the driveway. She looked at the time on her cell phone—nearly an hour after her mom normally left for work on Mondays. She felt it in her gut: something was wrong. Brenna pushed open the front door and let it slam behind her.

"Mom," she called. "What's wrong?"

"In here," her mother said, her voice strained.

Brenna rounded the corner into the kitchen quickly and stopped. Seated at the counter with his back to the doorway was Colin, wearing that same washed-soft T-shirt, the hole just visible.

Had he known, somehow, how it made her hurt to see it? Her mother was leaning on the counter across from him in her gas station uniform, her visor curled in her hand.

"What's going on?" Brenna hissed. She meant the question for both of them. Colin, who'd appeared at her house. Her mother, who'd invited him in.

Colin turned slowly on the stool and smiled sheepishly. Brenna shook her head wildly, as though that would separate whatever still connected them.

She turned to her mother. "What is he doing here?"

"He stopped by and insisted on waiting for you, so I thought it was best if I waited too."

Brenna hugged the straps of her book bag. She wanted to be angry at her mother for letting him in, but her mom was also protecting her. If she'd said no, Colin would have found another way.

"I just thought we should talk," Colin said. He glanced over his shoulder at her mother. "In your room maybe?"

Her mother shook her head. "You two stay here. I'll be in the living room."

Brenna glued her eyes to Matthew in the *Last Supper* print above the counter. He was incredulous. *What is this?* he seemed to be asking Simon. As a preteen, Brenna had had to name all the disciples in Spanish before she could have one of her grandmother's empanadas—her abuela's way of trying to make up for Brenna's lack of religious education.

"I just wanted to say I'm sorry," Colin said, when her mother had left.

"For what? Hiding your Jeep a few blocks away so I wouldn't know you were here?" Brenna asked, scanning the painting for the surprised Judas. So young. So taken aback. He couldn't imagine what was going to happen.

"For that night at the concert. I shouldn't have done that."

"Done what exactly?" Brenna asked. She wanted him to speak his guilt out loud.

"Put you in that position while I was still with Tara." He was being careful with his words, Brenna knew, because her mother was just on the other side of the wall. "Yeah, Tara and I broke up," he continued, as though she'd asked a question.

"Good for her," she said.

He paled and ran his fingers through his hair. "I just wanted to say I'm sorry," he repeated.

"You already did," Brenna said. "Anything else?"

He exhaled loudly. "I'm sorry for hurting you before. You know, the first time."

Brenna nodded.

"Can you forgive me?" he asked.

Brenna's eyes found Christ in the print. His peaceful face, his downward gaze. She thought of the way Colin had said *pals* and given that flimsy peace-sign gesture of goodbye. She began to laugh. Cackle, really. Colin was trying to keep his options open and wanted to know that Brenna would still be there for a hookup. Otherwise, he wouldn't have bothered with all the apologies. It was hilarious.

Her mother returned to the kitchen, a worried look on her face, and shooed Colin out. He slid off the stool and, through her laughter, Brenna was aware of him looking at her one more time—surprise, confusion, maybe even hurt on his face. He would try again; she was sure of it. Someday, when her mother was gone. Or via text. Or even through his friends. But Brenna felt more secure now. She held up the two fingers of her right hand. *Peace*, she thought, though it was all for her.

52

C allie walked home from the first cross-country practice she'd attended since the tornado, the sweat cooling too quickly on her skin, her teeth chattering. The temperature had continued to drop since the storm, and she no longer had flesh to insulate her. She wasn't sure how much weight she'd lost, but in the locker room mirror, she'd seen her skull: the white of her brow bone, the sockets of her eyes, her jaw and cheek. *You're buried deep down*, Mrs. Vidal had said. And she had been. She'd started looking like her mother again, chasing the resemblance to death.

She considered stopping at St. Theresa's to warm up and ask Mrs. Vidal a million questions about hearing Celeste after she died, about whether Callie could expect to hear her own mother, or if her mom would be able to return in a storm to watch Callie like Mrs. Vidal had. But she was also afraid of the answer—that maybe that could never happen again. Who made the rules about which ghosts came back? Callie broke into a jog home. When she reached their driveway, the whir of the leaf blower alerted her that her father was in the backyard. A year ago, or even a few months ago, Callie would have walked around the house to say hello. Instead she headed into the house. All she wanted was a shower and her fleece-lined pajama pants.

Midway upstairs, she heard mumbling. It was her mother's voice.

Callie paused and stood still for a moment, until a gut feeling that something was really wrong propelled her to the door.

"I want to know when," her mother seemed to be saying. Callie didn't hear a response. Was her mother on the phone?

Callie knocked lightly. "Mom?"

Nothing.

"Mom?" Callie tried again louder.

"It's the house," her mother said. Or maybe: "It's a ghost."

Callie shook her head, trying to understand what was going on. Her mother was clearly alive. Everything was okay. Callie grabbed the knob, turned it, and pushed the door open in one quick motion, like she might catch the talkers midsentence.

The reek of shit slapped her. Sharp, sour, fungal. Her mother was on her side, eyes closed, a thin string of yellow liquid connecting the corner of her mouth to the pillow. Her skin was the color of putty.

"Mom?" Callie repeated. She watched as her mother's eyelids struggled to open. "Are you okay?"

Callie willed herself to enter the room. Gingerly, she lifted the corner of her mother's comforter and gagged. A black stain blossomed beneath her mother's hip. Callie heard sobbing and realized it was coming from her own throat. There were no tears—just loud gasping noises forcing their way up again and again, like hiccups.

"Mom, wake up," Callie pleaded. She imagined her mom laughing when she realized what had happened in her sleep, masking her embarrassment about the whole thing. She'd apologize profusely to Callie and tell her to take a shower while she cleaned up the mess herself.

Instead her mother asked, "Where's my lunch?" It was accusatory, like Callie had eaten it.

"I don't know. I'll ask Dad."

Callie backed out the door and crossed the hallway to her bedroom. She shut herself in. Monty, her stuffed brontosaurus, watched her from his perch on her pillows with his plastic-bead eyes. Maybe this wasn't an emergency. Maybe it was just the way things were now. She tried to slow her breathing, tried to swallow back the dry sobs, but they shook her like earthquakes. She wanted a moment of stillness in her room, a moment where she could pretend nothing had changed—that she was still a little child.

Her mother wailed loudly from across the hall. *Caaaa-llliieeee.* Long and high, like a farmer calling in the pigs.

Callie's first instinct was to jog downstairs to tell her father, and then retreat to the cellar, letting the chill and silence seep into her, while he took care of the mess. Another wail, this one sounding more painful. Something was hurting her mom. Callie walked to the window and watched her father blow leaves from the base of the tree. He had already sacrificed so much of himself to care for Callie and her mom. Throughout Callie's life, her parents had given her everything so that she could live a life rich with history and opportunities. For them, Callie could take responsibility. She would.

Callie returned to her mom's room. There was someone else in there, standing at the foot of the bed: Mrs. Vidal. Her blue eyes were glassy and her perm was loose, frizzed, her head a dandelion gone to seed. If it had been any other moment, Callie would have asked if she was okay, what she was doing here, and how she had gotten in. But this time Callie didn't need to; she knew all the answers.

"You can do this," Mrs. Vidal said. "You'll need to bring her to the bath." Callie nodded. She removed the blanket and worked her arms under her mother's thighs and shoulders, trying to ignore the wet and warm material on her skin. She clamped her teeth tightly, swallowing back bile. Her mother was straw-light, her head lolling back, eyes half-lidded. Even hollowed by hunger, Callie could carry her to the bathroom.

"Yes, you're doing just fine," Mrs. Vidal murmured, steps behind Callie.

Callie leaned in as she carried her mom, desperate to hear her words—even if they were nonsense—because she'd waited too long to listen. Her mom's breath smelled surprisingly sweet, like butterscotch. She combed her fingers through Callie's hair, snagging the ends, and then let her hand hang limply. As a child, Callie had loved the feeling of her mother doing her hair—standing in front of the mirror while her mom created fishtails and French twists, bobby pins clamped between her teeth, her own hair pulled back in a sloppy bun.

"Prop her on the toilet so you can get her clothes off," Mrs. Vidal said.

Callie did so before tossing the clothes in the sink and starting the bath.

It had been years since she'd seen her mother naked. Her breasts had flattened. The flesh beneath her armpits appeared too taut, like an imaginary hand was pulling it. But the sores on her mother's belly, red and wet like open mouths, were the most disturbing part. No one had told her about them. But they'd been right not to. She would have pulled even farther away, would have failed at hiding her disgust.

Callie wet the cloth, not worrying that the shower was raining on her, too, soaking her hair and clothes. She started with her mother's face, blotting away the yellow crust on her lip and cheek. Her mother weakly slapped Callie's wet neck.

"Stop," she gasped. "It's hurting."

"You have to keep going," Mrs. Vidal said. "Even if it hurts."

"I'm sorry, Mom," Callie whispered, and she meant for all of it, for her mother's pain, for this inexpert bath, for shuddering at hugs, for holding her nose for the past few months so she wouldn't breathe her own mother.

Callie lifted her mom under the armpits, but she wailed and slid back against the wet tiles. Planting herself on her knees, Callie held her mother with one arm and used the other to clean. She realized she was out of breath, that tears were running down her face.

She knew what to do next without needing to be told. She grabbed a towel and gently dried her mother's skin.

"That's right," Mrs. Vidal said. "Then clean pj's and clean sheets and you're done."

Callie grimaced as she shifted her mother's weight back onto her own shoulders. Her head lolled into Callie's neck, and Callie could feel her breathing there, steady and deep like she'd fallen back asleep.

Callie followed Mrs. Vidal's instructions: resting her mother in the recliner, balling the soiled sheets, throwing them into the hamper, retrieving new ones, stretching them over the mattress and on and on. The steps were largely intuitive, but it was easier with someone guiding the way. Joshua had been right: Mrs. Vidal was what she needed.

Callie lifted her mother one last time and placed her back on the clean sheets. Her mom's nose crinkled—like she'd smelled something terrible—or, more likely, like she'd felt a bolt of pain.

"You've done well," Mrs. Vidal said. "Now. Where's your father?"

Outside, Callie's father sat in the grass beneath the tree, the leaf blower across his thighs. He held a screwdriver—he was always repairing the thing—but now he seemed to be cradling it, exhausted.

"Dad?" she called.

"What?"

"It's Mom," she managed.

Her father looked up and Callie watched him take her in: the wet T-shirt and running shorts, shit stains, and tearstained face. He stood abruptly, the leaf blower rolling off his lap with a clatter.

Upstairs, he swung open the bedroom door so it smacked the

wall, and her mother's eyes fluttered open. She smiled at him. Callie was close behind. Her father took in the scene: the open window, the basket of soiled laundry, his wife's wet hair on the fresh pillowcase.

Mrs. Vidal was gone.

Her mother mumbled Callie's name. Callie moved to the bed, leaning close, as though she could swallow every last word. Her mom didn't say anything else—just gripped Callie's hand to her chest with surprising strength and looked into her daughter's face with what felt like understanding.

FREDERIC VIDAL

Frederic Vidal, who is ours too now, remembers his wife standing on the porch, glaring past the clock tower and band shell, watching the clouds form a shelf across the sky.

Eleanor wanted Frederic to call Celeste's boss and ask him to send her home. He could make up some sort of emergency. But he kept delaying, sure they were about to cancel the movie and she'd be on her way home to them in the Chevy. He didn't want to make waves—not in a town that only tolerated him because he had married into its oldest family.

His carefulness, his softness, was something we'd all observed. When we stopped into his shop for French chocolates, he'd lift the dome off the pyramid of candy with precision. If we were making a racket with Celeste, he'd smile and quietly retreat upstairs. We often wondered how someone whose whole town had been shelled, who'd hiked hundreds of miles to cross a border and survived off rotten mule meat in a barn for a winter, could be so gentle.

That night, the rain stopped suddenly and it felt like all the air had been suctioned away. The sky was gray and green. The maple's leaves were a slick black. Even Frederic, who hadn't grown up in the Midwest, knew how to read the signs.

Of course, Frederic and Eleanor never saw it—not the actual tornado. Like many of our parents who found our beds empty that night, they simply understood.

Frederic took the old spaniel under his arm and then grabbed Eleanor's elbow, guiding her down to the storm cellar. She was shrieking, *No, we have to find her!* Digging her heels into the wet grass like a toddler, like she wanted the storm to take her to Celeste.

When the storm cleared, Frederic borrowed the neighbor's truck and went looking for their daughter—though it would take nearly three days before her body was distinguished from the others in the snack shack. Mrs. Vidal waited for him on the porch steps, scraping them with her fingernails—as though she could rid them of a century's worth of dirt, atone for clinging to the old ways at the expense of her relationship with Celeste.

But it was too late.

C allie decided that she wouldn't go back to school while her mother was still alive. She already felt the weight of regret for squandering the ten months she'd been given. Because she'd been selfish. Because she'd been afraid.

She cracked her mother's door and stuck her head in.

"Come in," her father said softly.

The room smelled like warm bodies and sleep with a sourness lingering from the day before. Callie flipped on the frankincense diffuser, and her dad nodded at her appreciatively. He was sitting on the edge of the bed with a book in his lap. His eyes were sunken and tired. Her mother was curled up beside him, as small and tight as a cat. Her skin had a purplish hue. Callie sank into the nearby armchair.

"I'm not going to school anymore."

She expected a protest, but her father just nodded again.

"Okay. I'll talk to your teachers about sending your work home."

She was relieved he understood. They couldn't afford to waste energy now on anything but being there for each other.

"What time is her appointment?" Callie asked. He'd been on the phone with the doctors for an hour after the incident the day before.

"In about forty-five minutes." He moved his hand closer to her mother's nose on the pillow, waited a second, and then relaxed. Callie wondered if he'd been there all night, testing to see if she was breathing.

"Has she been awake at all?"

He shook his head. "Not since you went to bed." Callie heard the catch in his breath. "We used to do this when you were a baby," he went on. "Sit and watch you sleep." *And check that you were breathing.* But that he didn't say aloud.

"What if we talk to her?" Callie said. "Maybe she can hear us and she just doesn't have the energy to say anything."

Her father studied her. Callie didn't blame him. After all, until now, she'd avoided as many opportunities to be with her mother as possible. "Okay," he said finally.

Callie thought for a second. Maybe it didn't have to be anything heavy. Maybe her mom just needed someone to be the jolly one, since her dad couldn't manage it anymore.

"Mom, Dad and I are playing hooky. We're going to eat ice cream for breakfast and even—gasp—sit on the chaise in the living room."

Her dad smiled, catching on. "We'll put our feet up on it—with our shoes on."

"And leave damp towels on the bathroom rug."

"And a knife in the peanut butter jar."

Then Callie's smile faltered as the painful reality set in: they *could* do all those things now without her mother even noticing. The rules they followed and the way they lived together would change. It had already.

"We'll save the house, Mom," Callie blurted. Her father looked at her sharply—a look that Callie understood to mean *Don't make promises you can't keep*. But Callie did intend to keep it.

"We'll register it as a historic place," she said.

"Callie, that won't pay a mortgage."

At that, Callie's mom woke, rolling onto her back and wincing in pain.

"Here, Cath." Her father gently lifted her mom's shoulders and shoved another pillow behind her.

"How are you feeling?" Callie asked.

"Okay," her mother croaked.

"Do you need anything?" her dad asked.

"I'm thirsty." She rocked her shoulders back and forth, trying to sit up more.

"I'll go get you some water. And you should eat a piece of toast too." Her father headed downstairs.

"Did you hear us talking about playing hooky?" Callie asked, perching on the side of the bed.

"No." Her mother patted her head. So she probably hadn't heard Callie say that she would save the house, either. "Where is my hair?"

Callie laughed, surprised by her mother's sense of humor. Maybe the day before had been an anomaly. Maybe they still had plenty of time.

Callie found the green scarf on the bedside table and started to wrap it around her mom's scalp—something she wouldn't have done even a few days ago. But her mother batted her hand away. "No. Where's my hair?"

"You lost it, Mom. With the treatments."

Her mother narrowed her eyes at Callie, but then her face relaxed and she nodded, remembering. Callie tried again to tie on the scarf, but her mother bobbed her head away. "I hate that thing."

There was a knock on the bedroom door then, and Mrs. Vidal appeared. Apparently in the habit of letting herself in.

"The damn ghosts don't let us have any peace," her mother said.

Callie froze. Had her mom heard—and seen—Mrs. Vidal? Or did she just associate the knocking with the usual haunted house sounds?

"Mom, can you see her? It's Eleanor Peterson, who owned this house before the Gallaghers." Callie gestured in the direction of Mrs. Vidal, who was dressed in the same floral dress, now hopelessly wrinkled. There was a patch of scaly red skin on her forehead, like she'd had an allergic reaction to something. Was something wrong? Could ghosts become ill?

"No, I can't see anyone," Callie's mom said. "But I heard something."

"She is closer to us now," Mrs. Vidal said.

"There, I heard that. Quiet as a whisper." Her mom grabbed Callie's elbow and lifted herself into a sitting position. She focused her eyes in the direction somewhat to the right of the woman. "What will it be like? The after?"

Mrs. Vidal frowned and seemed to be chewing something. "The problem is that I can't describe it. Or maybe I can't remember it clearly enough. I know that I wasn't myself—not the person I am here. And it's not a physical space. More like a sensation. What are you afraid of?"

Her mother shook her head and looked to Callie for help. "I couldn't catch it all. It's so quiet. Could you?"

Callie nodded and repeated what Mrs. Vidal had said.

"I'm afraid of being alone," her mother said. Tears sprang to Callie's eyes. The thought of her mother alone made her feel like something was tearing inside her. She'd been so focused on deflecting her own feelings, on avoiding the pain of losing her mom, that she hadn't considered how scary it was for her mother to face losing everyone.

"You won't be alone. This is Mercer," Mrs. Vidal answered. "All our parents' souls and grandparents' souls are here, holding this place up. Watching over it. You'll be right there with all of them."

Callie's mother was leaning forward, her eyes now closed, as though it would help her hear better. "What about God?" her mother asked.

Mrs. Vidal looked at Callie like whatever she was about to say was for her especially. "Oh, I'm sure He's a big fan of the place." This acknowledgment of the possibility of God flooded Callie with nostalgia, a desire to go back, to return home.

Callie's mother heard Mrs. Vidal and laughed. A brash bark, loud and clear and as much her mom's laugh as always. And then Mrs. Vidal laughed, clutching her belly. Callie watched the two women in wonder. This, too, was a lesson in dying. And, she realized, in living.

54

Joshua finished tacking up flyers for his LGBTQ + group at lunch before finding Brenna in the cafeteria. She was at a table with her yellow-haired friend, a grungy dude who wore kilts to school, and a girl who looked like a vampire with green eyes. The past few months had taught Joshua to expect even outsiders like Brenna's friends to ignore him. But he decided to push past the invisibility and do what he needed. For himself.

"Hey," he said.

"How's it goin'?" said Brenna.

"Callie wasn't in pre-calc today."

Brenna twisted on the bench. Yellow Hair glanced at Joshua, but then returned her attention to the conversation that he was interrupting.

"Did you text her?" Brenna asked.

"Yeah, I just asked if everything was okay and if she needed anything. She said no."

Brenna nodded. "Come sit," she said, gesturing at the bench across from her. "Dutch and Jade, scoot so Joshua can sit."

His stomach flip-flopped in excitement. This was the chance he'd imagined the moment Brenna had picked him up in her car. No, the one he'd been imagining since before the first day of high school.

Brenna introduced the group. Her friends glanced up from their lunch trays or stopped their conversations long enough to meet his eyes. A baby step, but still a step.

"We should do something," Joshua said, when Brenna was finished with the introductions.

"Like what?"

"Maybe go visit and bring her something. She might need a break from whatever's happening."

Joshua didn't remember the days following his father's death; hell, he could barely remember the man. He only had a sense of what it felt like to have a father and then to not have a father: an ache he associated with dropping a string of beads onto the tile, watching them scatter beneath the couch and under the table, knowing that you'd never reassemble them the same way, that some would always be gone, while others would grind into the heel of your foot when you least expected it.

He could more clearly remember the days surrounding his grandparents' deaths, years later. Tyler had come over, and Joshua had been so grateful to have a reason to read comics and think about something, anything else.

"Good idea," Brenna said.

Joshua flushed with pride. "Oh, I wanted to give you something." He opened his binder and slid out the hand-drawn flyer he'd copied and posted earlier.

"'Safe space for LGBTQ+ and allies,'" she read aloud. "Our school needs something like this." She passed it to Amy, who gave it a cursory glance and nodded.

"Will you come?" Joshua felt as though he'd unzipped his chest so that everyone at the table could see his stupidly hopeful heart.

"Sure." Brenna smiled, and a wave of relief washed over Joshua. She snatched a few French fries from his tray. "Friend tax," she said with a grin.

He offered her every last one.

After school, they stopped at the Fill Station to buy candy bars using Brenna's mom's employee discount before walking to Callie's. They found her sitting on the porch, bundled in a jacket several sizes too large. She looked so pale, so lost.

"Hey," she said. "You came." She said it like she'd been hoping they'd come all along, her smile tentative but bright.

Joshua fanned out the three candy bars, offering them to Callie. She shook her head. Brenna sank onto the step next to Callie and draped her arm around the girl's shoulders. It came so easily to her, being close to someone else without awkwardness. Joshua sat on Callie's other side.

"Mrs. Crawley was asking the class where you were," Joshua said.

"What'd you say?"

"Oh, just that you'd decided to winter in the French Riviera."

Callie laughed. "I'm sure she's very jealous."

"Nothing to be jealous of. She gets to spend her summers teaching driver's ed. So it's pretty much the same," Brenna said.

"Ouch," said Joshua.

"Well, she once told me that remedial math was better for someone like me," Brenna said.

"She said that to you?" Callie asked.

"Yeah, you'd be surprised what people say to my face."

"I wouldn't," Joshua said, thinking of Tyler. Brenna met his eyes, and he thought he could see his pain mirrored there.

"No, you probably wouldn't," she said. "How is your mom, Callie?"

"She's starting home hospice."

Joshua had heard the phrase often enough to know that her mother would die soon.

"Do you need anything?" he asked.

Callie shook her head. "My aunt and some of my mom's friends are helping with meals and cleaning and stuff. And Leslie's mom called to say she'd drop off my homework."

"But, like, do *you* need anything?" Joshua pressed.

Callie looked at him as though it had never occurred to her that there was more than food and homework. "Like what?"

Joshua thought for a second before unzipping his backpack and pulling out his sketchpad and a pencil. That was what he would do if he were feeling sad. He handed it to Callie. Brenna smiled over Callie's head at him.

"I'm terrible at drawing," Callie said. Still, she opened the sketchpad and began to flip through. Joshua regretted the gesture, ashamed of the drawings of himself in thinner X-Men bodies. She laughed out loud at the drawing of Mr. Nelson as Beast and paused at him as Nightcrawler. He wondered if she recognized his likeness, could see him in the hero's body. She brushed the page gently with her fingers, and Joshua felt something drop in his throat. Whether or not she recognized him, he wanted to cry—surprised by and grateful for her tenderness when her own world was so shredded.

On a fresh page, Callie lifted the pencil and began to outline what appeared to be a house. Brenna removed her arm from Callie's shoulders and dug through her own backpack. She pulled out cigarettes and offered them to Joshua, who shook his head. Brenna began to write in a lavender notebook, cigarette hanging unlit from her lips.

Joshua leaned back against the steps and savored the moment, the scratch of graphite and pen on paper, the closeness to these girls who not long ago were strangers. It felt like a miracle, like a gift from Mercer.

Callie's drawing was beginning to take shape, to resemble the very place where they sat—except there was a man on the stoop—lanky and bearded with a top hat.

"Is that your house?" he asked.

She nodded. "The medical bills are too much, and my dad says we have to sell it."

"And who is that on the stoop?"

"Lincoln," she said. "He's going to save the house."

"How is Lincoln going to save your house?"

"If I can prove he visited, I can show the historic significance of our house and no one can tear it down."

Inspired, Joshua rubbed his hands together, pulled out a spiral notebook, bit into his chocolate bar, and started solving his own problems.

Tomorrow would be the first meeting of his club. Then he'd see. Surely, he wasn't alone. Surely, there were others who felt like ghosts of themselves. Together, they'd have power. Together, they'd be a community. It was what Luke and Eddie had needed so many years before.

What Joshua needed now.

55

B renna left Callie's early to attend her aunt's birthday party with her mother and brother. Her mother's family lived in the Cities in a neighborhood that made Brenna yearn for Houston: panaderías, churches with tall spires and names like Sangre de Cristo, and, at this time of year, sugar skulls for Día de los Muertos. They parked outside the resale shop Brenna's uncle owned. The family now lived above the shop in two spacious apartments. As soon as they got out of the car, Brenna could smell the carne asada her uncle was grilling on the back patio and hear the accordion from the norteño he loved. It filled her with nostalgia for the few family celebrations she had attended as a child, when she didn't yet understand how complicated her mother's relationship with her abuela was.

Her grandmother greeted them at the top of the stairs, kissing Brenna's cheeks and pinching the fat above her hips with a cluck.

The woman was the height of a child and thin, too, like Manny. All Brenna's life, she'd bragged about being called flaca.

Manny smirked at Brenna, but wasn't free from their grandmother's judgment for long. After releasing him from a hug, she made a scissor motion with her fingers and told him he had the hair of a woman. She patted down the flyaways that framed Brenna's mother's face and clucked about the bags under her eyes.

Brenna kissed the air near her aunt's ear with a whispered *Feliz cumple*. Her tía was much taller, like Brenna's grandfather had been. Saint Camila, as she and Manny jokingly called their aunt, was a pious, gentle woman—too gentle, in Brenna's opinion, to live in a household with five children who walked all over her.

Manny slunk into the living room—a room that reeked of male body spray and was papered with school photos of the cousins arranged haphazardly above the couch. Amid the collage, there were two wallet-sized pictures of Brenna and Manny that their mother had sent when they were kids. Their actual cousins were sprawled across every piece of furniture: two on the couch, one balanced on the coffee table, and another two squeezed in the armchair. Manny snatched the remote, settled onto the floor, and flipped the channel. "¿Este quién se cree?" *Who does he think he is?* Mariana complained. Manny didn't appear to hear. Or he simply ignored her, as he did all their cousins.

Brenna slipped through the room, muttering greetings and ignoring the smirk on her cousin Tomás's face, which was usually a response to her standard wardrobe—torn jeans, ribbed tank, flannel, and boots. She wedged herself into the corner of the room, her elbow against a bookshelf filled with old VHS tapes, and took out her notebook.

On Callie's stoop, she'd started imagining the parts of Dot's story she didn't know yet, all the moments that weren't overshadowed by her terrible father. For the first time, her writing pulsed and beat. It practically bled. She hadn't had to force anything. Instead a vision of Dot—or the Dot she imagined—came to her and her pen didn't stop until Callie had to go inside. The Dot she'd described roller-skated across hardwood floors while her parents were out. She bit the first boy she kissed, holding on to the pink underbelly of his lip with her incisors. She cheated at pool. She could hear a song once and sing it back to you.

She wanted to write more, to hear more from Dot herself, to ask about auditions and first songs and inspiration. She wanted to record her life. Not as the talk-show proof Joshua had imagined, but for the sake of their town's history. An archive for the shelves of the historical society museum. Here was a person who lived and breathed and wrote beautiful music for far too short a time. And then Brenna could write Luke's and Mrs. Vidal's stories too.

She would share a new kind of ghost story with the world.

Brenna was thinking of what to write next when Tomás ripped the notebook out of her hands and fanned the pages. Brenna leapt up.

"¿En serio?" she said. "Are you twelve?" She tried to snatch it back.

Tomás was just a month younger than Manny, taller and much wider than Brenna. He used his ass to block her, and held the notebook out of reach. "Whatcha keeping from us?"

She tried to swivel around him, but he ground a hip into her pelvis.

"Who is Dot? You a marimacha?"

Brenna dug a knuckle into the soft flesh where his kidney must be—buried beneath the fat her grandmother never commented on. Not with Tomás, who Díos had smiled upon with football talent when he was in high school.

"Fuck you," she growled. "So what if I were gay? Why would it matter?"

Manny was watching her coolly from across the room—as uninterested now in protecting her from Tomás as he'd been as a kid. Brenna managed to get in front of Tomás, but he moved the notebook behind his back, leaving his crotch exposed. Brenna grabbed his shoulders and kneed him in the groin with one swift motion. Tomás doubled over, dropping the notebook and gasping. The cousins were all on their feet, shouting, like his balls were all he had. Manny slow-clapped, his face twisted in a wry grin.

The adults appeared in the doorway. "What's happening?"

Mariana just pointed at Brenna, her mouth hanging open. Brenna blew her hair off her face with her bottom lip and readjusted her flannel. She grabbed the notebook off the floor and held it to her chest, still catching her breath.

"A girl fighting like that," her grandmother said to her mother in Spanish. "What a shame. Truly your daughter."

"Leave her alone," Brenna said.

"Brenna, don't." Her mother shook her head.

"No, Mom. You don't deserve to be spoken to like that."

"Ma-hm," Tomás parroted. "Such a gringa."

"All of you, stop. I'm sorry we're not the family members you want us to be." Brenna turned to her grandmother. "Abuela, you want us to visit more often and we want to be here, but you make it really hard. I know it must have hurt a lot that Mom got pregnant and left, but that was a long time ago. It's got to be okay to make mistakes," Brenna spoke in English—not sure if her grandmother even understood, but her mom smiled at her proudly.

"I just want what's best," her grandmother replied in Spanish. "That's all I've ever wanted."

"I know, mamá," Brenna's mother said. "We all do, but nobody is perfect."

"Why don't we pray together and eat?" tía Camila said softly, ever the peacemaker. If anything had the power to heal their family, it would be food: her uncle's charred tenderloin, Camila's fresh tortillas, her grandmother's salsa verde, and Mariana's tres leches cake.

Mariana turned off the TV, and the cousins bowed their heads—even Tomás, whose hands were still cupped over his balls. Camila's prayer was for forgiveness, for love, and grace. Brenna's grandmother punctuated each word—*perdón, amor, gracia*—with a nod, though Brenna was not convinced she was any nearer to understanding. Brenna was, though. No matter how difficult, she would keep trying to be closer to this family, to be closer to who she was within it.

Brenna's mother caught her hand and squeezed it a moment. "You and Manny were never a mistake," she whispered.

Across the room, Manny was lolling his head from side to side as though stretching his neck. "Are you sure about Manny?" Brenna asked.

Her mother grinned and elbowed her playfully.

"I don't want us to end up like you and Grandma," Brenna whispered.

"We won't."

And Brenna felt sure this was true.

EDDIE DIDN'T WANT TO LOSE

Eddie didn't want to lose Luke after the incident with Carolyn at the shop—especially when there was no one else in Mercer who could understand the yearning deep inside his abdomen, which wasn't for Carolyn, never had been for Carolyn, but for Luke: all muscle and bone and sweat and grease. This, Eddie can share with us here, in the after.

When Eddie arrived at Luke's, Luke was burning brush and leaves in his backyard, standing way too close to the fire. He wore his mechanic's jumpsuit, unzipped to the waist, and Eddie's Mercer Fire T-shirt, a gift, underneath. From his vantage point, the flames were licking Luke's face. Eddie panicked that Luke's features were melting, like the Mercer fire chief's, who didn't have a nose or eyelids and always stared, unnervingly, at his men.

Eddie called out, and Luke looked up, seemingly unsurprised

that Eddie was there. He stomped out the fire. The knees of his jumpsuit had blackened.

"I thought I was going to have to call the truck," Eddie said. He expected Luke to flirt back or tease him, but Luke walked toward him slowly, as though stalking prey.

"What do you want?" Each syllable was sharp, cutting.

"To take you to the drive-in." It was the moment Eddie would wish he could erase for the rest of his life.

"Like nothing happened?" Luke asked.

Eddie was always nervous near Luke's house. He'd never been hated before, and Luke's dad certainly hated him. "Come on. We can talk in the car."

They were silent driving to the country. Eddie spun the radio dial obsessively—never landing on a song for more than a few seconds. Luke leaned against the window, his face tight and still, except for the slight movement of his jaw clenching and unclenching.

"Listen," Eddie said when he had parked. "I want to spend time together, but I can't just up and leave Carolyn. And I can't go west with you."

"Why not?" Luke asked gruffly.

"People expect certain things of me."

"Like they don't of me?"

It was raining by then, pinging loudly on the roof of the Pontiac.

"You're braver than I am, Luke. Dumping Connie like that."

He shrugged. "It's what was fair. What was right."

Eddie watched the movie for a moment. The smell of Luke was overwhelming: fire. He wanted to taste it, wanted all of Luke in his mouth. When he brushed his lips against Luke's neck, Luke didn't push him away, but he didn't respond, either. He just sat there, waiting for Audrey Hepburn to appear. Eddie moved downward, closing his teeth, finally, on the zipper. Luke grabbed Eddie's hair, pulling his chin up, and Eddie felt a rush of excitement.

"Do you love me?" Luke asked, his grip tight in Eddie's hair, his eyes still glued on the windshield.

Eddie had never considered a question like that before. Attraction, certainly. But love? Like his parents' love? That meant marriage, a house, children you raised to play baseball like you. With Luke, he'd never have that.

Finally Eddie spoke, carefully. "As much as men can love each other."

Luke released his hold on Eddie's hair then, opened the car door, and climbed out. Just like that.

"Where are you going?" Eddie called, suddenly desperate. "It's too far to walk, and it's pouring out!"

Luke didn't turn around. He walked with purpose, as though he'd cross cornfields and keep walking straight through the storm to California.

As the tornado screamed toward the Pontiac, Eddie shook in his seat, but he kept the car in park, waiting—hoping—for Luke to return.

Days later, when Luke was identified among the dead, Eddie proposed to Carolyn. He'd wed himself to that future the moment the words *As much as men can* had left his mouth—whether or not he truly believed what he'd said. Because, in the end, Eddie's words had sealed Luke's fate.

56

At the impound lot two days before, Joshua had promised Luke he'd sneak a sleeping bag and a few candles into the house across the street.

"I want you to feel welcome and comfortable somewhere," he'd said, and Luke had looked grateful. Joshua had hoped he'd be able to see the flicker of the candles from his bedroom, but last night the house remained dark.

After school, he parked himself on the couch with the curtains open, still hopeful. Ruthie plopped on the couch next to him and started talking about her teachers. Joshua had a feeling his mother had put her up to talking to him. It was annoying because he wanted to watch for Luke, but he missed how they used to talk for hours, their imaginations spinning out.

Ruthie was theorizing that two of her teachers were dating. "I bet Mr. Fulton takes Ms. Jones on dates to Victorian Harbor. He orders duck à l'orange and she orders a Cobb salad, dry, because she's 'watching her figure.'"

"And a nice bottle of chianti," Joshua said, making a sucking sound with his teeth like Hannibal Lecter.

She laughed. "And he'll want to split the check. Teacher salaries and all."

They fell silent, and Joshua chewed on his cuticle, staring out the window. There'd been no sign of life for a few days.

"What's new with you?" Ruthie asked—clearly searching for something to keep him talking.

"Not much," Joshua answered. "I've been hanging out with two girls from school—although one of them was out today." He paused. "Her mom is sick. I think she's going to die soon."

Ruthie was silent, probably thinking of their grandparents, since she had no memory of their father. Joshua shifted so he was seated sideways, a more comfortable position for keeping an eye on Luke's house.

"Ginger ball, there's no one there. And even if there were, he'd be way out of your league."

"So now even imaginary people are out of my league?" Joshua asked.

"Pretty much," she said.

Joshua pulled her into a headlock and licked his finger to give her a wet willy.

"Ew. Mom! Lawrence!" she squealed.

Lawrence rounded the corner from the kitchen, a can of beer in his hand.

"Do something!" she shrieked, slapping Joshua's head.

"Ow! Lawrence!" Joshua shouted.

"I have to remain neutral." The man's eyes were twinkling, mischievous. He set the can down carefully on the end table, pressed his fingers into the condensation, and launched himself at Joshua. The sweat from the cold can in Joshua's ear felt as though someone was tickling his nerves. He squirmed away, releasing his sister.

"What's going on down there?" their mother called from upstairs.

"Nothing," all three called back in unison, muffling laughter.

Ruthie popped up from the couch, finger-combing her hair back into place, and jogged up the stairs—flicking Joshua off on the way up. But Lawrence remained, waiting—it seemed—for them to be alone. Then he dropped his head, the folds under his neck spreading so his face was framed by fat.

"Hey, Josh, I'm sorry about the other day. In the hardware store. I should have said something after he called you that . . . name. I'm not the best at thinking on my feet."

Joshua looked at the man beside him. For so long, he'd been in such disbelief that his mother had chosen this man. But here was Lawrence—shy and gentle beneath all that linebacker bulk—and trying to learn how to be a parent—*his* parent, which made Joshua feel an unexpected swell of tenderness.

After dinner, Joshua migrated to his drawing desk, listening for the soft click of Ruthie's and his mother's doors, which signaled there'd be no further interruptions. He liked to imagine a world where he snuck into Luke's house for secret romantic trysts. Where Luke's hard shell had peeled away—not just momentarily, like at the impound lot, but regularly. He'd say vulnerable things—*Age doesn't matter. Death doesn't matter. Love is forever. Etc., etc.*—before pressing Joshua up against a wall.

As though on cue, Joshua saw Luke walking down the street in his mechanic's uniform. He looked different: smaller and less muscular, his shoulders bowed so his chest was concave, the hollows of his face more pronounced, the skin orangish and pale.

Joshua scrambled out of his room and down the stairs, flinging open the door. He met Luke in the yellow pool of a streetlight.

"Hey," he said. "I put some things in the house for you."

Luke smiled, that tight half grimace he made. It was even more pained than the first time Joshua had seen it.

"Are you okay?" Joshua asked.

Luke nodded, but his eyes told another story. They seemed dim, like a light inside the pupils had been extinguished.

"What have you been up to?"

"Wandering," said Luke. "Visiting old places. My dad. The cemetery. Even the drive-in again."

"Are you looking for something?"

"Probably. But I don't know what. Just feel like I have to keep going."

Joshua wondered about his own family, the ones who had passed long ago. Were they this restless too? "Can I ask you something? About before"—Joshua paused—"before you were back here?"

Luke nodded.

"Did you see other people who'd died? Like, maybe some of my relatives?"

Luke's face softened. "It's a good place," he said. "We're all together."

It wasn't exactly the answer he'd hoped for, but it made Joshua feel a little better. Before he could ask another question, he heard his mother's voice.

"Joshua?" She was leaning out the front door with a look of concern. "What are you doing outside, barefoot?"

Luke gave a slight shake of his head. *Don't acknowledge me*, he seemed to say.

"I thought I saw a lost cat," Joshua said.

His mother looked puzzled. He'd never been a pet lover. "Come inside, you goof," she said.

Joshua walked back up the driveway and climbed the steps. Before he went inside, he glanced back at the street. Luke still stood in the yellow cone of light.

Joshua lifted his chin in goodbye. The same gesture Luke had made the day they met. Luke returned the nod.

Joshua smiled. Though he alone could see Luke, it didn't matter.

Luke saw Joshua.

57

B renna had looked up where the River Bandits were playing, and then she'd driven to the Cities, convinced Dot would be there. The band was already on when Brenna arrived, so she slid into a seat near the back. And then, there Dot was, tripping onto the stage in front of the band. She wore the same outfit, polka-dot shirt wrinkled and untucked. Her hair was loose and matted around the crown of her head. Her eyes were vacant, staring at some indiscernible point at the back of the bar. Brenna glanced around, still half expecting others to see her, to be shocked by this intrusion, but the audience sipped their canned beers and bobbed their heads unwittingly. Every time the lights moved, Dot followed them, stopping only when she was bathed in yellow. Right in front of the lead singer, she closed her eyes and started belting the lyrics: "*Every lonely moment, I think of you.*" Her voice sounded raspy, torn, like she'd been sobbing.

Brenna pushed her way through concertgoers, murmuring apologies, until she was at the foot of the stage. "Dot," she called.

The girl's eyes fluttered open, and she blinked, confused.

"The River Bandits are performing. Please come down." Someone elbowed Brenna in the ribs, but she still managed to reach out, beckoning Dot to take her hand. Out of the corner of her eye, Brenna spotted a bear-sized bouncer moving toward her. "Dot, this isn't the Rock-a-Gals. This is after—after the storm." Dot sank to her knees, then sat, dropping her head into her hands. She was keening, a high-pitched whine.

"Back up, miss," the bouncer said, stepping in front of Brenna and crossing his arms.

"Please," she said. "I'm just trying to help my friend." But to him, of course, there was no one there. Brenna backed away, watching until Dot lowered herself off the stage and stumbled toward the bathroom. Brenna followed.

Inside, Dot was gripping the porcelain basin, the water running hot and steaming the bottom of the mirror. She was so close to the mirror that her lips were almost touching it. Her skin was scallop-white and wet. Her hair had lost its luster. Brenna stared at her own reflection. The dyed tips had faded to a cotton-candy pink. Amy would not approve. Beside Dot, though, she looked clearer and more substantial, as though Dot had become a fuzzy hologram.

Dot smelled, too, something Brenna couldn't quite put her finger on. The scent left in the air following a lightning storm?

Dot met her eyes in the mirror and Brenna saw desperation. "I don't feel right," she said.

"Why? What's wrong?"

"I feel like something is pulling on me constantly. It's hard to move. Hard to think."

Brenna thought of one-armed Gretta, of her insistence that she was caught in the wrong place, that her arm was trying to pull her to the other side.

"Can I drive you home?"

"No." Dot shook her head. "I just want to be—" She flexed her fingers as though the motion would help her come up with the word.

"Alone?" Brenna asked.

"Alone," Dot repeated.

What would happen to a ghost who was being pulled from the other side? Would she disappear? Could she die all over again? "I can't leave you like this," Brenna said, knowing how scared she sounded. "At least let me take you home." She grabbed Dot's hand, hoping for that fortifying warmth and strength she'd felt a week ago in the parking lot, but her hand was cold.

It felt like death.

THE ROCK-A-GALS

The Rock-a-Gals were in the VW. Beth and Bex on the floor where the back seats once were. Kitty up front with Detonator Dorothy beside her, blowing smoke out the window, a blank lavender notebook in her lap, ready for new songs. It was the Rock-a-Gals' first time in Mercer, their first time at a drive-in. Like many of us, they ignored the smell of rain.

Celeste took Dorothy's order at the drive-in. That night, everyone was calling Celeste over just so she'd lean in their windows, all pink and perky. The wind was making her hair wild and lifting that red-and-white-striped uniform collar. We felt a little sorry for her—everyone having fun and there she was, working her ass off. She didn't mind, though. Not our sweet friend.

Dorothy was a few years older than Celeste, but she must have been feeling magnanimous that night, because she invited Celeste to her first show. We heard Celeste say she'd ask her mom.

We were so full of hope and excitement, so sure that if Dorothy could look happy, if she could be grinning out her window and chatting easily with Celeste, anything could happen.

When the rain started, Celeste had to hold a tray above her head and run for the snack shack. The movie was only a few minutes in. Audrey Hepburn flapping out her white scarf and mincing down the empty street. Celeste would never return with our Cokes, popcorn, and elephant ears. We'd never lick the grease off our fingertips.

The Rock-a-Gals opened the back doors of the van and beckoned a few of us who were on picnic blankets to pile in. They had a tarot deck, and Kitty was reading the cards for Dorothy. We could tell Dorothy wasn't paying attention, though, that her mind was far from swords, cups, wands, and that fool. She was probably imagining the show. We can imagine it too: stage lights on your face and a crowd at your feet that you can't quite see but you can feel—their heat and anticipation, a yearning.

Dorothy sang, face placid, as though the sound of the storm was the applause. The song yawning out of her was huge and strong and new.

Kitty was the first one to see the tornado plotting its course for us. *Holy fuck holy fuck holy fuck*, she said, and some of us thought *holy, yes*, meaning the song, before we saw the spinning beast for ourselves, before we screamed at Kitty to drive, before we squeezed our eyes shut, before we said our last prayers.

58

Joshua brought doughnuts to the first meeting of his group. He arranged the desks in an optimistic circle, wrote *Welcome LGBTQ+ Alliance* across the board, and was two doughnuts in when Brenna arrived. She was ten minutes late and looked worn-out, but she sank into a desk next to him and fished a bear claw out of the box.

"It looks like it's just us two."

She scanned what he'd written on the board and chewed thoughtfully for a moment. "So why'd you want to start it?"

"I want to create a safe space and get to know people who are like me. It's so lonely in a town like this for us. I mean, I learned that I was gay from watching a TV show and being like, 'Oh yes, that's what I feel.' I had to watch YouTube videos to learn how to talk about it. I don't want others to go through that. I don't want them to feel so alone."

Brenna nodded sympathetically.

"And I really thought they'd come if there was a place that offered a little comfort," Joshua continued. "If I was brave enough to make it." He scanned the empty desks. "Guess I'll have to wait until college."

Just then a boy, lean and sandy haired and wearing a letterman jacket, poked his head into the room. Joshua had seen him around before, one of the quieter popular kids, blushing at the attention of girls and grinning self-consciously whenever addressed by his teammates. Joshua wondered if Luke's Eddie had been something like this boy: golden and beautiful. Not like him, fat and ginger with torn jeans and toe-holes in his shoes.

"Come in," Joshua said with deliberate cheer. "I'm Joshua. What's your name?"

"Beau," the boy answered.

Brenna introduced herself, patting the desk next to her.

The boy sat, but his eyes darted to the door.

"Don't worry; you're safe here," Joshua said, trying to sound welcoming, but there was part of him that was wary, suspicious of this gorgeous boy's intentions. Joshua had been bullied too long to trust anything right up front. "Is there anything you want to talk about? Anything going on at home or school?"

Beau began to trace words carved into the desk. "Nothing is going on," he said. His voice was surprisingly gravelly, like a smoker's.

"Okay, I'll share something, and if you think of something later, just let me know."

Beau stiffened visibly in his chair, eyes on the hallway. Joshua looked over his shoulder.

Tyler.

He was lurking just outside the door, his face twisted like he'd sucked a lemon.

Beau's chair scraped as he stood up. Wearing that jacket, Joshua knew, would make him a target for someone like Tyler. Brenna stood too, her lip in a snarl. Fear coursed through Joshua— for himself, and for his little alliance with its nervous new member. But something else flooded him too. It was bright, this new thing, and white-hot.

"It's okay," he said. "I'll handle this."

Joshua walked out the door, and closed it behind him. "It's important that you respect our privacy," he said to Tyler. Joshua's hands were hot, blood beating into them. He opened and closed his fingers, trying to relieve the pressure. He managed to keep his voice calm.

"Privacy?" Tyler snorted. "You're meeting in a public school with the door open. You advertised the meeting with posters."

"It's important that we do," Joshua said. "But our stories, our coming out, they belong to us. Does that make sense, Tyler?"

Tyler's arms were locked tight across his chest, though he appeared to be leaning away from Joshua, like he couldn't decide if he was being the aggressor or the casual passerby. His face was set in an expression of bored distaste.

"What'll you give me?" he asked.

"Nothing. I'm not even going to appeal to our former friendship, because clearly you don't value it. I'm just asking you, human to human, not to out anyone you saw here today." Joshua readied himself to be hit again, though this time with his arms at his sides and his eyes on Tyler's face.

Instead Tyler took a step back, something cracking his expression—a small ray of understanding? Or regret? Or sadness?

Joshua stepped into the space that Tyler had surrendered. Tyler backed up again, putting his hands up like he expected Joshua to hit him.

"I'm not going to hit you, Tyler," Joshua said. "But I will go to the principal, the police, and anyone who will listen to stop you from hurting anyone else."

"Okay, okay," he said. "Jeez. I won't say anything."

Joshua watched, bewildered, his once-friend back away. Had Joshua actually become that powerful? That strong? As the shock subsided, he felt a wash of pride.

And it felt better than he'd imagined.

59

A hospital bed was installed in Callie's living room in place of the sofa and coffee table. There was a blood-pressure monitor where there'd once been a lamp, and a CPAP machine to help her mother breathe while she slept. Aunt Toni bought a walker and it sat, unfolded, beside the bed, though her mother never used it. Callie had become an expert at maneuvering her mother's weight onto the toilet, at lowering her underwear and helping her wipe—all things she'd never imagined doing before that day in her mother's bedroom. Now she would do it over and over. Because it was for her mom.

Callie began to mark time by the arrivals and departures of hospice care workers. Nurses to begin and end the day. Aides in between. A new doctor who would visit three times a week. A bereavement specialist named Deb who helped her father "make a plan." The house, which had once felt unnecessarily large, now felt crowded with strange people and machines, cramped with the nearness of death.

Callie spent the mornings with her mother in the hospital bed, which was wide enough for both of them. Their father had set up the TV so they could watch *Gilmore Girls*. Her mother slept—the CPAP whirring—through most of it. Occasionally she woke enough to remove the mask and ask, "Who's that man with the ball cap?" "Why is that old woman so mad?" "Can you check the weather, love? It feels like a storm is coming." Callie checked, but saw nothing but a cool, crisp fall ahead. "For once, I agree with your father. The weathermen are wrong," her mom said before sinking back into sleep.

One morning, while her mother slept, Callie managed to complete the form she'd found online for the Illinois Historic Preservation Agency. She wrote about the house's history and significance, about Margaret Peterson and Lincoln, the stories her mother and Mrs. Vidal had told.

Around lunchtime, Callie peeked into her dad's office to ask if she could scan the illustration of Lincoln in front of their house for the application and saw her dad slumped in his office chair, eyes almost closed, watching family photos cascade across the laptop screen. To the right she saw the bills stacked neatly beside the keyboard. Registering the house wouldn't erase those bills, but it would ensure that, when sold, the house would be protected from damage and destruction, and that, Callie knew, would make her mother happy.

She stood there for a moment, watching her father, and froze as a photo of Niagara Falls—she and her mother hunched together—flashed across the screen. Callie was grinning and her mother's mouth was open, the name *David* on her lips.

Breathless, Callie backed out of the room. She jogged downstairs, flung open the door, and stepped onto the porch. It was only outside, breathing the crisp, fall air, that she began to cry until her throat felt raw and her eyes burned. There was no way she was going back inside, but she needed to move, to warm herself. So she ran in what she was wearing—house slippers, a long-sleeve T-shirt, flannel pajama pants—to the canal. Everything was gray: the sky, the water, the ground. A mile in, the crowding trees cleared for an abandoned city golf course so overgrown, it looked like a prairie laced with broken concrete cart paths and errant cornstalks. A mile farther was the tree with the heart-shaped knot that her father always managed to reach first.

Running, Callie became the rhythm of breathing and footfalls. She became the twinge in her knee or the dull ache along the arch of her foot or the heaviness knuckling her sternum. Being a body and its pains was fullness, awareness—not emptiness. She'd been wrong, which meant that maybe she was wrong about other things too. Like God. Maybe there was a house with many rooms in heaven, a replica of her house, and her mother would wait for her there. Maybe it wasn't stupid, but beautiful, to believe that.

Back at home, Callie stood in the kitchen and regarded the contents of the fridge. *Bodies need fuel*, her father had said. There were Gatorades at the back, the blue kind that had once been her favorite. Callie opened one and sipped it. She felt something lurch inside her—hunger. She swung open a cabinet. Her mother hadn't made granola in months, but there were a few granola bars. A little stale, but passable. Callie took a tentative bite, swallowed, and waited to see if her body would reject it. Instead of nausea, she felt ravenous. She took another bite and another until the bar was gone.

Callie showered, checked on her mother, who was still asleep, and waited on the porch for Joshua and Brenna. They hadn't promised to come, but she sensed that they would. Elbow-nudging each other, sparring with sharp jokes. Callie couldn't offer them any more friendship than she could offer Leslie, but there was something about the experience they shared that was enough for them to show up for her. And it was enough for her to show up for them too.

But it was Leslie who turned onto Main, walking slowly and alone, her curls pulled back in an elegant braid, wearing a tweed coat, and with a tote bag over her shoulder. They hadn't spoken since the pizza party nearly two weeks ago. Leslie blanched when she saw Callie, her fingers going to her teeth. It was Leslie's tell. She chewed the tips when she was nervous—each finger had a tiny pink callus like a crown.

Callie wasn't sure what she felt about seeing her old friend walking toward her house. There wasn't room for resentment or anger. And she'd felt affection when she'd recognized her in the distance, acting in such familiar ways. But had she actually missed Leslie over the past few days? No. Too much had changed.

"Hi," Callie called out as Leslie crossed the street.

"Hi." Leslie was out of breath. "I have your assignments. I was just going to leave them so I didn't interrupt." In other words: *Sorry I arrived when you were here.* It occurred to Callie that Leslie didn't know what else to say in the face of real loss.

"It's not a problem at all," Callie said.

Leslie held out the homework. "I color-coded the assignments. I thought it might make things easier."

"Thanks."

"Do you have anything I should bring to school?" Leslie asked.

"No."

Leslie nodded.

Callie nodded back, and then realized how goofy the two of them were—bobbing their heads like a pair of pigeons. Callie giggled, and Leslie's face flushed—embarrassed or still angry. But then she started laughing too.

"How are you?" Callie asked when they'd stopped.

Leslie shrugged. "I'm okay." There was a silence. "Hey, look, I should get going."

"You can stay," Callie offered, warmed by the nostalgia of laughing with her old friend, "and do your homework here. My mom is asleep."

Leslie smiled, her lips snagging on her braces, and shook her head. "My mom is expecting me." But that smile, Callie thought, contained forgiveness—for Callie's behavior at the birthday party—and acceptance that even though they wouldn't be the kind of friends they'd once been, that was all right. As Leslie turned and walked away, Callie sank back onto the steps to wait for Joshua and Brenna, lightened by relief.

60

As they walked to Callie's house, Brenna and Joshua crossed paths with the curly-haired, sour-faced girl Brenna had seen Callie with at school. Today the girl's energy was less sour, and she smiled when Brenna nodded at her.

As usual, Callie was waiting for them when they arrived. Brenna sat on the porch steps and pulled out a cigarette. Joshua nudged a bag of French fries toward Callie. She shook her head, but as soon as Brenna grabbed one, Callie reached for the bag, taking a few. It was the first time Brenna had seen her eat. As she did, Callie's cheeks bloomed pink. Only her eyes—puffy and red—revealed her grief. Brenna thought of Dot, how dreadful she'd looked at the concert.

"Have you guys seen Mrs. Vidal or Luke lately?" Brenna asked.

"About a week ago," Joshua said.

"Was he okay?"

Joshua shrugged. "He said he was fine, but it looked like maybe he was sick."

"I saw Mrs. Vidal a week ago too," Callie said. "She looked like she had a skin rash and was shedding or something."

"Dot said she felt like something was pulling on her constantly. Weighing her down. She seemed desperate."

"What do you think it means?" Joshua asked.

"I don't know. But I know someone who might. Do you have time for a quick field trip?" Brenna asked.

Callie shrugged. "I guess I need something to do while my mom sleeps. And it's not going to be homework."

She disappeared into the house to ask if she could borrow the car.

"Shotgun," Joshua said when she reemerged with the keys.

"Um. No," Brenna said. "It goes by seniority."

At that, Joshua took off running to the car. Brenna was just a few steps behind, but he boxed her out and grabbed the passenger door handle.

"Asshole," she said with a laugh.

"Hate the game. Not the player," Joshua said.

Brenna pretended to sulk but couldn't hide her grin as she climbed into the back seat. In the rearview mirror, she could see that Callie was smiling too.

*　*　*

Brenna was worried about bringing Callie to a graveyard, but the girl appeared unfazed. Maybe she'd started to come to terms with her mother's imminent passing?

"That's Celeste Vidal," Brenna said when they arrived before My Sky's stone.

Callie bent down over the stone, as though wanting to read something carved behind the letters. "I can't believe she lived in my home," she said.

A small, wiry figure approached from the distance then. Brenna recognized the wild hair before she saw the empty coat sleeve pinned at the elbow.

"Callie, Joshua, this is Gretta," Brenna said. "She was at the drive-in that night. One of the only survivors."

Gretta pulled her hand out of her pocket and made a smoking gesture. Brenna patted her jacket and found one of Manny's packs, which she tossed. The woman stuck one cigarette in her mouth, then took another and tucked it behind her ear. Normally, Brenna would have been annoyed—she was too broke to hand out cigarettes—but it was Gretta. Somehow, everyone in town owed her for being the voice of the survivors, for always telling their stories.

"What are ya up to?" Gretta asked, allowing Brenna to light her cigarette.

"I was showing Callie Celeste's grave. They grew up in the same house."

"And?" Gretta asked.

"And?" Callie repeated, unsure.

"You're not just here because you lived in the same house. Let's see: another tornado, that car, the whispers. She came back, didn't she?"

Callie shook her head. "Not Celeste, no. Her mother. And two others, too. They've been trying to help us."

"But they're not doing well anymore. It's like they're falling apart," Brenna said.

Gretta blew smoke and appeared to be mulling over the information. "What'd you say they were whispering again?"

"'Find them. Save them,'" Callie said.

"And have you?" Gretta pointed her cigarette at Brenna, an indictment. "It sounds like they found you instead."

"And saved us," Callie said. "Or me, anyway. Mrs. Vidal helped me face my future."

Joshua was nodding, and so was Brenna. Dot had given her a future packaged as a small lavender notebook.

"Dot said she felt like she was being pulled from the other

side. It must be because they don't belong here." Brenna knew it was hell when you didn't belong. She had a feeling Joshua and Callie did too. Now they belonged together.

"So we have to help them somehow," Callie said.

"Gretta, you said before that they're always whispering about their regrets, sorrows, and goodbyes, right?" Brenna asked.

Gretta dropped her cigarette and crushed it under her boot. "Yeah. But you can't take them back in time."

"No," Brenna said. "But I think we can help them face their pasts and make peace."

FACING THE PAST

Facing the past? Making peace? We scoff at the idea. If it's closure you mean, we all need it. So why them? Some fateful matching? When the next tornado comes, will more of us get a turn to help and be helped?

Again, we tug at the threads of our memories. We try to separate ourselves. Who were we when we were fully ourselves?

Andy, whose girlfriend's skull was crushed in his lap by the steering wheel. Frances, who kept her pregnancy a secret from Donald because she wanted to graduate. Donald, who'd figured it out and already had a ring—a temporary dime-store bauble—in his pocket. Pamela, who'd asked her forever-crush to the drive-in for the first time. Ernest and his brothers, who came on foot from a nearby farm and watched from outside the fence. Harold, who had inherited his father's failing restaurant. Trudy. Charles. Sandy. Celeste. The list goes on.

We all wanted more time.

But our jealousy is misplaced. As much as we'd like to visit our remaining families, we know that we'd curl up like dried worms on a sidewalk when we were no longer needed, just like them.

We don't belong with the living anymore.

61

Brenna knocked loudly on Dot's garage door. It was the first time she'd been able to borrow Golden Girl for a trip to the Cities since dropping Dot off at her house nearly a week ago.

"Dot," Brenna called, knocking again. Her heart thumped. What if she'd gone without saying goodbye? What if she'd already been pulled to the other side?

But Dot slid the door open and shielded her eyes with the palm of her hand. Her lips were cracked with tiny dots of blood where the skin had peeled away. The whites of her eyes were streaked with red vessels.

"Can I take you somewhere?" Brenna asked.

Dot shook her head. "I'm not up to it."

"I think it could help you feel better. Maybe not immediately, but soon."

Dot squeezed her eyes shut as though the sun were giving her a headache.

"Dot, I can't pretend I understand how you're hurting, but I think I know how to help you get back to where you're supposed to be."

Dot looked at her dully but was silent.

"You do know you can't stay here, right?"

"I know." Dot seemed resigned to hear this, but relieved, too. Brenna reached for her hand and led her to the car. Soon she would lose Dot. Soon Dot would find her peace.

Brenna drove Dot downtown. Once parked, she peered through the Fill Station window on her way to the library, trying to see her mom. When she remembered her mom kicking her out, and the girl who'd actually left that night, who'd spent the night in the Pontiac, she felt like she was remembering someone else's past. Because of Dot, and Callie and Joshua, too, she was assembling a new self that was strong, brave, capable, and sure.

Inside the library, a few perm-haired women sat in a circle, each clutching a book in their laps, an old man had a newspaper spread on a table in front of him, and another sat at the microfilm machine with a notebook.

Brenna chose a computer in the back corner behind the magazine racks, where no one would see her talking to herself and think she was crazy.

"I think if we can figure out where your parents are now, that will help. What was your father's name?"

Dot shuddered. "Richard Healy. Goes by Rich or Richie."

Brenna looked for death announcements first, and found one from Terre Haute, Indiana.

Dot leaned in, trying to see the picture better. The man was nearly bald, and fat had gathered under his neck like a turkey's wattle. His ears stuck out, one corner clipped like someone had bitten him in a dogfight. There was no family resemblance except in the eyes: dark and bright. Brenna glanced at Dot, whose lips were a straight line.

She nodded. "That's him."

"I'm glad he's not hurting anyone else, but I'm sorry, too. I'm sure your feelings are complicated," said Brenna.

"Yeah, I think I already knew he was gone on some level, but I was kind of relishing the thought of scaring the bejeezus out of him. A good old-fashioned haunting, you know?"

Brenna laughed. "It says he's survived by his wife, Sherry. Is that your mom?"

"No. That must have been after—" Dot swallowed. "Are there—are there other kids mentioned?"

Brenna shook her head, and relief washed over Dot's face.

"Can we try my mom? Her name is Mildred Healy. Maiden name: Goddard."

Brenna typed it in with the word *obituary*. Nothing came up. She scrolled through a page of living Mildred Healys. "What about this one?"

Dot shook her head.

"This one?"

Again, a head shake. Brenna changed her search, trying the maiden name. Then the hospital where she was born. Then Mercer High School. They landed on a picture of an elderly woman with a cribbage board. Brenna looked at Dot and then the woman. She was blocky, but with a long, elegant neck and a sharp chin—just like Dot's. They both had small, pinched noses.

"That's her," Dot said. But Brenna found Dot's expression impossible to read.

62

Callie drove to St. Theresa's, thinking of Brenna's words: *I think we can help them face their pasts.* She snuck by reception and peeked into the puzzle room. Mrs. Vidal was on the couch in the empty room, her face blotchy, her eyelids rimmed in red. Each time Callie had seen her since the day at the impound lot, she'd looked more and more ill.

"Mrs. Vidal, what's wrong?" Callie asked.

"Oh, Callie," Mrs. Vidal said. "I'm so sorry."

"Why are you sorry?"

"I didn't visit you and your mom today. I just—felt so tired."

"That's okay."

"I just wanted to have something to bring you after all this time." The woman's fingers wrestled with one another, winding and unwinding. Her perm was unkempt and frizzy.

"To bring me?"

"A win-win: so that you'd get to stay in your house and it would be cared for."

Callie thought of her house and waited for the inevitable ache, but all she saw was her mother, years ago, stretched out on the warm floorboards and beckoning her to join. "Just because there isn't any snow doesn't mean we can't do angels," she'd said, making rainbows with her arms and legs.

"What if the house were generating money?" Mrs. Vidal continued, tugging her messy curls. "Then it wouldn't be a burden and you could keep it. Just think: it could be an inn again."

"I don't know that we could take care of an inn, Mrs. Vidal. I have school and my dad has work."

Mrs. Vidal's face fell. "Of course. Of course. How silly of me. I'll think of something else. I have to help. I owe you that," she said. She didn't seem to recognize how poorly she was doing, that her time was nearing its end.

"You have helped me, Mrs. Vidal," Callie said gently. "You were there when my mom was sick, and you made me see that I could be there for her, that I could be strong enough to lose her. And I'm applying to register the house as a historic place because of you, so it can be preserved even after someone buys it."

Mrs. Vidal smiled weakly. "I helped with all that?"

"Of course. Now let me help you."

"I just have too many regrets, Callie. I told Frederic I wasn't well enough to go to Celeste's funeral, but really I was ashamed. Like she'd judge me for even showing my face after treating her how I did." Mrs. Vidal put her face in her hands.

"Why didn't you talk to her after you"—Callie searched for the right words—"joined her?"

"It's not like here, Callie. There are no individuals; you can't have a one-on-one with someone. Everyone is jumbled together, and all our thoughts and memories and voices are shared."

"Have you tried visiting Celeste's grave and talking to her since you got back?" Callie asked. "Maybe she's listening. You were."

Mrs. Vidal's nervous fingers went to her hair again. Callie caught her hand and held it. "There may not be much time left," she said, thinking of her parents when they'd said nearly the same thing to her.

Mrs. Vidal looked at Callie as though she finally understood and nodded. The nod felt firm and final—as though it were the last thing she vowed to do.

63

Joshua still felt invigorated by his success with Tyler. It filled him, lifting and squaring his chest until he could imagine himself—not crouched like Nightcrawler—but Superman-like, cape swirling behind him. If he'd been able to stand up to Tyler, Joshua could certainly help Luke. The easiest thing, he decided, was to bribe Ruthie to cover for him and plant himself in Luke's driveway after school—even if it took all night. He might not return to the house, but that was a risk Joshua was willing to take. He buttoned his coat up to his chin, crossed the street, and sat on the cold pavement with his sketchpad. He flipped it open to the sketch of his neighbor as Wolverine on top of the Pontiac. Inside the driver's seat, he began to draw what he remembered of Eddie from the yearbook photo he'd seen—the light hair, the Ken-doll smile, the letterman jacket, and MERCER FIRE like a superhero's emblem on his chest.

Fifteen minutes later Luke rounded the corner in his gray jumpsuit. His hair seemed greasy, curling out from behind his ears, and his face was drawn, the pallor of his skin even more pronounced in daylight. He was walking slowly, the comic book hero depleted of his strength. How much time did they have left?

Joshua tore the drawing out of the sketchpad and stood, brushing off the seat of his pants.

"Hi, I made you something," Joshua said. "As thanks." The sketch wavered in the air between them, its soft crinkling betraying just how much Joshua's hand was shaking. Luke took the drawing and unfolded it. In those seconds that the man looked at the drawing, Joshua's heart was trying to force its way up his throat and past his tongue so it could flop onto the driveway at their feet.

"This is me?" Luke asked, his voice soft, ragged.

"How I see you," said Joshua.

Luke gave a sad smile. "I wish my father had seen me like that."

At the impound lot, Joshua had repeated Luke's story to Callie and Brenna; he could be Luke's voice again. "Maybe he still can."

The ancient tree that stood in Luke Senior's front yard had lost its leaves early. No one had raked, so Joshua crunched up to the front door, Luke hanging back like a shy puppy. The cigar-smoking man Joshua had seen from the bus many times before answered the door. He was small with yellow skin, stretched earlobes, and a spine that buried his chin in his collar. He looked at Joshua, eyes beady like a frightened rodent.

"Who are you, boy?"

"I'm Joshua Calloway. Are you Mr. Winters?"

The man didn't answer, just narrowed his eyes, and Joshua saw Luke in the crinkle of skin.

"That's him," Luke said from behind Joshua. The man's head jerked like he'd heard something, and he looked over Joshua's shoulder before fiddling with his hearing aid.

"Would it be okay if I ask you a few questions about your son?" Joshua asked.

The old man grunted but shifted in the doorframe and held the door open just wide enough for Joshua to enter. Mr. Winters tried to close the door after him, but Luke stopped it so he could squeeze through. "Thing keeps getting stuck," the old man grumbled.

Inside, the house was so humid, the floorboards and walls were slick. Damp spots like coffee stains spotted the ceilings. The warped doors hung on their hinges as though they were in a fun house. Joshua squinted at a wedding photo propped against the wall. The groom must be the man leading him through the house. Back then he'd been much larger, muscled and tall like his son, hair military short and face clean-shaven. There was something Wolverine-like about his face, something resembling Luke.

On the mantel there was a graduation photo smoke-stained yellow. No mistaking Luke, mischievousness in the glint of his eyes and the way his lips were pressed together, as if he knew a secret about the photographer. Joshua glanced at Luke, whose face had since thinned, his eyes saddened.

Joshua and Luke sat on the sagging tweed sofa, and Mr. Winters shuffled to and from the kitchen to deliver a warm can of Coke and a plate of crackers with a lump of canned tuna in the middle. The tuna smelled sharp, and Joshua had to resist the urge to plug his nose. Out of politeness, he took a cracker and tipped it—just barely—into the fish. Mr. Winters shoveled tuna onto a cracker and then munched thoughtfully, looking up at the ceiling.

"I had a dream Junior came back, that he was following me everywhere."

"I know it sounds crazy, but it's true. He's here."

The man grunted. "How is he?"

Not a *Have you lost your mind?* or *How the hell is he here?* Mr. Winters clearly knew the lore and believed it.

"He doesn't seem to be doing well," Joshua answered

truthfully, looking directly at Luke when he said it. Luke's eyes dropped to his large hands, but he didn't say anything.

Mr. Winters looked at the ceiling again. "That boy always seemed a little off to me." He sounded disgusted, cruelty flaring as red as the belly of a robin. Joshua winced. Luke grimaced like he'd been punched in the stomach. "Always running off with that Eddie kid. Sitting alone with him in the car. Like I didn't know what was going on in there."

Again, Joshua was surprised. Luke looked surprised too, his head lifting with a jerk. "If you knew, why didn't you stop him?" Joshua asked.

Mr. Winters shrugged, popping the tab on his Coke. "He reminded me a lot of his mother." Joshua followed Luke Senior's gaze to the old wedding photo. In black and white, she'd been reduced to extremes. Skin and dress white. Hair black. Her lips the only gray.

The man noticed Joshua studying the photo. "No, no. Not like that, not literally. I mean, happy."

Tears welled in Luke's eyes, and Joshua smiled at him. This man knew his son was happy and wanted to preserve that—despite his beliefs. Why hadn't he been able to make this known to Luke at the time?

"Here's what I don't understand," Luke Senior said,

interrupting Joshua's thoughts. Joshua prepared himself for questions about being gay, about how the sex worked or how one man could love another. But instead Mr. Winters asked: "Why didn't Junior just stay inside the car with that Eddie kid?" He sounded angry and hurt and sorry, all at once.

Joshua thought of the story Luke had told him about the tornado, about his unwillingness to settle for anything less than open, outright love. "He was being brave," he said.

"Brave?" Mr. Winters grunted. "Sounds like he was being foolish to me."

Luke's jaw clenched. "He left Eddie because he was standing up for himself. For what he needed," Joshua said.

"Brave, huh?" Mr. Winters said again, but this time, the words weren't meant for Joshua. He was looking where Luke sat on the couch—not focused on him exactly, not really seeing him, but aware, Joshua thought, that he was there.

Luke's eyes welled with tears. "Yes," he said firmly, and Joshua saw a note of recognition in his father's face. He'd heard.

WE WATCH

We watch the three who escaped us with anticipation, watch their drawn, nervous faces and the way they shift, bounce their knees, bite their cheeks as they embark on their journeys. We forget what it was like to occupy physical space, how the human body aches to express whatever is inside.

We find ourselves rooting for them, though we're not sure what we're rooting for. For a storm to whip them back into the skies? For them to stay? For our turn?

No matter what, we hope for happiness and wholeness. How can we not?

64

I t's going to storm. Can't you smell it? It smells like an ice rink," Callie's mom said.

Callie checked her weather app again and shook her head. "Still no sign of a storm. More *Gilmore Girls*?"

"I can't take any more of that fast-talking."

"How about a story?"

Her mom smiled. "I'd love that."

Callie smiled in return and began. "Back when Mercer was no more than a few farmhouses, there was a woman named Margaret Peterson." Callie proceeded to tell the story exactly as her mother had when she was a child. "And when they died, they still came—"

"To sit by her fire, eat her bread, and curl up under her blankets," her mother finished, tears glittering in her eyes.

"They'll still come, Mom. I promise. I'm making sure the house will be preserved. I'll get it on the National Register."

Her mother pulled the Kleenex from under her watch and blotted her eyes. "You're a great kid, Cal."

"Preservation is important. Mrs. Vidal taught me that. And you did too. I mean, look at this room."

The living room was now as much her mother's as it had been Margaret Peterson's or Mrs. Vidal's. She'd hung drapes that were heavy and rich—like an aging starlet's. All the furniture was equally elegant and old: daybeds upholstered in champagne pink, lamps with stained-glass shades, end tables with curved legs and lacquered tops. Only the hospital bed—a great metal-and-plastic beast—seemed out of place.

"Ha. I never thought I'd die in our living room. It's so—antique."

Callie laughed. "You picked all this out."

"For the Victorian Christmas tours. Not to die with."

"Well, I can move it. What would you prefer in here?"

"The farm table."

"I can't move that."

"I know." She smiled. "That's exactly the point. This isn't the way I want to go, but none of us can stop this thing. It's happening exactly as it is. Tassel lamps. Velvet chaise. Vases and all."

Callie's mom closed her eyes, a signal that their conversation was over. Callie blotted her mom's forehead with a washcloth and stood up. She walked into the dining room and stared at the farm table. Its blocky legs, which she'd bumped her knee on so many times. Its surface—scratched by Callie, the Gallaghers, Celeste, Mrs. Vidal, her mother, her mother's mother, and the mother of them all, Margaret Peterson. She liked that this table would never move, that when they sold the house, the new owners would live with this reminder of previous lives. It was possible to preserve a legacy, even in death.

Mrs. Vidal was waiting outside St. Theresa's when Callie arrived. She looked like someone had wrung her out until there was nothing left but wrinkles, bones, and dry hair. Callie opened the door for her and then helped her into the seat. The car filled with Mrs. Vidal's scent, a mossy, wet smell, like earthworms.

While Callie drove, Mrs. Vidal cleaned her glasses over and over on the sleeve of her floral-print dress.

"Are you nervous?" Callie asked.

Mrs. Vidal shook her head but didn't stop buffing the lenses.

Callie parked on the street right beyond Brenna's driveway and led Mrs. Vidal into the cemetery, the woman leaning shakily on Callie's arm.

"Frederic picked out the pink stone, but I was the one who

insisted he get a plot near a tree. It's a good one, don't you think?"

Callie nodded. "Why'd you engrave *My Sky*?"

"That's what we called her. She was our sky. And everything else, too." Mrs. Vidal shuffled closer to the stone. "Can you help me sit? I'm feeling a little—" Mrs. Vidal held up her hand so Callie could see the tremor.

Callie walked her closer to the stone and then held on as the woman lowered herself toward the ground. She was heavier than Callie had expected, or Callie had just grown accustomed to her mother's lightness. Mrs. Vidal scooted until her back was against the stone and her legs were out straight. She tilted her head back and looked up at the ancient oak. Its leaves were yellow with a few blazes of red. Behind it, the sky was chalky and heavy.

"These trees are older than us and they still haven't learned that they can't hold up the sky," Mrs. Vidal mused. "Come on; sit with me."

Callie hesitated. She'd never touched a grave before; it seemed sacrilegious. But soon a stone would mark her own mother, and she wanted to be able to touch it if she needed to.

Callie sat on the other side so that the stone was sandwiched between them. She tilted her head back, following the oak's branches to the gray sky beyond. The wind blew, and Callie felt an underbite of ice. The branches dipped in the gust, leaves fluttering.

A few let go, lifting once, twice, and then floating to the ground by Callie's feet.

The coldness from the stone seeped into Callie's back. She shivered, and Mrs. Vidal reached for her hand, intertwining their fingers. Callie tried not to shudder at the waxiness of the woman's skin.

"What should I do?" Mrs. Vidal asked.

"Try talking to her."

Mrs. Vidal was silent at first. Then, quietly, she began to speak. "I'm sorry I didn't come to your funeral," she said to the fall breeze, to the tree, and the leaves above them.

Callie waited—not sure what to expect. There was no Ouija board for Celeste to spell out her forgiveness. What signs would she send? Birds? Snakes? Lightning?

"I'm sorry I didn't teach you to love Mercer. I'm sorry about the dog and the comments about your weight. I'm sorry I didn't see you off for the dance. I'm sorry I didn't support your dreams. I'm sorry I wasn't the best mother for you." The woman was sobbing. "I'm trying to be better now."

Just a couple of weeks ago, this would have been agony for Callie. This intimacy. These feelings of regret.

"It's her," Mrs. Vidal said suddenly.

Callie looked around, but the cemetery was unchanged. The

bluish stones amid the gray and white and My Sky's pink. The old stones still jagged and broken, their inscriptions worn away by wind and rain. The dry leaves rustled in the breeze, but it was otherwise silent.

"It's her," Mrs. Vidal said again, and Callie closed her eyes.

On the wind, she could smell buttered popcorn and caramel. A laugh bubbled out of Callie before she could clap her free hand over her mouth.

"She's delightful, isn't she?" said Mrs. Vidal. "So much joy."

"I wish I'd met her," whispered Callie.

Mrs. Vidal squeezed her hand. "Me too," she said.

65

The facility where Dot's mom lived was beige brick, mesa-flat, and long. There was a fenced-in shuffleboard court to the left and a few trees to the right that had lost their leaves and were clawing at the sky, bare-branched and sad. Dot closed her eyes and took deep, shuddery breaths.

Inside, the home was equally dingy, yellowed wallpaper peeling at the seams and gray floors. There were depressing Halloween decorations on every door, pumpkins made of construction paper that seemed to be wilting, black cats and bats missing their googly eyes, a vampire who'd faded to a pale purple.

Brenna asked for Mildred Goddard, and a nurse pointed Brenna toward a door with a wrinkled ghost. Dot stopped in front of the door, looking skeptical. "My mother never decorated," she said.

Brenna knocked.

"Come in," a woman called.

Dot's already-pale skin blanched. "It's her voice, isn't it?" Brenna whispered.

Dot nodded. "I haven't heard it in so long."

Brenna swung open the door. Dot's mother was perched on the bed, her hands folded over her belly, a book of large-print crossword puzzles nearby. She seemed like a benevolent Buddha to Brenna, her flesh a gentle mound resting in her lap.

"Hi, I'm Brenna. I'm from Mercer."

"For a second I thought you were my Dotty," the woman said. "I could have sworn I heard her voice outside the door."

"Actually, you did. I'm here with her," Brenna said. "With Dot. She wants to talk to you."

"You're with Dotty?" The words were small, barely audible. "Are you foolin' me? Trying to take advantage of a dying woman?"

Brenna looked at Dot for help. "Is there a way you can help me prove you're here?"

"She made a pumpkin pie the day after he left," Dot said. "It was his favorite."

Brenna repeated the message, and Mildred shut her eyes, a tear sliding down her cheek. "Am I dead? Is this the judgment?"

"No. Dot just wants to talk to you."

"I prayed for this moment for so long," the woman said, her

eyes roving around Brenna, as though she were hoping to catch sight of her daughter. "I'm so sorry, Dotty. I think about you all the time. How I was blind. How awful he was. How I didn't do anything to help you. How I just let him walk right up to our door after what he did to you." She spat the word *how* each time, like she might get the poison out. "I was foolish and lonely. And you were—"

"I was your blood," Dot said, her voice choked.

Mildred wiped her eyes, and sat up straighter. "I heard her. It was very quiet—practically a whisper," she said to Brenna. Then, in the general direction of where Dot was standing: "You *are* my blood, Dotty. You *are* my blood."

"Was," Dot repeated. "I don't belong here now."

"You'll find where you belong. I've always known it. Come here." She patted the bed beside her for Dot to sit. Reluctantly, Dot moved to sit beside her.

"She's there," Brenna said softly.

"I saved up and fixed the VW. Toured the US after I quit the diner. You always wanted a bigger life for yourself. I thought I could try to live a little of it for you." She smiled, as though remembering a sweet time. "The VW broke down in California, and I had to sell it to pay for a bus ticket back home. I was old by then anyway." She turned toward her daughter. They were so close, their noses almost touched. Mildred began to sing what sounded to Brenna like gospel music:

Soon we'll come to the end of life's journey
And perhaps we'll never meet anymore.
Till we gather in Heaven's bright city
Far away on that beautiful shore.

"You learned to sing for me," Dot said. "You hated music." She traced her mother's cheek with her fingertips, and Mildred tilted her head as though she could feel it. Dot began to sing softly along with her. Her mother's voice was thin and high where Dot's was warm and low, but still pleasant and sweet. Dot didn't seem to know the lyrics, but somehow she wrapped her voice around her mother's, knitting it with hers, until they both fell silent and the air hummed on without them.

66

Joshua lied to his mom about having a daylong event with his newly founded LGBTQ+ club. Ruthie looked suspicious, but his mom was thrilled and kept asking him if he needed her to buy snacks for their event. He accepted, pleased to have Goldfish crackers and Oreos for his road trip.

After their visit with Luke Senior, Joshua had sat with Luke on the curb while the man pulled tufts of his hair out and held them in his palm like they were clues to what was happening to him.

"I think it might be because you don't belong here," Joshua had said.

"I don't know how to leave."

"Is there something else you need to do? Someone else you need to talk to?" Joshua asked.

Luke had chewed his lip, staring at the wolf fluff in his hand.

"What if we went to Indiana?" Joshua said. "What if we found Eddie's grave?"

Before leaving, Joshua printed Eddie's obituary, which listed the town and the church. From there, they'd rely on small-town friendliness to find the exact house. Joshua rode his bike downtown to avoid Ruthie's spying, and met Luke at his father's. The old man had agreed to loan them his truck without even bothering to ask Joshua if he had a license yet. Maybe, after hearing his son speak from beyond the grave, he didn't see the need to bother with earthly things like laws. Joshua wasn't worried either; he had driven around his grandfather's farm as soon as he could reach the pedals.

"I printed this for you," Joshua said, and handed Luke the obituary.

"He collected cars? But I was the one who knew about cars. He could barely keep the Pontiac running." Luke was wearing the mechanic's uniform unzipped so the fire department shirt—Eddie's shirt, Joshua realized—was visible.

"Maybe he kept them to stay close to you. Or maybe it was a message to you."

Luke looked doubtful. "Let's get going. Just warning you, the truck shakes like a sinner on the highway, so you should take the country roads."

As they drove, there was a metallic, oily smell that seemed to be emanating not just from the truck, but from Luke. Joshua tried to focus on the landscape. Indiana wasn't that much different from Illinois: the yellowing corn, the flat land, the courthouses like monuments. When they got closer, Joshua noticed that the Indiana town's Main Street was lined with antiques stores and bars, just like Mercer's. There were churches at every corner, and it didn't take them long to locate St. Benedict's. It sat across from one of the new cemeteries, the kind with flat stones for easy mowing.

Eddie's plot was right next to Carolyn's. They shared a white stone with their names and dates. Luke was silent the whole time, but Joshua couldn't help feeling a little disappointed. In Mercer's Blue Light cemetery, where all the tornado victims were buried, everything felt connected—the Mercerites in the ground and all those walking on it and even Luke, who seemed to be doing both. There were trees pushing their roots through the coffins. Everyone's bones were mingling down there, becoming one great soup of history. In Eddie's cemetery, there were no wilting flowers, tiny flags, or trees.

"I hope he didn't feel like he had to," Luke said.

"What?"

"Marry her. Carolyn. Out of guilt or shame or something. I hope he wanted to. I hope they were happy."

Joshua looked at the stones again. Wanting the best for someone even if your heart had been broken by them? That sounded like more than just love. It sounded like forgiveness.

When they left the cemetery and found the farm, there was a FOR SALE sign up. But the land was unkempt. Trash from the road was caught in the high brown grasses. The trees needed trimming, and the house was missing some siding. There was a pole barn, and a newly constructed building that seemed to be the garage.

Luke tried a side door first, but it was locked. He tried the garage door next, and it slid up easily. No wonder people thought the Pontiac had been stolen.

Right up front was the spot where the Pontiac seemed to belong—the car-shaped pad of still-white concrete. No oil stains. No dirt. Along the back wall were army-green motorcycles. On each side of the Pontiac's space was a much newer car. One a deep shade of blue. And another black. The Pontiac must have stood out: white, glimmering chrome, the size of a boat.

Unselfconsciously, Luke dropped to his knees and then rolled onto his back on the clean space the Pontiac left. "I was a little glad the Pontiac got destroyed in this last tornado," he said.

"Why?"

"I felt like the storm had left the right person standing this time."

"He hurt you," Joshua said. "That seems like a natural thought."

Luke sucked his teeth. "Maybe." He splayed his legs and arms, and Joshua thought of a wild cat stretching. "I wasn't around long enough for the pain to stop, you know. I think I wouldn't have been so angry if there'd been time to—" He stared at the rafters, seeming to search for a word.

"Heal?" Joshua suggested.

"Yeah. I imagine it feels something like this."

Luke patted the floor beside him. Joshua lay down. The concrete pressed into his spine, but the space above and around him felt wide-open—and all his.

WE HEAR THE WIND

We hear the wind gathering itself: shrill and bitter. It tunnels through Mercer, whipping the leaves off trees. This storm is pewter, slate, and flint. This storm is nails. Is bite. No one expects it. Not when summer stayed so late. It seems too providential. Too well-timed.

But time is a tricky thing. Sometimes it skips by, smooth as a river stone. Sometimes it crawls. Vast empty beds of it, desert-dry.

It's been well over fifty years since 1961. A blink in the scheme of the universe, but enough time that we'd now be retired, losing ourselves in crossword puzzles and fumbling with technology we don't understand. Grandchildren would climb into our laps, weaving their tiny fingers through our thin hair. We'd be taking them for ice cream and blotting crumpled napkins against their sticky chins.

For Callie, time has been freight-train fast, tornado fast. Each day speeding toward the inevitable end. One uneaten piece of toast closer. One visit from Aunt Toni. One moment of confusion. One moment of lucidity. One hospice nurse. Another.

This storm takes its time, shifting from wind to rain to sleet. We're tempted to chorus and whisper and call our storm song. But tonight we are silent. Tonight we are still.

67

The night nurse, a freckled Irish woman, woke Callie and her father to say that her mother was having a hard time breathing and that her pulse was erratic. *It* might be coming, she said, and Callie briefly thought she meant the storm her mother had been predicting. Despite the weather app's clear skies icon, the windows were shuddering in their frames and the wind whistled through the chimney.

The nurse pulled two antique chairs alongside the hospital bed. She'd tied the green scarf poorly, and Callie pinched the tail of it, rubbing the silk between her fingers. Callie's mother hadn't been awake since the day before, when Callie had spoken to her before leaving for St. Theresa's. Just one day later and her mother's face wasn't recognizable anymore. The mask over her mouth, the sharp slabs of her cheekbones, the temples that had become valleys, the wishbone jaw. She'd been sleeping fitfully, her legs and arms jerking violently.

"You can take her hand," the nurse said softly. Callie took one and her father took the other, and they tried to tame her movements, tried to hold on as best they could.

Her comforter had been removed and folded on the armchair. Only a thin blue sheet covered her. The room smelled like rubber gloves, and there was gentle music punctuated by wind chimes playing—something her mother never would have listened to. Callie wanted to pay attention to her mother, to these final moments that would be her last forever, but she was distracted by everything that was wrong: the scarf, the jerking hand, the sheet, the smell, the music.

Callie half expected Mrs. Vidal, with her impeccable timing, to appear. She would tell Callie what she was supposed to do and say, what she herself had done when Frederic stopped talking to the people in the television and started "actively dying."

The wind howled outside, and Callie felt like the house was wheezing in and out like an accordion around them. She wasn't aware of the passing of time, but at some point, the light outside became gray and ice balls started tapping their windows. At some point, the jerking stopped. At some point, the CD ended and no one chose another. At some point, Callie retied the scarf and her father dragged the comforter back onto the bed. At some point, her mother's eyes opened, but they were vacant and dilated. At some point, with a few words to Callie's father, the nurse switched off the machine helping Callie's mother breathe.

Callie waited for her mother to wake—at least once—so they could collect some final words that they'd be able to repeat later to Toni and her mother's friends. Something meaningful and thoughtful. But maybe *Tassel lamps. Velvet chaise. Vases and all* would have to be enough.

The nurse moved around, checking vitals, administering morphine. Callie's mother didn't appear to be struggling to breathe anymore. Instead her breaths were slow and shallow and, at times, barely visible.

"If you have anything to say," the nurse prompted, "now would be the time."

"I love you," Callie whispered. The words were a handful of coins in her mouth—metallic and too large—but she forced them out anyway. Her father murmured the phrase too, like they were at Mass and she was the priest leading prayer. Her mother was the one who'd always known instinctively how to provide comfort, and Callie had never asked her how to be the one who lives. How many more times would Callie think, *If only I'd asked my mother when I'd had the chance?*

Callie knew there wouldn't be another chance for granola and Gatorade and the shuffle of newspaper. For driving lessons. For her mother's fingers in her hair. For her mother's arm around her, dotted with waterfall spray. For her mother's arm around her, period. For hearing her mother inhale when she arrived home, a breath as soft as an eyelash on Callie's cheek.

And then quietly, "She's gone." The nurse's words snapped Callie out of her thoughts. She sat fixed on her mother, hoping for something discernible: the light leaving her mother's eyes or an exhalation that announced itself with a final rattle—like books said. Except there wasn't a sign. So Callie listened to the house instead, hoping to hear a knock upstairs, a creak of its warm floors, a door slamming as her mother's spirit passed through. But she heard only the storm.

What had the nurse seen that she hadn't?

The nurse tugged on the sheet, straightening it needlessly. Callie wanted to push her hand away, to tell her they could do whatever else they needed to do on their own, which wasn't the least bit true. Because Callie didn't know what it was they needed to do. And because her mother was—had been—everything.

"Take as long as you need," the nurse said, and left the room.

Her father started to cry and Callie felt her own tears respond, heavy in the corners of her eyes.

"I forgot to tell her we'd be okay," he whispered. "She wanted to hear that."

Callie nodded, understanding how regrets stung. But if Mrs. Vidal had been watching and listening all along, maybe her mother would be too.

"We're going to be okay," Callie said loudly.

Her father looked at her with deep sadness, but also gratitude. "We're going to be okay," he repeated.

"We're going to be okay," Callie said again.

"We're going to be okay."

"We're going to be okay."

Over and over. A prayer for her mother to hear.

WE WATCH IT SNOW

We watch it snow—flakes so tiny, they're like dust in the air. It melts as soon as it settles on bare necks, black suit coats, gloves. Even on the casket, like this, too, is warm, as warm as the yawning hole beside it.

In our day, you'd stay for the lowering of the casket, you'd contribute your shovelful. Now it's all machines, and so they usher the people away before the tamper chatters sledgehammer-loud, packing the dirt on top. We've watched our share of burials—our friends and lovers and parents joining us and wanting, as they always do, to see what they've left behind. Tearstained faces. A flat plane of packed dirt.

We watch as Callie stands beside her father, face drawn, eyes down, as everyone filters back to their cars. And we know it's Eleanor: the reason Callie managed to be here, the reason she remains beside her father. And maybe it's because of them, too:

Joshua and Brenna hovering on the path nearby, hair shining from melted flakes, torn jeans damp at the hem. We know Callie trusts that they're there. We can feel it, this trust. And we watch when her father beckons her toward the car, as one of Callie's hands goes to the pearls at her neck and the other skims across the mahogany-colored casket—a touch so light, like the falling snow.

68

Well past midnight, hours after the funeral had ended, Callie padded down the maid's staircase to the cellar. She couldn't sleep. She couldn't cry, either, because sobbing made too much noise and she needed to listen for her mother's voice, or the shuffle of her feet, or her cough, door slam, knock. Callie wasn't positive she'd be able to find her mother in the house, or that the spirit would even be her mother, but she had faith in her ability to recognize the sounds of her mother anywhere: the murmur of her voice from the other room, the unfolding of a newspaper, the jingle of her key chains.

The daytime hadn't been much better. When she descended the stairs that morning, the wood was warm under her feet—despite the frost on the windowpanes. When she opened the front door to pick up the newspaper—her mother's job for so many years—the house sighed contentedly. When Callie slammed the door, the windows chattered back at her. The house wasn't just alive, it was desperate, like it already missed her mother's attention and needed someone, anyone, to throw open its drapes and wax its floors. Callie would try her best.

Someday soon she and her father would have to go through each box and plastic bag in the cellar. They'd have to thin out the possessions for the move, sell the nineteenth-century chairs, donate the clothing. It would mean holding little pieces of her mother and deciding which ones could be preserved. She sank onto her knees next to the plastic bin with the photo albums. Upstairs was the historical society book that Callie had pulled off the top and shared with her mother on that last fully lucid day.

Callie closed her eyes and listened to the house. If she heard a sound, she planned to find the source and talk to it, starting with how very *in* love with her mother Callie was. The *in* made the love more active. It returned Callie to childhood, at church, when she'd had time to marvel at her mother, to trace every blue vein, to encircle every knobby knuckle with finger and thumb, to pinch and rub her pulled-dough earlobes. Except now Callie was marveling at what was inside. How her mother had been brave to fight. How she'd been brave to stop fighting. How she'd been wise to gather history beneath her roof and polish it gleaming. And patient enough to wait for Callie to accept her illness, never doubting, always offering Callie a way back.

Callie shoved a box off the sofa they'd moved downstairs from the living room to make room for the hospital bed. She brushed off the cushion, intending to sit—maybe even to sleep—while she waited for a sign from her mother.

Above, a door hinge creaked and something thudded. The hair prickled on the back of her neck. Was it her mother? There was a scraping sound, like a chair moving across the hardwood above Callie's head, and disappointment flooded her, dense and sodden. Her mother, who loved this house more than almost anything, would never scrape the floors—even as a ghost.

Maybe it was Mrs. Vidal? Callie hadn't seen her since before her mother died, and, given her unusual sense of timing, it wouldn't be out of the question. But the light flicked on at the top of the stairs and Callie recognized her father's shape.

"Hello?" he called down.

"It's me, Dad."

"Oh." He sounded disappointed. Maybe her father—the nonbeliever—was looking for her mother too. He trudged down the stairs. In the shadows, his face looked wan and weathered. His stubble was growing in blondish-red patches. His eyes were sunken behind hills of blue puffy skin. "Why are you sitting in the dark?"

"Just thinking about Mom and how much she loved this house."

At that, her father's eyes fell to his slippers. "I'm failing."

"Dad, stop. No, you're not," Callie said.

"There's so much to do," he said. Aunt Toni had taken care of the funeral and the food train. But Callie knew there were more adult tasks her father was expected to do: paying the pile of bills, returning to work, making repairs to the house before they could sell.

"Can I do anything?" Callie asked.

He inhaled, and in the half-light, she saw his eyes glittering. He was shaking his head. "You're doing great. You really are. You know that, right?"

He wrapped his arm around her shoulders, drawing her to his chest. "Though you have to go back to school at some point, my little slacker."

"I will when you go back to work."

He laughed. "It's a deal."

It was then, wrapped in her father's arms, that Callie smelled her mother as discernibly as she'd smelled Celeste. The *before* smell, the one Callie had thought she'd lost. She felt her father inhale and knew that he smelled it too. Callie imagined the oxygen molecules carried by her blood, imagined her mother's scent pumping through her heart. And she knew she'd carry her mom with her—wherever they moved.

69

Joshua wanted to visit Callie after school, but her text said she was on a long run to the next town and back. Selfishly, Joshua was disappointed that he had to take the bus. Tyler was riding too, and he didn't make eye contact with Joshua, but he didn't knee his seat either. Respectful distance was something Joshua could accept. He'd mourned the end of their friendship long ago.

Joshua and Ruthie walked home from the bus stop together. She was moping, pissed about some test she'd failed. "Mr. Hershel marks the whole problem wrong if you skip a step—even if you get the answer right. But, like, there are just some things I can do in my head. I shouldn't be punished for that."

Joshua nodded sympathetically, but his eyes were trained on Luke's house. The FOR RENT sign was down and there was a moving van in the driveway. A thin woman with bobbed hair was standing in the yard, holding a phone to her ear. At her feet, a toddler in overalls pulled up handfuls of dead grass and stuffed them into his mouth. His face scrunched up in disgust, and the dirt and grass dribbled down his chin. Who were these people?

Joshua tried to remember the last time he'd seen Luke. After the trip to Indiana, they'd had that freak ice storm. That was the day Callie's mom had died. Joshua's mom had driven him over with a Tupperware of brownies, and he'd left them on the stoop with a drawing he made of Callie as Rogue. The next few days had been busy: a test, the second meeting of the LGBTQ+ club with Beau and Brenna, the funeral. Each night, he'd looked for the flicker of a candle across the street but had seen nothing.

"New neighbors," Ruthie observed. "Wonder if they need a babysitter."

"But he just got here," Joshua said. Disappointment fluttered in his chest again. Finally he was beginning to understand Luke, to see what was under that muscle and pelt, and he was gone.

"You're worrying me, ginger head." Ruthie tugged at his elbow and dragged them toward the driveway.

"Look, just tell Mom I'm going to Brenna's to work on a project."

"Hold up, I'm not your messenger. Besides, aren't you still grounded?"

"Fine. I'll text her. Why don't you tell her about the test you flunked instead?"

Ruthie grimaced. "I won't say anything. Just be careful, okay?"

Joshua surprised himself by pulling her into a quick, fierce hug. She laughed and shoved him away playfully.

Joshua unchained his bike and rolled up one of his jean legs so it wouldn't snag in the chain. The air stung his ears and froze the hairs in his nose. He rode desperately, remembering his ride after the tornado weeks before. That night, his entire world had grown to include Brenna, Callie, and Luke—his Wolverine, who made sure that Joshua couldn't hold on to his hurt and anger any longer. If Luke really was gone, Joshua swore he'd be happy for him, because it would mean that the man had found what he needed.

By the time Joshua reached Brenna's house, his exposed calf was red and burning from the cold. Brenna's porch light wasn't on, but Golden Girl was in the driveway, and Joshua could see lights through their blinds.

A slim, thin-haired guy who Joshua took to be Brenna's brother answered the door. "What?"

"I'm a friend of Brenna's."

Joshua allowed his teeth to chatter, hoping that the guy would invite him inside to warm up, but he kept his dark eyes locked on Joshua and shouted, "Brenna, your prince is here!" A few seconds later Brenna shoved him aside and stepped onto the stoop, pulling on a jacket.

"He has his asshole friends over," she said, and gestured toward the cemetery. "Wanna walk?"

By now it was dusk. Dull stars and a sliver of moon were just visible in a lavender sky, transforming the trees into black silhouettes. The pair weaved around the stones, not following the dirt paths but some route only Brenna knew. She paused for a beat at the foot of certain graves, as though greeting the residents below. Joshua tried to read the stones each time they paused, but the text had been worn away on many.

"Did Callie say anything to you about Mrs. Vidal?" Joshua asked.

"No. Why?"

Joshua stomped his feet to get some feeling back into his frozen toes. "I haven't seen Luke since we went to Indiana. It's like he never existed. Have you heard from Dot?"

She shook her head and snaked her hands into the sleeves of her jacket. "Manny's had Golden Girl a lot, so I haven't made it to the Cities. And it's not like she has a phone."

"Do you think he's gone for good?" Joshua asked. "Just like that?" He tried to ask this casually, but his voice sounded ragged, its bare underbelly exposed.

"I mean, I hope not. But I hope so too. Maybe you helped him face the past or whatever." She shrugged weakly, resigned. "We could go look for Dot to check it out. You can stash your bike in the car again."

"Technically, I'm still grounded."

"But your mom doesn't seem to take that very seriously, does she?"

He laughed. "No, I think she's probably glad I have somewhere to go for once. Anyway, what's she going to do? Double-ground me?"

"That's the spirit." Brenna smiled. "I'll steal the keys from Manny."

The sky had become a velvety navy and the darkness had settled around them like a quilt. A blue light—frosty and ethereal— glowed near Joshua's feet.

"Brenna. The stones."

"The stones," she repeated, the words barely a whisper. They spun in a circle.

Blue lights spotted the darkness around them in a mysterious constellation. The lights were steady but also appeared to float.

Lanterns of the dead. The color, Joshua imagined, of glaciers.

He exhaled, aware now that he'd been holding his breath. So much was possible. Finally, all that hurt and sadness at the way he'd been treated had been replaced by something altogether different: wonder.

70

The warehouse's mural had been repainted—this time as a representation of Notorious RBG, the crown on the justice's head a neon pink. Brenna knocked on the sliding door and then pressed her ear against it. She couldn't hear anything. She pulled on the handle, and the door slid open easily. Inside, the warehouse was dark. Brenna used her phone flashlight, but the measly light didn't reach the corners of the cavernous room.

"Dot," she called.

No one answered.

Brenna took a breath and slid inside. "Stick close," she said to Joshua. He grabbed the shirttail of her flannel, shuffling like a duck behind her, and she laughed, shaking him off. He flicked on his phone flashlight too, adding the light to hers. The room was empty.

"She's gone too," Brenna said.

"No goodbye."

"No goodbye," Brenna repeated, a lump in her throat. She hoped Dot had made her way back to where she belonged, but she also wished they'd had more time together. Time to ask more questions. To write with Dot's encouragement. To listen to her sing.

"Wait—what's this?" Joshua's light landed near the center of the room, illuminating something on the floor. The candle Dot had lit, broad and white, left behind like a sign or message. Brenna picked it up and rubbed the wax that had dripped and hardened along the sides.

"Maybe it's up to us," she said.

"What is?" asked Joshua.

"Saying goodbye."

Somewhere in those howling hours of the first winter storm, our three slipped back in, like kids sneaking home, tumbling into their beds weary and wind-kissed, and we became whole again.

Now we watch as Callie jogs down the stairs of Mrs. Vidal's inn and climbs into the back seat of Golden Girl. There's a FOR SALE sign in Callie's front yard, a smaller placard that reads HISTORIC HOME perched on top.

"It should probably say *haunted* too," Callie says.

The three teens laugh and debate if haunting is something that realtors must disclose, if the people who move in will think the mysterious sounds are mice and a settling foundation or visitors passing through from one world to the next.

Across from Callie's house, the park has transformed into Halloween Land. Jack-o'-lantern string lights dance in the wind, and children climb hay bales. A zebra with mittens licks a candied apple. A toddler-zombie drags a pillowcase full of candy. A ladybug tries to catch an old man dressed like a wolf. He lets her.

Golden Girl passes the cemetery and the impound lot where the Pontiac still sits, glistening abalone in the moonlight.

In the country, the turbines are motionless, but they pulse red, warning off airplanes and scaring birds. Stadium lights illuminate Heinrich's Haunted Maize Maze, and the teens hear intermittent screams, the buzz of a chain saw, the barks of coyotes.

There's a sense that Brenna, Callie, and Joshua are time traveling, heading into a before-time kind of darkness. Golden Girl's headlights carve their path. But in the rearview mirror, they can see the present—bright and blinking.

At the roadside memorial, Brenna pulls onto the shoulder and leads them into the field, lighting their way with her cell phone. The stalks are golden and dry, ready to be cut for the winter. They stop near the center of the field. Brenna pulls up the opening scene of the movie on her phone, and they watch Audrey Hepburn walking down the street, in her sleek gown and sunglasses, with her pastry and coffee, white scarf fluttering over her arm. The movie is on mute, and they listen to the breeze hissing the dry tassels.

We can imagine picnic blankets, rickety lawn chairs, rows of cars around them. A wide whitewashed wall as the screen. The smell of popcorn, of cinnamon and sugar, of rain and lightning. Us, laughing and chatting and loving and living.

The night is cold, but stormless, and they're wearing coats, gloves, and hats. Joshua holds Brenna's phone while she finds her lighter. She's brought the candle from the warehouse and positions it on the ground between them. They hold hands and huddle close, to protect it from the breeze. They keep it simple, but ritualistic—a ceremony, a service, a séance.

"Thank you," Callie says.

"Goodbye," Joshua says.

"Be at peace," Brenna says.

Thank you. Goodbye. Be at peace.

Thank you. Goodbye. Be at peace.

They repeat their lines again and again, until it sounds like a chant. They watch the flame, a tiny pinprick of light at their feet. Finally they fall silent.

We fight to be heard. At first, our whispers are soft and breathy, but we crescendo like crickets in the summer.

You will be okay. You are *okay,* we tell them. *We are too.*

71

Thank you.

The sound of the voices became a waterfall—not Niagara-violent but steady and calming, filling Callie's ears until she could hear nothing else. Callie had a feeling this was the last time she'd hear the voices, that she'd search her whole life, hiking up mountains and following streams for this exact sound.

All their names—the loved ones and lost souls of Mercer—chanted over and over: *Erma Thomas. Luke Winters. Gordon Fife. Sally Jordan. Chester Lewis. Dorothy Healy. Jeanette Gillespie. Stephen Turner. Edward Milton. Delores Tanner. Celeste Vidal. Warren Worley. Trudy Miller. Eleanor Peterson Vidal.* And on. And on. And on.

Of course, one name thrummed in Callie's heart. It was for the woman with pulled-cotton hair and crystalline eyes that Callie said *thank you.* It was because of Mrs. Vidal that Callie had the courage to be present in her mother's final days; to feel the weight of her mother in her arms, her grip on Callie's hand, her mechanized breathing on the back of Callie's neck; to participate in conversations, brief and sometimes confused, but hers to keep.

Catherine Keller. Catherine Keller. Catherine Keller, Callie thought, and soon the voices took up the name, whispering it back to her. Her mother's name. A breath on the wind, forever a part of Callie, forever a part of Mercer.

72

*G*oodbye.

Joshua once asked his grandfather about the night of the tornado. His grandfather remembered crouching in the storm cellar with his parents. He could hear the tornado, knew that it was close and dangerous. But what his grandfather remembered most clearly was the feeling that all the air in the cellar, in his lungs, was being sucked away from him. Now the voices around Joshua felt like the opposite, like being filled with air—enough to lift off and float away.

If Joshua concentrated on the voices, picking a thread and following it through, he heard encouragements. *It gets better. Be yourself. Anchor yourself in history, yet sail forward. Take courage. The power is yours. Don't let them get you down.*

When words become as used and worn as a child's blanket, do they cease to have meaning? he wondered. *Or are they more pow-erful? Do they make you stronger?*

Joshua did feel stronger, as though he'd redrawn himself in Mercer, darkened his outline, filled himself in. Joshua, as himself, was possible because of the queer people before him, the Eddies and Lukes and so many more, who hurt and loved and struggled and succeeded and died and lived happily and were invisible and visible both.

Discover new landscapes, the voices said.

Joshua nodded. He would, for himself, and for Luke.

73

Be at peace.

Inside, Brenna didn't feel peace, exactly. Instead she felt something live-wire bright and humming—electricity in her gut where there had once been a magnet. The pull replaced by a pulse. But the feeling was a comfort. It was desire—to live and write and love—and maybe that was her own brand of peace. She clutched her notebook, felt her heart beating against it.

She wished peace for Dot, who'd carried her hurt for as long as she was alive, as long as she was dead. She wished it for all the Storm Spirits, and, if she listened carefully to the voices, she thought she could hear apologies, confessions, stories.

Emma, thank you for sitting near me that day at recess so long ago. Daddy, we will never come to an understanding. I don't want or need you. Luke, I am so sorry I never got a chance to tell you that I love you. Frederic, I will always remember meeting you at the train station, standing beside your trunk, lost, and I knew—just knew—that you were my future. Mama, I was so proud to be your daughter; I never wanted to hurt you.

Brenna squeezed her friends' hands, and they squeezed back. She'd tell their stories, all their stories, and bring them what peace she could.

In time, the voices quieted, the candle wavering as though it had been fueled by their breath. Then, in silence, the flame snuffed out.

Still, Callie, Joshua, and Brenna stood, hand in hand in hand, as the world continued to spin.

ACKNOWLEDGMENTS

Thank you to my agent, Sarah Davies, for believing in me and finding a good home for this novel. To the entire team at Philomel Books and Penguin Random House, thank you for your guidance and expertise. Thanks to Mark Oshiro for being a shrewd reader. And thank you, especially, to my editor, Liza Kaplan, for incredible insight and for loving Joshua, Brenna, and Callie as much as I do.

I'm deeply grateful to the Purdue University MFA program for welcoming me into its writing community and to all my workshop companions for their clear-eyed critiques as this book was born. Thank you, especially, to my teachers throughout the years: Maxine Clair, Peter Marks, Faye Moskowitz, Patricia Henley, Porter Shreve, Bich Minh "Beth" Nguyen, Chinelo Okparanta, Janet Alsup, Sharon Solwitz, and my thesis adviser, Brian Leung. You challenged me to be truer to myself.

Thank you to the fierce and brave women who stood by my side as I grew into a writer: Priya Ramanathan, Emily Ryder Perlmeter, Justine Williams, Maria Maldonado, Denise Varughese, Rhiannon Killian, Kyrlyn Chatten, Megan Gibbs, Sarah Murphy Traylor, and Kelsey Ronan. And to my forever wolf pack—Julie Henson, Bethany Leach, Katie McClendon, Rebecca McKanna, and Emily Skaja—thank you for giving this book its heart.

I'm grateful to my family—Mary and Charles Lund, Frances Lund and Troy Randall, Jennifer Lund and Dan Ross, Gus and Maxine Ross, Julie Lund and Jonathan Wheaton, Owen and Cora Wheaton, and the Acevedos—for their unwavering support. I'm proud to have been shaped by your hands.

Thank you to my husband, Johnny Acevedo, for all the love and encouragement. You fortify me every day.

And finally, to the town that raised me, your ghosts are always just beneath my skin.